BRASS PONY

BRASS ♠ PONY

two novellas

by

Marsh Cassady

E-Book Division
GLB Publishers   San Francisco

Published in the United States by
GLB Publishers
P.O. Box 78212, San Francisco, CA 94107 USA

Cover by GLB Publishers
Cover photo by Rogelio Guizar
tioroge@hotmail.com

This is a work of fiction. Names, characters, places, and incidents are either the products of the author's imagination or are used fictitiously, and any resemblance to actual persons, living or dead, events, or locales is entirely coincidental.

ISBN 1-879194-82-1

Library of Congress Control Number:

2001089490

2001

To Randy Gray

In Memory of Barbara Allen Zeigler

And, as always, for Jim

TO RIDE A WILD PONY

A Novella by

Marsh Cassady

CHAPTER 1

Coast Boulevard is a narrow street stretching along the rocky shoreline. A number of small houses, greatly overpriced, perch along the eastern edge. When the sun is bright, the sea calm, waves lap gently into the beach. Yet often the sea is angry, smashing again and again, in thunderous claps against eroding earth.

La Jolla itself is more constant. It is a moneyed area, where even the people behind the grocery carts in Vons project an air of wealth. Here in the Village one rarely hears of the day-to-day struggle. Rather, the talk is of investments, the stock market, weekend jaunts to Cancun or the Riviera.

La Jollans do not often admit to being a part of San Diego. They attempt to mislead the unknowing into belief that the Village is an entity unto itself. Many residents actually believe this myth, fostered and nurtured by the United States Post Office Department which allows them to use their own separate name, rather than that of the city of which they are a part.

Dennis Thompson had lived in the Village for more than thirty years; yet he knew he didn't belong. He had no pretensions of belonging. His roots were in the tenement houses of Brooklyn, with the perpetual smell of cooked cabbage, and cardboard thin walls that made neighbors' business everyone's business. That was where Dennis was spawned and where he grew to young adulthood. Only his talent for sketching got him out, gave him a scholarship to whatever university he chose to attend. He chose San Diego State. He was tired of the humidity of summer, the freezing sleet of winter in New York.

Now he'd wasted his talent, traded it for security ... and for love, a rare commodity in the tenements of home, where people screamed and beat each other as a matter of course.

Dennis was an early riser. He liked nothing better than to watch the sun float into the sky and slowly burn the morning mist from the sea. Before the sound of traffic and the awakening city intruded on the morning, he loved to walk along the sand and rocks, listening to the *scree, scree* of the sea gulls, the roar of the waves. When he closed his eyes, he imagined those waves to be sheets of rain, beating on the roof as it had in his youth. It was a comforting sound, perhaps the only comforting sound he remembered.

In memory's eye he saw himself huddled under thin blankets, sketching, drawing, inventing cartoon knights who would ride their white horses up the tenement stairs and carry him off.

On mornings such as this he would sigh for what might have been but now wasn't. Yet Dennis knew he was lucky. Most kids with beginnings like his never got out. And yet here he was, Thanks to Menolaus. Maybe that should be enough, he thought, but deep down inside knew that it couldn't be.

Dennis was fifty-five years old and believed he'd pretty much wasted his life. When he was being particularly honest, he realized he couldn't blame anyone else but himself.

He walked along the beach now as was his daily custom. Stocky, well-built, his body hard like a boxer's, he rarely gave his physical condition a thought. When he did, he chuckled at the fact that his and his lover's friends often expressed envy for his having to do so little to stay in shape. He wore running shorts and T-shirts, often torn and faded, in the summer, and baggy sweats in the winter. He wore them not as a reverse kind of snobbery as people were wont to do in a place like the Village, but because they were comfortable. He was an active man who loved to walk and run for the joy of it. Staying in shape was merely a side benefit.

He was a physical man who loved to work with his hands, whether tinkering with a motor or touching his brush to canvas. Yet it had been so easy not to touch that brush to canvas.

He half-walked, half-ran for what he knew to be just under seven miles, winding in and out around the coves and crannies of the beach, doubling back upon his own trail several times. He looked overhead, the sun still young and white in the sky. He knew his lover would soon be up. He wanted to be there today when he came downstairs.

He reversed direction and headed home. Nodding to one of many dark-suited surfers whose cars now lined the sidewalk, he jogged across the street and up the three steps to the porch.

to ride a wild pony

He stooped to gather up *The Union-Tribune, The L.A. Times* and *The La Jolla Light.* Tucking the papers under his arm, Dennis slipped off his running shoes, banged them together to dislodge damp sand and opened the door.

Once inside, he set the shoes under a small table in the hallway and tossed the newspapers onto the coffee table. Menolaus apparently hadn't come downstairs. Dennis crossed through the living room, his feet sinking in the deep pile of the carpet, a frothy blue.

He spread the thin curtain at the bay window overlooking the ocean and watched the surfers, like shiny black crayfish, crawl with their boards toward the water.

He sighed, turned, ran his fingers across the mantle of the marble fireplace, filled with bleached driftwood. Idly, he recorded the fact that it needed dusting. He thought to take a quick shower in the downstairs half-bath, so as not to waken Menolaus, in case he still lay in bed.

It was only Men's second day home; the doctor had warned him not to overdo, yet not to become inactive. Dennis thought that later they'd go somewhere for lunch. They hadn't done that in ages. La Valencia Hotel maybe; he knew Men loved the paella there. Dennis made a mental note to check Men's diet, to see if that was all right.

He worried about Men. He never took care of himself. Even in retirement, he seemed to keep pushing. He could never simply relax, not for more than a minute or two. There was his book on the evolution of Greek government, his correspondence with dozens of former students. Dennis had always felt jealous of that. But finally he accepted that it didn't mean much. And it occupied Men's time.

Sometimes Dennis wished they owned a television set. But they didn't; the only one they'd ever owned had worn out years before. And that was okay. Occasionally, of course, there was the PBS program on art and artists Dennis read about. And there were plays and other cultural programs. But he and Men had both agreed long ago that for the most part television was simply pap for the masses.

As he stepped from his clothes — which though dirty, he folded carefully and lay on the back of the olive-green commode — and then into the shower, he thought of all those times in the past, when he was stuck at home all day. Sometimes he was entertaining Boris; at other times he found he couldn't paint, and turned on the ancient black-and- white set in his and Men's bedroom.

He'd become addicted to the soaps and was fearful that Men would discover him, eyes glazed over, listening to all the problems of the world in each of these tiny microcosms. As he turned on the water, first as hot as he could stand it, and directed the spray directly against his chest, he wondered if that were redundant. Tiny microcosms. Micro did mean tiny, after all.

Soaping himself, he thought then of the microcosms of his life: the encapsulated universe of his few blocks of Brooklyn; the few weeks in greater New York; his three semesters at San Diego State, and finally, his years with Men. And he felt somehow that he'd never experienced what he should have.

That was silly, he told himself. Many people he'd known in the past would give anything to live as he and Men now lived, never wanting for anything material, able to do as they pleased. Before he'd met Men, even before Men had made full professor, Europe and Asia and the rest of the Americas were places from fairy tales. They existed only in the imagination as did the handsome and virile knights of his fantasies. Now he'd visited foreign countries on all three continents.

Using a sponge instead of a washcloth—because it was rougher and more likely to sand away scales of dead skin—he vigorously rubbed his body from face to toes.

He adjusted the spray till it became lukewarm and finally stinging cold. He turned it off and grabbed a fluffy bath towel from the rack.

After drying off, he toweled away the steam in the center of the mirror, opened the bathroom door to dispel the mist and glanced at his reflection. He was pleased with what he saw: craggy features, dark blond hair, a lightly furred body, the hair more brown than the blond of his head. He squirted shaving cream into his palm, rubbed it over his face, took out the razor that matched the one in the full-bath upstairs, and scraped away his day-old growth of whiskers, the only place where grey showed.

He rinsed his face, splashed himself with lotion and a hint of Aramis. He placed his clothes into the hamper, tiptoed upstairs and into his and Men's bedroom. He heard water running in the bathroom, knew his lover was finally up, hurriedly dressed in loose-fitting slacks, light brown, and a yellow knit shirt, his concession to any dress code La Valencia might have.

He trotted down the steps and into the kitchen, where he filled the Mr. Coffee with decaf and water for Men, not the real stuff since his heart attack, and set the kettle to boil for tea for himself. He reached into the cupboard, pulled out the copper canister, and decided on Lemon Zinger.

He popped four slices of sourdough bread into the toaster to wait till Men arrived downstairs. He took a moment then to collect his thoughts. Bill Rizzo had asked him to stop by the gallery. He didn't know why; he hoped, of course, that Rizzo would finally consent to take some of his paintings. But it was a private kind of thought, at least up till this point.

Rizzo had called while Men was still in the hospital but out of danger. He'd said there was no rush, but there was something he wanted to discuss. Dennis tucked the thought into a cubbyhole somewhere in the recesses of his mind, and took it out only for an instant or so two or three times a day. The thought was to be savored, not worn out by constant use.

But now that Men was better, nearly himself as Dr. Stevens had told Dennis yesterday, he held the thought of Rizzo's request a little longer. Yes, today would be the day he decided. When they were out to lunch, he and Men would stop by. The gallery was on Girard, only a few blocks from the hotel where they'd eat. Men could wander around and look at the paintings while Dennis and Rizzo went into the office.

The teakettle whistled; Dennis grabbed a stoneware mug from the cabinet beside the sink. He poured the hot water and then began to dunk the bag. He remembered what Men had told him the first time he'd seen him make tea.

"Dunk it, Denny. Up and down and up and down. Infuse the water with flavor. Don't try to drown the damn bag by dousing all that water on top."

That's what Dennis had always done, tossed in the bag and filled the cup with water. Now it had become a habit to do it as Men had suggested. But frankly, Dennis thought, he couldn't tell a bit of difference. But it was such a little thing, and if Men felt it was best, why not? Wasn't that what a relationship was all about? Pleasing your partner? Making little concessions that hardly mattered?

As he raised the cup to his lips, he heard Men coming down the stairs. "Morning," he said as he walked into the living room. "Sleep all right?"

He felt a rush of tenderness, as if he wanted to protect Men from all the bad things that could ever happen. And yet he knew Men was the one who had protected him for more than three-and-a-half decades.

But now it was the thought of Men's mortality, of Dennis' own mortality, that intensified his feelings. Most times he could block out those feelings, replace them with the mundane. But not now. He realized for only the second or third time ever that Men was old; he was really getting old, his face deeply lined, sagging pouches under his eyes.

Maybe Men's physical size contributed to the feelings of protectiveness. Men was a little under five-feet, five. But in all the years they'd been together, Dennis never thought of him as a little man. Not until lately.

He wore a pair of grey slacks that hung loosely. He'd lost weight in the hospital, at first unable to eat, translucent liquid in tubes running into his arm. Even his shirt was outsized now, a blue, button-down with the ever present tie. Just as Dennis always wore "comfortable" clothes, Men said he felt naked without his tie. Broadly striped in shades of gray and blue, the one he wore today was drawn too tight at the neck, accentuating the shirts ill-fit, making Dennis think of a little boy dressing up in his father's clothing.

"I put on the coffee; it's almost done. Would you like me to bring you a cup? And some toast."

Men sat in the white rattan couch, picked up the *Times* and glanced at the headlines. "It scares me," he said.

"What does?" Dennis asked, stepping briefly into the room, arranging magazines on the end table beside where Men sat—*San Diego Magazine, Newsweek, The Advocate*. There was a time, Dennis thought, not so long before, when the latter would have been kept out of sight. It no longer mattered.

"The state of the world. The way things are."

"Don't read the paper."

"Bury my head in the sand? Goddamn it, Dennis, be serious. All my life, all my life I've been concerned. I just can't turn it off."

"All right, all right, I'm sorry." Why did this always happen? Why did they always bicker? No matter what he said or Men said, it always ended like this. He wanted to drop it; it was too late.

"Christ, Dennis, what's wrong with you?" Men asked. "Don't you know we could be blown to hell or get radiation sickness from some damn nuclear plant?" He shook the paper angrily, the wrinkles disappearing.

Dennis sighed. He didn't want to stir things up. Not now, not with Men just home. "It could happen," Men continued. Dennis realized there was no stopping him, and despite himself, he began to get angry. "San Onofre's not that far away. Suppose there was an accident—another Three-Mile Island. Or just plain air pollution. Sometimes now you look out the window and see a filthy yellow mist hovering over everything. Some morning we'll walk outside and not be able to breathe."

"Come on, Men, let me get you some coffee."

"I'm sorry." He folded the paper, placed it beside him and shook his head. "I thought at my age I was supposed to accept. Remember, remember that poem, Dennis?"

"Yes," Dennis answered. "I remember." It was Men's poem, one of his many poems. Layers upon layers, exposed one by one over the time they'd known each other. They'd been together nearly five years, or was it more, before Dennis even knew Men wrote. He knew immediately the poem Men meant. "This Easing" it was called, written a decade before. Dennis claimed the sentiment as his own. Maybe because it was so foreign to his nature. Maybe because it was something to yearn for.

"I see it in their bearing," Dennis quoted.
"hear it in their voices.

They nod, smile;
in wrinkled faces a certainty.

They follow patterns—
the geometry of snowflakes,
concentric circles in a pond."

Men joined in for a line or two, then stopped.

"Similar, so similar,
they talk on street corners,
rest on benches.

Is it a contentment I see,
a wisdom?

Old women, old men
(quiet ones who helped to build
this path)
will time instill in me as well
this easing?"

Men chuckled, the sound surprisingly deep for a man his size. "How do you do it?" he asked. "Your memory—your memory's phenomenal. Sometimes I can't even remember the names of our closest friends."

"How about that coffee?" Dennis asked.

Men smiled. "Okay, Mom," he kidded. "But let's forego the toast. I can't quite face food yet."

Dennis walked back to the kitchen, grabbed a mug exactly like his, a unicorn etched on the side. "Later then," he called as he poured the steaming liquid. "I thought we might go to lunch. Would you like that?"

"No, Dennis, I don't really think so. I just want to sit and do nothing." Dennis handed him the mug, pulled out the chair to the secretary desk in the corner and sat down, occasionally sipping his tea.

"Dr. Stevens says it's okay, if you don't overdo."

"I'd rather stay home." Men's voice was clipped, the last word spoken at a higher pitch. Dennis knew he was being obstinate. Is that what old age was then? Obstinacy, not "easing," not acceptance.

"It'll do you good. To get out and see people. To be among the living." Dennis was frightened; Men had always been so active.

"No." He picked up the newspaper once more, opened it, folded it in half and placed it on his crossed knee. He looked so frail.

"I thought we'd go to La Valencia."

"I don't want lunch. Can't you understand?" His voice had almost a pleading quality.

"I want what's best for you."

"I have no appetite." His eyes were clear, light blue, a contrast to his dark complexion, his skin the golden color of roasted fowl.

And because he cared so much, Dennis lost his temper. "Just going to give up and die, are you?" And immediately he was sorry; the effect of his words were like a physical assault. Men's face drained of color, his mouth drew down at the corners.

"I don't want to go anywhere, damn it," Men finally said. "If that's what you mean by giving up and dying, then that's what I'm going to do."

Suddenly, Dennis shivered. Men really could die; he almost had. And that would mean—What would it mean? Dennis asked himself. And for the first time *the thought* touched him, barely into his consciousness. Quickly, he pushed it away.

"I figured we could stop at the gallery as well."

"The gallery? What do you mean?" Men's voice held a hint of petulance, a new thing, like that thought that had almost surfaced, and Dennis wanted to push it aside as well.

"Bill Rizzo's." Dennis voice was patient. "Remember when he stopped in to see you last week at Scripps? He told you he'd called me and said he wanted to talk." There was no response. "I thought we'd eat and walk to the gallery. Dr. Stevens—"

"The hell with what Stevens thinks. Damn it, Dennis, you're

treating me like a three-year-old." He shrugged. "Again, I apologize. I'm sorry." He smiled, or tried to smile. "Why did he want to see you?" he asked.

"Who?"

"Rizzo, isn't that who you said?"

Dennis stood up, took his own mug from the desk, reached for Men's. "More coffee?"

Men ignored the question. "What do you suppose he wants?"

Dennis tried to breathe in; his chest felt tight. "I'd hoped he'd want to see some of my work."

"Don't get your hopes up."

As quickly as it had come, the tension in his chest was gone. What he felt now he could deal with: anger. He strode to the kitchen with the mugs. "Why should I get my hopes up, huh?" He turned on the water, hard, splashing the front of his shirt and pants. Quickly, he turned it off, went back toward the living room. "Nothing I've ever done has amounted to shit."

"Come on, Dennis. Come on."

"Yeah, I know." He walked to the window, glanced outside without really seeing anything. "I'm fifty-five years old, Men." He turned. "Look at me."

"So go see him; I guess it can't hurt."

"Will you go along?" He felt vulnerable; he knew he was close to pleading.

"To the gallery? What for?"

"To lunch, damn it. And then to the gallery." He expelled a harsh breath of air. "I thought you could look at the paintings while Bill and I talked. I didn't want you to hold my hand."

"What is it, Dennis? What's wrong? I've never seen you this way before."

He didn't answer at first; then his voice was quiet. "You might have died. You might die." A sob escaped before he knew it was there.

"My God, don't you think I know that?" Men's voice had the slightest of quivers. "Jesus, I lay there for days, unable to do anything for myself, except think. Wonder. Would I live through this? Would I get better? And even if I did, what about the next

to ride a wild pony

time?" He pushed away the papers, giving up any pretense of further interest. "I'd look at those monitors; I didn't know what the hell they meant. But I was fascinated by them. What were all the little secrets they held? Did they know I was going to live? Did they predict I was going to die?" He clasped his hands between his knees.

"I didn't mean to remind you— I didn't mean—"

"There's nothing to think about. Except how old you are and how much time you have left. You can't exert yourself. You can't even shave."

Dennis' mouth felt dry. "I'm not trying to be selfish. You know that. But this may be my last chance. Thirty-five years, Men. And I've really gotten nowhere. Who else do you know who'd stick to something for thirty-five years without getting anywhere?"

"You did other things, Dennis. My God, you almost single-handedly raised Boris. I'm not the fatherly type; you are. He was more your son than mine."

"That's nonsense."

"Is it? Who did he always come to with his problems? Who did he kiss first thing every morning? Who did he ask to tuck him in at night?"

"I never thought about it; I didn't."

"I'm not blaming you; don't you see I'm grateful?"

"I could have done more; I could have done so much more."

"Couldn't we all?"

"I can't talk you into going to lunch."

"No, Dennis, you can't."

"I only want what's best."

"Give me some credit, for God's sake. I just don't feel like it, okay?"

"Jesus, Men. I'll go by myself. To the gallery. Not to lunch."

"You'll do all right."

"Sure, I always do, don't I?" He heard the sarcasm in his own voice. From feeling so good this morning, his mood had completely shifted. He had wasted his life. He'd quit school in his sophomore year. He didn't need college, he thought. He could take art classes, and that would be enough. He could use the time to paint. And to take care of Boris. Then the caring, the parenting, became the excuse for not doing anything else.

His paintings were stacked in the extra bedroom upstairs. He'd go look at them, figure out which were the best. Which Rizzo would like.

He trudged up the stairs, leaving Men to his papers. Was Dennis fooling himself? Probably. They'd known Rizzo for years; he'd never expressed an interest before. He tried to avoid the topic of Dennis' art every time he or Men brought it up.

He thought then of Men's parents, Nikkos and Theodora Aradopolos. They got along; they always got along, never seeming to fight or bicker. And they were accepting of his and Men's situation. He'd been tense when he met them, worried that because they were from the Old Country, from Greece, they wouldn't understand. But they had. They'd treated him like their very own son.

They'd died long ago. He hadn't thought of them in years. He wondered why he had now, and then he knew. There were parallels, Nikkos and his son; Theodora and Dennis. Not the obvious parallel, not that Dennis had become a wife. Not by any means; he was too much of a man for that. Straights often had trouble accepting the fact that there wasn't always one dominant and one submissive.

No, it was more that Nikkos and Men were the prosaic ones, Theodora and Dennis the dreamers. But was that fair? Wasn't it oversimplification?

He opened the door; the room was filled with paintings. Where should he begin? He didn't know. He decided the rational thing to do would be to wait and see what Rizzo said. After that would come time for decisions.

He closed the door, walked to the bedroom, picked up the phone and dialed the number he'd memorized immediately after Rizzo's call.

CHAPTER 2

San Diego, unlike the cities of the East, is a collection of neighborhoods and localities rather than a unified whole. Each area has a different flavor. Ocean Beach is Bohemian; Hillcrest gay. La Jolla is an entity unto itself. Although wealthy, it is an area where wealth in large part does not hide in secluded mansions. Rather, the locality has maintained to a degree the atmosphere of the Village it was in the thirties and forties.

Young and old stroll the sidewalks, fill the many restaurants and cafes. The business district has more bookstores per capita and more art galleries than any other section of town.

Dennis loved to stroll the sidewalks, just as he loved the beach. He called Bill Rizzo and arranged to meet him at the gallery, La Casa del Arte, on Girard. Women in summery dresses, men in shirt sleeves and ties mingled on the walkways with those wearing shorts and little else. He dodged around a young man in bright orange pants and a Beethoven T-shirt pushing a side-by-side stroller with red-haired twins.

The gallery sat a lawn's width back from the street beyond the public library. A proud Painted Lady, the Victorian house was small by standards of the period, yet solid-looking.

Rizzo had retained as much of the original interior as possible, only modernizing the kitchen. Each room downstairs held a different style of artwork, from the minutely realistic to the abstract. Dennis' work was closer to the latter, more concerned with color and light than with detail. It hadn't always been that way; rather his art had evolved.

Like most young artists, he'd imitated, perhaps unconsciously, his own favorites. Later he worked to develop a style of his own. He knew, despite everything, that his work not only had gone through drastic change but had greatly improved. He considered that largely a matter of maturity, rather than talent.

Beginning with oils and acrylics, he'd gradually changed to water colors, delighting in the patterns and effects created by various kinds of texturing, from crumpled rice paper to glue and shredded fabric.

He knew he'd wasted much of his time; he rarely painted when Boris still lived at home. And that was an excuse. But for what? He wasn't really sure. He thought maybe it had to do with his beginnings. Artists were sissies where he came from. And he'd realized at an early age, that already he was different enough. So he didn't often show his sketches to others, just a few interested teachers at the public school he attended. It was their encouragement that kept him from destroying everything he did.

He remembered a time when he was six or seven. Even then he'd drawn his knights on horseback. He'd shown one of his drawings to his father, a sullen man as Dennis remembered him, always smelling of stale beer and sweat, not the clean sweat of running on the beach, but the days' old sweat of poverty.

His father snatched the drawing from his hands, scrutinized it, laughed and crumpled it into a ball, tossing it in the direction of the trash receptacle with the broken foot pedal that squatted eternally unemptied in the kitchen.

Dennis remembered that kitchen vividly, and his wadded up drawing lying on the cracked linoleum floor.

"What the hell am I raising, some kind of faggot?" Dennis looked out the window, tears blurring his vision. Down the street a dozen tall smokestacks belched grey smoke into the air.

"Don't you like it, Daddy?" the little boy had asked.

"Why the hell ain't you outside playing ball, instead of screwing around with this kind of shit?"

Dennis shook his head as if to clear away the memory. Jesus, he told himself, I'm fifty-five years old. My father's been dead for more than forty-five years.

When he'd died, Dennis was shifted from one set of relatives to the other, all of them doing their Christian duty for poor Celia and Frank's boy. He didn't even remember his mother; his youngest brother was twelve years older than he.

The gallery was empty, except for a young couple looking at prints in a bin. "Bill?" Dennis called.

Rizzo strode from a back room, arms outstretched, hands ready to grasp whatever part of Dennis was available. Maybe the thought was unkind, but Rizzo had yet to prove otherwise. He'd been interested in Dennis for years.

He was a tall man, his body padded with fat, his lips thick, his eyes always appearing half-closed. He looked more like a defensive lineman gone to seed than the art dealer he was. Yet Dennis knew he'd never been an athlete. A one-time practicing CPA, with a penchant for collecting, he'd decided to make his hobby his business. And he seemed to be successful. He and his ex had opened the gallery years before, just after Men bought his house on Coast Boulevard.

Bill and his lover at that time lived just down the street. It was by chance they met and recognized each other for what they were. Neither Men nor Dennis knew anyone in town. Bill and Tom were newly arrived from Cleveland. For a time they became a foursome, until Tom left and Dennis let Bill know beyond any doubt that he simply wasn't interested. They'd remained friendly, but at least on Dennis' part it was a surface friendliness. Yet Dennis had the idea that if he'd given in, his paintings might now be on display in La Casa del Arte.

Rizzo grabbed Dennis' forearms, just above the wrists and squeezed. "Come on back to the office," he said. "We'll have our little talk."

"What about—" Dennis indicated the young couple.

"Oh, them." Rizzo laughed. "They come in at least once every couple of weeks. They've never bought a thing." He turned toward them. "Mr. Agostino, Tony, if you and Liz need any help …" He let his voice trail off.

"We're looking, just looking." The young man's voice was high, contradicting his husky build.

"Well, if you need me—" Rizzo spoke in an aside to Dennis, "not very damn likely," then once again to the Agostinos, "we'll be in the office. You know where that is?"

The woman, blonde hair cut short as if to fit the rim of a bowl, smiled. "Just beyond the … the facility."

Rizzo snorted, as he grasped Dennis' shoulder and led him toward the back. "Facility, you get that? She wouldn't say shit house if she was drowning in one."

They entered what once must have been a downstairs bedroom, now dominated by a large walnut desk with a marble top. "Sit." Rizzo gestured toward a chair in front of the desk.

"So," he said, lowering himself onto the seat behind the desk, elbows planted on the top, hands clasped, beefy arms extending from folded back sleeves. "Melvin's home," he said, more a statement than a question. "And everything's copesetic."

Melvin, Dennis thought. Bill was the only person who called him Melvin. But then, of course, Dennis was the only one who called him Men. With everyone else, it was Mel. That's what Dennis used to call him too, after first, of course, calling him Mr. Aradopolos. Like everyone else, Dennis thought his name was Melvin. But it wasn't.

"I just couldn't go through life," he once had told Dennis, "being some damned Spartan king. Can you imagine me giving a hoot in hell for the face that launched a thousand ships?"

They were on their way home from a bar, the first gay bar they'd gone to together. It was in L.A. Men was too frightened then of being found out to risk being seen in any bar in San Diego. That was back at the time San Diego State wouldn't even consider hiring men who weren't or hadn't been married.

They'd gone to dinner first and then to the bar, the Manhole. They'd joked about all the connotations in the name and how silly it was that the walls were hung with manhole covers. Men admitted on the way home that it was his first time ever in such a place. Dennis found that hard to believe. After all, he'd lived for years in Europe.

They were riding home in Men's old Nash, when Men reached over and drew Dennis close, his arm around his shoulder, steering one-handed. They'd just decided to live together; they'd met when Dennis enrolled in Men's intro to poly sci class. For obvious reasons, they'd wait till the end of the semester to share Men's apartment.

"You're one beautiful man, Melvin Aradopolos," Dennis had said.

"That's not my birth name, you know," Men had answered.

Dennis was surprised. "What's this mean? Have I been dating

to ride a wild pony

an imposter?"

Men had chuckled. "No, not an imposter. Just someone who didn't like his name. Someone who wanted to be an American, not a Greek." He'd told Dennis earlier that his parents had come from Greece.

"So what's your name?" Dennis asked.

"Promise you won't laugh."

It was early December, the night clear, the stars like sparked flint, the road nearly empty of traffic. It was years before the freeways were built. "I'd never laugh at you," Dennis replied. "I never would."

"Okay then, try this on for size. King Menolaus of Sparta."

"Menolaus is your name?"

"That's what it says in the birth records."

"Menolaus Aradopolos." Dennis turned and kissed him on the cheek. "God, that's wonderful. It's beautiful. Like … I don't know, like the tolling of bells, like … the most perfect painting."

Men had laughed then, long and hard. "You're an incorrigible romantic. What in the hell am I going to do with you?"

"I've got some ideas," Dennis had answered. "Menolaus," he said then. "I guess I'll call you Men, all right?" He glanced at the other man's profile. "Melvin's sort of … well, Melvin's daily business, paying the bills, taking the car in for a checkup. Menolaus is … starry nights like this one. Being together, isolated, not needing or wanting anyone else. Men is Mankind; it's a symbol; it's all that I ever want, in one person. All my Men."

"In-fuckin'-corrigible," Men had said.

"Ah, Men," Dennis had answered, then realized what he'd said. "Ah, Men. Amen. Amen. So be it; the answer to all my prayers."

He'd been young then. Yet the feeling … the feeling was still there.

He brought himself back to the present, forced himself to listen to Bill Rizzo's words.

"The thing is," Bill was saying, "I watched you. You didn't know that. Maybe I didn't even know it. But you were good. Boris adored you. So did all the other kids in the neighborhood. Everyone

---

gathered at your house."

What had he missed? Dennis wondered. What in the hell was Bill talking about?

"You were their father, confidante and guide. I saw you running along beside the kid down the street—what was his name?—because he was too scared of that two-wheeler to take off by himself. And finally, he did, Thanks to you."

Dennis shrugged. "I guess so," he said.

"So what do you think?"

"I'm sorry," Dennis said. "I must have been daydreaming."

Rizzo laughed. "I offered you a job, and you didn't even realize it."

Dennis didn't understand. "What do you mean? What kind of job?"

"My assistant's husband is being transferred. To Norfolk. He's a Seal or some damn thing in the Navy. So they're moving. You know, she keeps the gallery open for me a couple of evenings a week. Among other things, I'd like you to take over for her."

"What makes you think I'd want to do that?" he snapped, and immediately was sorry when he saw the effect of his words. Rizzo's whole demeanor changed, like a lid coming down on a box. He'd said it without thinking, because he'd hoped ... Hell, what right had he to hope? It was just that he was starting to panic.

Male menopause? A little late for that. He just hadn't accomplished anything. Exhibits at the art festival in Leucadia for a lot of years running. But, hell, anyone could get in there, the good and the bad.

He was like a goddamned housewife with no ambition. He'd taken care of the house and the kid while Daddy Men went out to work. Shit! Maybe there *was* the obvious parallel between him and Men's mother.

He wished he could apologize, but he really didn't want the job. And if he had to admit it to himself, he was a little bit insulted. Take the place of a young girl, damn it. Someone who didn't know a goddamned thing. He might as well work at McDonald's.

He stood up. "I'm sorry, Bill. Sorry." He turned without looking back and strode outside. It was the middle of September, the sun

to ride a wild pony

getting on toward the middle of the sky.

Shit! He *had* gotten his hopes up. How could he go home now? Not that Men would say "I told you so; I warned you," but he'd feel ashamed. He often had that feeling, like everything was his fault, and yet it was shameful to admit it.

After being passed among different relatives every few months, when he was thirteen, he went to stay with his Aunt Mattie. She discovered some of his drawings stuck under his side of the mattress on a single bed he shared with his cousin Max, two years younger.

He came home from school one day, and Aunt Mattie had them at the table. Three drawings. He'd progressed from his knights. One was flowers in a vase. He'd drawn it at school, looking at long dead mums on top of the bookcase by the window. He'd given them life again. Another showed a bowl of fruit, a couple of oranges, an apple, a bunch of grapes. That came from his imagination. There was never money for all kinds of fruit. And if there were, it wouldn't last long enough to go into a bowl.

The third one showed the old man who lived next door. Mr. Chambers. Ancient, wizened. Dennis had just learned that word from a fairy tale. The drawing showed him bent over the trash bin at the side of the building, rooting around with the stick he called his cane. It was a sad picture; the old man not wanting anyone to see him. Proud, yet needing anything he could dig out and hock.

"My God, Dennis," Aunt Mattie had said. "My God, where did you learn to draw like this? How did you ever capture a man on paper this way? At your age, how could you understand?" Her voice sounded hoarse, her face was red. She must be terribly angry, he thought.

He stared at the tips of his high-topped sneakers, the white part nearly worn away. "I'm … I'm sorry," he said.

"Dennis! Dennis! Look at me." He was afraid of what she would do. He looked up then and saw the tears in her eyes. "It's beautiful, honey. They're all beautiful."

The boy let out a long breath, as if he'd been holding it all his life. It wasn't bad; it wasn't wrong. Why did the other kids make fun of him then? Why did his father call him that name?

Aunt Mattie reached out and smoothed down his hair. "This

kind of talent," she said, "has to be rewarded. We'll see what we can do."

A few days later she told him she'd found out there were classes. Classes at the Y over in Flatbush. Somehow she'd find the money for carfare. Somehow things would all work out.

Two years later Aunt Mattie kicked him out.

Outside the gallery, Dennis glanced at his watch. It was nearly eleven. He'd have to go home soon and try to get Men to eat something.

He headed back down Girard and turned toward Scripps Park and on down to the Cove. When he and Men moved to the area, Dennis often cruised the guys who hung around there. He knew the ones to cruise, older men, by themselves, sun-brown bodies, lying on the sand.

He never got beyond the exchanged glances, held a second or two longer than necessary. It would have been nice … but there was always something better at home.

The beach was a mixture of sand and rock, miniature caverns, caves. He nodded to a few of the regulars, people who lived in the Village. God, how he'd screwed things up. From that great beginning with Aunt Mattie to—

Suddenly, without thinking about it beforehand, he came to the tree. Jutting here and there, twisted into angles, like an arm bent at the elbow. It stood by itself in an open space. Larger than other trees in the park, it dwarfed them, not by size but by sheer beauty. Dennis didn't know what kind it was. Someone had said he thought it was a Monterey Cypress, but it was much more noble than other trees of that species, and its leaves a deeper green.

In a philosophy class Dennis had taken his freshman year at State, the prof had talked about some philosopher who spoke of ideals. Objects in people's minds with which all other objects of the same name had to compare. But none could. Because what each person carried with him always was perfection, or at least his definition of perfection.

Then there was The Tree. Dennis felt that nothing in anyone's mind could match it. It was timeless; it was perfect, yet someday its twisted branches would die.

to ride a wild pony

He loved to view it against the Pacific. He'd painted it often. He could never capture it.

He didn't want a damn job; he wanted ... he wanted to be known. To have his paintings hang in galleries and museums and private collections.

Why? Why was it so important?

He walked to the tree, and leaned his head against the bark.

CHAPTER 3

Men walked to the kitchen and poured himself another cup of coffee. He brought it to the desk and spread the curtains. The street was filled with young people.

Suddenly, he missed Boris, missed him intensely. God Almighty, he thought, was it possible that his own son was middle-aged?

The coffee tasted strong, too strong, and Dennis had forgotten the cinnamon. Men couldn't blame him. His mind was on the meeting with Rizzo.

He sighed and let the curtains fall shut. It was like looking at a world he couldn't quite reach.

His heart was wearing out, that's what Stevens had told him, and he was terrified. He drained the dregs of his cup.

Why weren't things ever easy? Rinsing out the cup, he placed it upside down on the counter and turned off the coffee pot. Maybe he'd work on his book, try to do a page or two.

He walked to the desk, opened the drawer and pulled out the manuscript. "Although most authorities seem to agree that the City States of Athens and Sparta claimed the loyalties …"

Athens, Sparta. What did he have to say that anyone cared about? And why in the hell was he writing about Greece? Why had he written so much about Greece over the past forty years? Even his doctoral dissertation. It didn't make sense. In younger days, he'd tried to deny his ties to the country, even though he'd lived there for a time. Partly, it was his name. More than that, he didn't want to be different from his classmates in junior high and high school. But most of all, he didn't want to be what his parents were, in nationality, in temperament. He simply didn't want to be identified with them, not at all. Suddenly, his mind flashed back to his mother's deathbed, fourteen years earlier.

He'd arranged for a substitute to take over his classes, one of the new instructors, willing to please, to do what he could to achieve tenure. Then he and Dennis had flown to Boston.

In his mother's bedroom, with the flowered wallpaper, he'd

to ride a wild pony

held her hand, little more than veins and bones. Had those hands, now like the talons of a giant bird, ever really played Chopin?

Dennis had left the room, perhaps to go for a walk, Men didn't remember. Men's mother started to talk, her voice barely a whisper. He leaned close to listen.

"You cheated me; you've always cheated me. Out of a career, out of the daughter I should have had in your wife. I tried to understand; I tried to be a mother. But you made it so hard, Menolaus, even abandoning your very own name. You made it too hard. And here I am nearing death, forced to put up with you still."

Her lips moved, in a smile or a grimace? He thought she'd finished. "I know I've not been a mother to you. But you were never a son to me." She turned her head away and slept.

Men rushed from the room, down the steps and out onto the sidewalk, the October leaves brilliantly red and orange. He wandered down the street, tears blurring his vision, tears for himself, he thought, and not for his mother. As she had proclaimed he'd always done, he cheated her, lastly now of grieving.

He returned a couple of hours later, something inside him resolved. Dennis stood at the open door, his face filled with worry. "Where have you been? I went upstairs to her bedroom ..." Dennis threw his arms around him. "She's gone, Men. I'm so sorry, but she's gone."

Men fingered his manuscript, straightened the corners, laid it down. He thought then of Lucinda, something he rarely did anymore. He wondered why after all these years he felt such sharp pain at the thought of her. Beautiful Lucinda; he'd cheated her as well, that's why.

She'd trusted him, taken him at face value. And he'd totally messed up her life. Then his in-laws acted as if he didn't exist, as if their grandson didn't exist. He couldn't blame them, but he blamed himself for cheating Boris out of knowing these grandparents. The thought occurred to Men then that he suffered some sort of curse, wounding the lives of all those who loved him.

Dennis had always envied Men his childhood, his parents, his New England upbringing. Because his own childhood had been so adverse, Men never set him straight. Dennis, the romantic, seeing the world constantly through that sheer curtain at the bay window.

Hating his parents yet wanting to please them, Men had married Lucinda, not stopping to think of the consequences.

"Damn it," he muttered. It wasn't like him to dwell in the past. He was the one who identified with the young, who looked to the future. As he'd slipped into his middle years and beyond, he'd avoided people his age and older, courting instead the friendship of those much younger.

Then the force of it hit him once more. He was being betrayed by his body. He could drop dead at any time. How could he live with that, day after day? How could people with terminal illnesses live with the knowledge and still go on?

There was no god; the universe was too illogical. No supreme being could be such a joker, such an incompetent. So there was nothing. And since that was true, why should a void terrify?

He needed Dennis badly right at this moment. Instead, he reached into one of the cubbyholes of the desk and pulled out a deck of playing cards. He laid them out in an intricate pattern, a version of solitaire he hadn't played in months. It was a mechanical task, but it kept him occupied. The repetitious rhythm of turning over the cards seemed to impose a slower rhythm on his body and on his thoughts, providing calmness, dispassion.

Dennis never understood this effect. He'd never believed that the laying down of cards one by one provided a catalyst to rational thinking.

Ah, Dennis. What am I going to do? he thought. There are so many obligations, even among the old and the dying. The will's made; it's all going to Boris because that's the way it's done. Fathers are supposed to provide for their kids.

He placed an ace in the center of the circle of cards. Over the years he'd saved quite a lot. He threw down the cards and placed his head in his hands.

Once, nearly thirty years before, he'd come home from class to find his son in tears. Dennis held him, stroking his head, crooning softly. Men became aware of the song then, and couldn't help smiling at the idea. Here was Boris, seven or eight years old, and Dennis was singing: "Every evening baby goes, trot, trot, to

to ride a wild pony

town. Across the river and through the woods, up hill and down."

When Boris had been an infant, Dennis often crossed one leg over the other, set Boris on his foot and swung his leg up and down in accompaniment to the song.

"What hap—?" Men started to say.

"Later," Dennis mouthed silently.

"Okay," Men answered, going on upstairs with his attaché case.

That evening after Boris was in bed, the two men sat at the round kitchen table, Men with his coffee, the real stuff then, Dennis with his tea. Men again asked him what had happened. "They were calling him names, that's all."

"What names?"

"I'd rather not say." The light from the ceiling played through Dennis' hair with a halo effect.

Men remembered feeling afraid. "Tell me, Dennis," he demanded.

"They started in about his not having a mother—"

"And?"

"They made up this stupid rhyme. One of them made it up. They were kids a few years older."

"For God's sake, Dennis, what rhyme?"

At first, he didn't answer, then seemed to come to a decision. "Your father is a fairy; your mother has no box. She and your father suck each other's cocks."

"Oh, Jesus Christ, Jesus Christ Almighty." Men had slammed his fist onto the table top, stood up, stormed into the living room and back. "Who in the fuck would think of a thing like that?"

Remembering the incident, Men realized he'd been the emotional one when usually it was Dennis. But was that true? It depended on the circumstances. Small things set Dennis off. When majors problems arose, he reacted calmly, rationally.

Dennis took to parenting instinctively. In light of his background, that was surprising, Men thought. Where had he learned such skills, such a capacity for love? Men often regretted the non-parenting of his own son. It had been so easy simply to let Dennis take over.

Sometimes that seemed lifetimes ago; at other times just

yesterday that he was a young instructor, glad to be settled in a warm climate, thinking of little beyond getting tenure.

He sighed; he'd never been fair to Dennis in any way. Not that he considered himself an evil man, but that he had appetites and needs.

He thought he might write a letter to Boris. They hadn't seen each other in more than two years, what with Boris establishing his practice and Melissa back in grad school now that the two kids no longer needed constant care.

He sat at the desk once more, pulled out a couple of sheets of paper and picked up the pen from the desk set.

What would he say? he wondered. He didn't want to worry Boris with his condition. He hadn't even told him he'd been in the hospital. He wished he could see him, as well as his grandchildren and Melissa.

"Dear Kids," he wrote and then was stuck. There was nothing to say, no news. Maybe if Dennis found out something from Rizzo …

He put the pen down and picked up the deck of cards.

When Dennis came in a little later, Men felt ashamed that he'd wasted the morning. But that was irrational; there was nothing he had to do. The back of his throat ached. Self-pity, he thought?

Dennis stormed into the living room. "That damned Rizzo!"

"What is it, Denny? What happened?" He read hurt, anger, anguish on his lover's face. "Why are you so upset?"

"He offered me a job, can you believe it? A job?"

Men didn't understand. "A commission, you mean? A commission to paint something?"

"Hell, no!" Dennis strode to the kitchen, turned on the tap and returned with a glass of water, sloshing it over the side. "His assistant's quitting. He wanted me to take over for her."

"What's so bad about that?"

"What's so bad?" He took a gulp of the water, went back to the kitchen. Men heard him empty the glass in the sink. In a moment he was back. "Jesus, Men, you were right. I did get my hopes up. I thought maybe this was the time; maybe he wanted to give me a show." He walked to the couch and sat down hard. "Why the fuck don't I just give up? Why didn't I give up years ago?"

Men stood, walked over behind the couch and began to knead Dennis' shoulders. "It's all right, Babe, it's okay."

Dennis jerked away. "Don't you understand that all these years I must have been deluding myself? I'm not a goddamned painter."

Men sighed. He wished he could ease the frustration, tell him that overall it didn't really matter. Except maybe it did. Maybe that's why he himself wrote, obscure books published by little university presses. Books on Greece, for God's sake. What was he trying to prove? And to whom? What was Dennis trying to prove? "I know there's nothing I can say that will help."

"You were right, Men. I went there with too many expectations."

Men shrugged. "You're entitled; everyone's entitled."

"I feel I've wasted my whole damn life. I've never worked; I've never done anything."

"And I think that's mostly my fault." Dennis started to interrupt, but Men allowed him no chance. "While you were gone, I did a lot of thinking. And I finally admitted to myself that I've done many things wrong. A lot of things that have to do with you."

"I don't understand. I don't see much you did wrong."

Men sat in the rattan chair in the corner. It was the time for admissions; maybe there wouldn't be another time. "I'd expect you to say that, but it's not true."

"What the hell are you talking about? You gave me everything, freedom to paint, freedom from any financial worries. God, you gave me everything."

"I gave you nothing," Men said, finally bringing it into the open, something he'd rarely even let himself consider. "I was selfish. I wanted you and so I set out to get you. And once I had you, I never loosened the reins."

"Jesus Chr—"

He held up a hand. "Let me continue." His mouth felt dry. "I offered no objection to your quitting school, allowing you to continue to think it was the best course."

"Hell, Men, I was nearly twenty years old. I made my own decisions."

"Maybe I made it too easy," he said and knew he'd touched a sore point.

"Became my sugar daddy?" Dennis was on his feet. "Yeah, I've thought of that. I even admit it bothered me sometimes. But I pushed the concerns away. You were getting something in return for—" His anger seemed to burn out.

"I love you, Men. Don't you know I've always loved you?" Suddenly, he laughed. "Sure, at first I thought maybe I was a little weird for falling for one of my professors. What I started to say was that it was a kind of business deal. I took care of Boris, saw things ran smoothly from day to day."

"I made you a … glorified housekeeper? A baby sitter?" Men saw the anger was back, but he had to risk saying what needed to be said. "The truth of the matter is I did the same thing to you that my father did to my mother." He hurried on before he lost his nerve. "You romanticized my parents, Dennis. What a good relationship they had. How they got along."

"I think they did."

"Well, you're wrong. Mother trained to be a concert pianist, you know that. She was damned good. At least all the critics said so."

"But her family came first, what's wrong with that?"

"No." Men felt a bitterness, because he knew he didn't come first. Maybe it appeared that way, but it wasn't so. "Nobody works as hard as she did and then wants to give it up. You wondered where I went that day, that day she died. The last words she spoke to me, the last words, I'm sure, that she ever said accused me. Accused me of cheating her of the kind of love she wanted."

"Oh, Jesus, Men, I can't believe that."

"It's true, all right. Hell, Denny, they were from the old country. A woman obeyed. She did what her husband told her."

"You're implying your father forced her into it."

"You're damned right he did. Just like I forced you into your role."

"You didn't force me; I had my eyes wide open."

"Go outside, Dennis. Look around. How old do you suppose the kids at the beach are? The swimmers? The surfers?"

---

to ride a wild pony

"I don't know. Late teens; early twenties. What's that got to do with anything?"

"Take a good look at them the next time you go out. That's how old you were, Dennis." He let out a deep sigh. "I didn't deliberately set out to fuck you up; I don't mean that I did. I wouldn't do that. It was simply unthinking selfishness."

"You're saying those kids out there don't know their own minds?"

"Yeah, Denny, something like that." He walked to the window, stared out. "Look at them. They don't accept responsibility. For them it's eternal playtime. Jesus, Dennis, I know people that age. I taught them for nearly forty years."

Suddenly, he felt ancient, defeated. What he'd said to Dennis had as much meaning for himself. Those were the people he'd identified with. Like them, he hadn't accepted responsibility for his life, for his family. He'd accepted responsibility only for that part that pleased him—to be somebody, a scholar, an internationally recognized authority on Greek government. Blind, like his father had been blind. Grasping for achievement like his mother had wanted to grasp.

Dennis picked up a magazine, leafed through it without looking at the pages. "But you're wrong. All kids are different. I knew what life was like. Shit, Men, I grew up in the slums."

Men decided to let all of it go, like a great burden suddenly released. "Mother resented it deeply. That she had to devote her life to her husband and me. If you knew what to look for, you could tell."

"You're down on everyone today, aren't you, Men?"

He supposed he'd hurt Dennis' feelings; he didn't know. "For once I'm facing facts. It's about time I did." He sat by the desk, folding his hands across his chest. He shook his head. "I could lie to myself. I could say that I honestly believed your quitting school was the best move. I suppose I even talked myself into it." He bit his lip, remembering two separate sets of circumstances. "By the time I was in high school, Mom rarely played the piano at all."

Suddenly, he felt drained. Dr. Stevens had told him to avoid strong emotion. To avoid conflict and stress. How could he? Didn't living mean feeling? Unless you felt strongly, you might as well ... He'd go upstairs and rest. He needed very badly to rest.

"Look, Men, if this is the time for confessing things ... There's something I need to tell you." Men could see Dennis was struggling, had trouble getting his breath. He'd started to rise but sat back down. He wondered what was so momentous to affect Dennis this way. He was the most guileless man Men had ever known.

"I've been so scared, Men. I've never been so frightened in my life as I've been the last few weeks." He stood up, walked to the stairs and back. "Never in my life, before I met you, did I have anyone. For a time I thought my Aunt Mattie ..." He seemed to Men barely able to contain himself, and Men wasn't sure he wanted to hear this confession.

"Whatever it is you want to tell me, it can't be that important. Can it?"

Dennis stopped, completely still and stared at Men, as if what he'd said were completely irrational. "I can't stand the waiting and the wondering." His voice broke. "God, Men, I understand what you were trying to tell me. I understand too well."

His breaths came in rasps. "What's to become of me? You talk about being selfish. But what about me? You almost died, and I was thinking of me. My God, Men, I've never done anything. Never even held a job. I have nothing beyond what you gave me."

Men did know; what Dennis said was true. "The house. It's in both our names. It would be yours."

"Yeah, I have the house. I can't live on that. And I can't stand the worry, and I can't stand the waiting." He stopped for a moment and then continued. "And then I had this thought—" He shook his head. "I tried to push it away; but it keeps coming back. Maybe the anticipation is worse than the reality. And so—" He had trouble getting the words out. "And so I thought, no, a part of me wished—wished that it was over."

Men didn't understand at first. Then it was like an icy chill engulfed his body. "You wanted me dead. Oh, Jesus, Denny, you wanted me dead." His own voice seemed far away; it had a quality he didn't recognize.

"I'm sorry, Men. I'm so sorry." His arms dropped to his sides,

---

to ride a wild pony

he stood completely still. He rushed to Men and threw his arms around him. "No, Men, no. I'm dreading it. Dreading what's going to happen. But, yeah, there's that little part of me that sometimes wants it all to be over, so I don't have to worry anymore. So what do you think of me now?" He let go of Men, strode to the door and went outside.

Men turned to watch him, half running, half jogging down the street. And in that single moment Men knew that he loved Dennis more than he ever had before.

CHAPTER 4

Dennis trotted on down toward the Cove and sat on one of the benches. Jesus, he thought, he must be crazy. His words had shocked the hell out of Men; he saw it in his face. Why couldn't he keep his damn thoughts to himself? He buried his face in his hands. He supposed he'd done it because ... because he wanted the air cleared; he didn't want anything hidden.

The bench faced down the bank at a beach where kids played in the sand, where men and women, singly and in pairs, lay on blankets or towels. Occasional swimmers bobbed up and down in the distance.

Men didn't think Dennis knew what Stevens had told him, but Dennis knew. And that was stupid as well, telling Men his heart was wearing out. What the hell did that mean anyway?

"Damn," Dennis muttered. He felt like smashing things; but there was nothing to lash out at. He stood up, walked down a flight of steps to the sand and on out to the water. He knelt, let the water pour over his hands. It was cold, always cold. He hadn't expected that when he'd moved from the East. The water didn't match the climate. In New York the sea was warm.

He stood up, rubbed his hands down the sides of his pants. He'd always ignored the differences between his age and Men's. Anyway, seventy wasn't that old. A person that age should expect to have a long time left.

Without warning his eyes teared. He'd always realized that someday he'd probably have to face Men's death, but years into the future.

He wandered across the stretch of sand. Rocks formed caves and caverns, braced with supports. Signs forbade entry. He came to another flight of steps and climbed to the top, barely aware he was out of breath and shouldn't be.

He walked down Girard till it ended near the country club, cut over to Fay and turned left on Nautilus. He rarely walked this direction, away from the main part of town.

to ride a wild pony

He tried to think rationally of what he would do if Men actually died. There was absolutely nothing he'd trained for. Of course, he'd have the house, but what good would that do? It was worth quite a bit, of course, and he could sell it. Then what? Where would he go? He couldn't make the money last.

He walked toward Soledad Park. Up on the hill stood the Easter Cross, high above the town. Once it had nearly been destroyed by vandals.

The sun burned down; Dennis felt damp with sweat. Men wasn't dead, he told himself. If he took it easy, he could live for a long, long time.

He stepped up his pace. Maybe Men was right about making it too easy for Dennis to leave school. But it had been his own fault as well. His whole damn life had been all screwed up, and that was a chance to change it. But that wasn't all of it. He genuinely thought that getting a degree didn't matter. He thought he'd beat the odds and make it as a painter.

What the fuck had he been thinking of? In frustration he started to run. He'd turn on La Jolla Scenic Drive and start to circle back.

Painting hadn't been the reason! Hell, he knew that. He just didn't want to admit it. It wasn't even Boris, even though he played a part.

Dennis remembered his disbelief at saddling a poor little kid with a name like that. It reminded him of Russian statesmen, dressed in somber suits.

Boris was anything but somber. The happiest kid Dennis had ever seen, he seemed to find laughter in almost everything, going for a walk, playing with his toys. When Dennis and Men started dating, Boris was not quite three.

When they both agreed it might be getting serious, Men picked Dennis up at his apartment on College Avenue, a few blocks from San Diego State.

"Instead of going out to eat," Men said, "I thought I'd cook dinner. Greek food? Okay?"

All Dennis knew about Greek food was that it sometimes came in grape leaves and often involved lots of lamb, which definitely wasn't his favorite. He reluctantly agreed.

"Besides," Men said, "there's someone I'd like you to meet."

"Who?" Dennis asked.

"Another dinner guest."

No matter how much Dennis tried, he couldn't get Men to say more. At that time Men lived in an apartment, actually the bottom half of a house built on a slope, a mile or so from campus.

Dennis wore khaki chinos and a T-shirt with broad green and white stripes, casual clothes. He worried that maybe it would be inappropriate for a dinner party.

Back then Men drove a VW bug, bright red. They pulled to the curb, and suddenly Dennis felt apprehensive. He wasn't used to dinner invitations. He'd come from the slums; he felt he didn't have many social graces.

"Are you sure it will be all right?" he asked.

Men seemed surprised. "Getting cold feet, are you?"

Dennis flushed with embarrassment. "Maybe," he said. "You know my background, Men. God, even going to college for someone like me—"

Men reached over took his hand and raised it to his lips. "I'm sorry, Denny. I don't mean to make you uncomfortable." He shrugged. "I could say I want it to be a surprise, but … I really don't know what my motives are."

He released Dennis' hand and opened the car door. "Come on," he said. "It'll be all right."

A locked gate led to a yard filled with gravel and cactus plants. Men fiddled with the key, held the gate for Dennis and led him around the house and down some steps.

A woman met them at the door, grey-haired, overweight. Dennis wondered who she was. Men had told him he lived alone. Was she the other dinner guest?

Suddenly, a little boy darted around her, laughing, and leaped into Men's outstretched arms. Men picked him up and turned to Dennis. "Denny," he said, "this is Boris. Boris, this is Mr. Thompson."

"Hi," the little boy said and held out his hand.

"Hi, Boris," Dennis said, his voice light. The two of them shook hands.

---

to ride a wild pony

Men turned to the woman. "Mrs. Vasquez," he said, "this is one of my students, Dennis Thompson."

She gathered up a sweater and purse by the door. "Nice to meet you," she said as she came outside. "I'll see you tomorrow morning, Mr. Aradopolos." She hurried toward the side of the house.

"Well," Men said, "this is the other dinner guest. He's my son."

Thinking back, Dennis knew it was love at first sight. He'd told Men the same thing later. "And why not?" he added. "Like father, like son."

While Men fixed dinner, Dennis and Boris told each other stories, a talent Dennis didn't realize he had, and played hide and seek and catch.

After eggplant and lamb, covered with bechamel sauce, which changed Dennis' mind about lamb, all three sat on the couch. "So what do you think?" Men asked.

Dennis was puzzled. "What do you mean?"

"I guess I mean—does it surprise you? Does it shock you? Does it bother you?"

Dennis frowned.

"I hoped so much you'd get along. My two favorite men in the world. I want you to get along."

Boris crawled into Dennis' lap, stuck a thumb into his mouth and closed his eyes.

"I think that answers my question," Men said. He looked hard at Dennis. "Maybe it wasn't fair to spring this on you. You never even knew I'd been married."

"No," Dennis said, shaking his head. He hugged Boris tightly against him. "I think he likes me too."

"God, Denny," Men said, "where would I ever find anyone else like you?"

Dennis loved to spend the days with Boris, teaching him things, playing games. Often the three of them spent whole weekends together, going to the zoo or the beach, taking long drives, packing impromptu picnics. Men was an excellent cook.

Out of breath, exhausted now from his second long jaunt of the day, Dennis slowed to a fast walk. They'd shared so many things. Boris' growing up, starting to school, going into junior high, graduating, leaving for college, getting married.

It hadn't all been easy. The other kids found out about Dennis and Men. That first time came as a shock, though Dennis should have suspected. It was a spring day, early June, just before the end of the school year. Dennis looked out the window to watch for Boris. He saw him hurrying down the street, three or four older boys trailing after.

At first, Dennis wondered what was happening; he couldn't hear the words. When he did, the unexpectedness of it took his breath away so that he had to lean on the window sill.

He went out on the porch. They were in the La Jolla house by then. Suddenly, Boris bolted for the steps and raced into the house. The others, all kids Dennis knew, saw him then and tried to slink away. Dennis played ball with these kids, took them on hikes, so he knew they were basically good.

It must have been one of the parents, he thought. He doubted the kids were old enough to realize what the words meant.

Boris lay face down on the couch, sobbing. Dennis went over, rubbed his shoulders, picked him up, carried him to the chair and held him. He didn't know what to say; he simply tried to comfort him.

Once he calmed down, Boris asked what the other boys meant. He was a thin kid, dark complexioned, probably like his mother. Sitting on the floor now, arms around his knees, he gazed intently at Dennis.

Dennis avoided answering directly. It wasn't the time to go into his and Men's relationship. "People do mean things sometimes," he said. "Even people we think are our friends. There's not much we can do about it, except love each other." At the time Dennis had the fleeting thought that he and Men should split up but knew it wouldn't solve anything. It could give the impression that gays were weak, somehow not as good as straights.

The episode had blown over except that two of the kids weren't allowed to associate with Boris anymore. Apparently, their parents had found out what had happened.

Yet the house was still a gathering point for the neighborhood. Sometimes, Dennis saw, it bothered Men to come home and face a houseful of Boris' friends, and to have kids wandering in and out at all hours, but he never made an issue of it.

Back on the corner of Nautilus and Fay, Dennis looked at his watch. Despite what had happened, he should go on back and see if Men felt like eating. The sun sent up waves of heat from the sidewalk.

Hands in his pockets, he ambled toward the house. He'd always thought of himself as a person who had his head in the present. Yet for several weeks, since Men's heart attack, he found himself again and again meandering through the past.

In high school Boris had understood all the implications of Dennis' and his father's relationship. There'd been no repeats of the name-calling incident, at least so far as Dennis knew. Yet, by the time he was fourteen or fifteen, Boris was ashamed. Friends no longer came to the house. Dennis would hear them out on the sidewalk talking. But when he'd step outside, Boris would hurry past him and on inside, and his friends would leave.

That hurt. Part of it Dennis put down to the natural sequence of change, a teenager's need to seek independence. But it was more than that.

One day as Boris raced past him, he called him to stop. He didn't know why he'd felt a sudden anger. Maybe he and Men had argued; maybe his feelings had simply built up. He followed Boris inside.

"Why is it—" Dennis shouted. Boris turned. Dennis continued more quietly, still defensive, not allowing any cracks to show. "Why is it that suddenly your father and I are pariahs? Will you answer that, Boris? Can you tell me why?"

Boris had filled out, put weight on his frame. Black hair spilled over his forehead. On his face was a look of defiance. "I don't know what you mean," he said.

Men was off somewhere, probably at school. Dennis softened a bit, at the look of fright on Boris' face. Not that Boris could be afraid of anything physical; Dennis would never intentionally hurt him. But he apparently knew what was coming. He realized there'd be a confrontation. "Stay down here for a minute, will you please?" Dennis walked to the chair by the far wall, glancing over his shoulder to see if Boris followed.

He waited then for Boris to sit down, in the middle of the couch, space around him, as if consciously giving himself room to escape. He looked ready for flight.

"It's time we talk about it," Dennis said. "We simply can't let it go on any longer."

"I don't know what you mean."

"If we don't talk, it'll just keep eating away."

"All right," Boris answered, staring straight into Dennis' eyes. "Say what you want. I'll listen."

For a moment Dennis had doubts. Maybe it would be better not to go through with this. He paused, undecided. "People are like they are," he said. "Most of the time they can't do a great deal about it."

"Maybe ..." Boris looked away, bit his lip, looked back. "Maybe they don't want to do anything about it."

"Since we're talking in generalities, I'll admit that's true. But let's change that a little. In certain respects I have no control over what I am. At the same time I wouldn't want to change it even if I could."

"Oh, fuck," Boris had answered. "This is shit, man. Just plain shit." He stood up. "I know what you are; you're the kind of ... of person kids make jokes about at school."

Dennis refused to get upset, at the language—he'd never heard Boris use that kind of talk—or at the thought. "And what's your reaction when they do? Come on, damn it. Tell me. You're the one who brought it up."

"No. You're the one who brought it up. Not me, but you."

Dennis signed. "Okay. All right."

"May I go now?"

"Of course, you may go. I never meant to keep you against your will."

Dennis knew he lost a little that day. There was a stiffness after that, a holding back. Later, when Boris was on his own, when he'd finished med school, it would be hard for anyone else to find this stiffness. But it was there.

***

to ride a wild pony

After Dennis left, Men stretched out on the couch, something he rarely did during the day. He closed his eyes, thought he'd just rest for a time.

Something had to be done; something had to be reconciled about Dennis. He didn't know what.

For the second time then he thought of Lucinda, how they'd met, how under other circumstances their paths might simply have crossed and they might have forgotten each other in a day or a week.

After graduating from Harvard, Men had taken something akin to the Grand Tour, so popular in earlier ages. He'd gone to Europe, bumming around from one country to another, taking classes here and there, at whatever school suited his fancy at the time.

In Italy one of his classmates gave a party and invited him. In attendance was a young woman with piercing black eyes and an infectious grin. He knew only that her name was Lucinda. They started to talk, about nothing at all of importance, and found they enjoyed each other's company. Men had no thoughts that things would go further. He knew what he was, and his parents knew. He'd always thought that much of the reason for providing the money for his stay in Europe, beyond wanting him to discover the background from which he'd come, was as a bribe. We'll do this for you, they seemed to be telling him, if you'll forget all those ideas of yours.

But he and Lucinda became fast friends, meeting at cafes, sometimes at the theatre. Never would she allow him to call for her. Finally, she admitted the reason. She knew little about his background, only that he was an American of Greek descent.

They were walking down the street, hand-in-hand, a noisy street, filled with taxis and private cars, all impatiently blasting their horns. Gaps in the green leaves showed off a brilliant Italian sky.

She drew him to a little table at a sidewalk café; they ordered coffee. They would meet friends later for dinner. He could tell she was nervous. She kept patting he lips with the napkin, pulling on a strand of hair.

"I don't want to—how can I say it—push you away. But I have

---

to ride a wild pony

something I must tell you. What I've been avoiding." She blew her nose lightly on a lace handkerchief. "My family …"

"I've wondered about them," he said, apprehensive about what she might tell him.

"Yes," she answered. "I didn't want to frighten you. I do not know much about you. Only that you are an American. And perhaps such things mean more to Americans."

"What things, Luce?" he asked, puzzled by her nervousness.

She told him then. "My family is titled. I myself am titled."

Men had laughed. "So? You're certainly not a princess, are you? My Princess Lucy."

"Oh, Melvin," she said, "you make a joke."

He spread his hands, palms up. "Do I?"

"I am the Countess Lucinda." He started to speak but she hurried on. "I didn't tell you, not because I'm ashamed of you. I would never want you to think such a thing. But I know so little of Americans. I thought—"

"That the title would scare me away."

"Yes." He could see the mist in her eyes.

"Oh, Lucy," he said. "You must know I love you." And in that moment he was sure he did, despite the other thing, the other feelings. The young men he'd known. Beautiful men with handsome faces and gorgeous bodies, always a little younger than he. Usually Scandinavian or at least blond.

"And I love you," she answered. And he began to think it might work. His mother and father always questioned him about young ladies in his life, hoping perhaps that he was going through some sort of phase. He'd always had to tell them there were none.

He met her parents, who offered only a slight objection to the romance. After all, his family was, if not wealthy, at least respected and well to do, his father a surgeon.

He decided that afternoon at the café that someday they'd marry. He'd picked up a European degree; he wanted to teach, but there was no hurry. He still had money. He'd intended to return to the States, find a job as an instructor and enroll in a doctoral program.

But what would that mean to Lucinda? He ignored the

practicalities; so did she. In a few more months they were married. And then she was dead.

Remembering, he sighed and sat up.

Why had he ever let the marriage happen? It was wrong; wrong for him, wrong for poor Lucinda who trusted him, who was willing to risk the censure of her family's friends, and marry him. She'd even follow him to America, she said, although that had been far from settled.

Suddenly, another memory intruded. He and Dennis had been together maybe a couple of years. Already Men had begun to stray. He'd had good intentions, but he couldn't follow through. Dennis was everything he wanted, but still …

The risks were great, he knew, but he couldn't help it. And he didn't fully understand. He loved Dennis, would never want to lose him, but there was always that student. Blond, well-built— to be honest about it, almost replicas of Dennis.

It was more than a need; it was as if he were driven. Maybe, he thought, he wanted acceptance. He could never live up to what his parents wanted. No matter that he learned five languages, could converse intelligently on a hundred different topics. It was never enough. But if that special student accepted him, wouldn't that prove his worth?

Actually, it didn't. There was always the next one. Anyhow, the answer was too pat; it smacked of pop psychology.

He'd come home late, expecting Dennis to be asleep, since he rose so early every day. Instead, Dennis sat in the living room, the light from the kitchen throwing shadows across the carpet.

Men thought at first Dennis had forgotten the light, so he started toward it to turn it off before he went upstairs. He was startled when Dennis spoke. He sat by the window, the chair turned toward the street.

"What's your excuse this time?" He swung around, snapping on the desk light. In the harsh glare, his features looked pasty white. "Was he cute? Well-hung? I bet he was tall and blond and good-looking. And who knows what you promised him?"

"What the hell are you talking about?" Men asked. He blustered because he was frightened.

"I'm familiar with the routine." He stared out the window, away from Men. "I called the school to ask you to stop at the grocery store. And I knew it had happened again. Every time the department secretary becomes evasive about your whereabouts ..."

"Hell, Dennis, for all you know—"

"No, Men, no more bullshit."

Men had gotten angry. "Why don't you come right out with it then? Instead of spouting innuendos." He reached for the light switch on the wall. "And for Christsake, why does this look like some goddamned interrogation room?" He flicked the switch; diffused light glowed from the ceiling.

"All right, damn it, I want to know where you went."

"That's none of your goddamned business." He shrugged out of his sport coat, strode to the hall closet and hung it up.

"You weren't working this late. It's not the end of the term. There are no papers that need grading. No exams to plan."

Dennis sat there, hands dangling between his legs. Men wished he could go over and pull him up and hold him. "So I'm home late. So what?"

"I want to know where you were."

"Jesus, am I on trial in my own home?"

"If so, I'm sure you're guilty."

Men sat on the couch opposite Dennis. "What makes you think I was with anyone?" He didn't want to lie, but he couldn't admit it. Dennis was too important to him to risk losing him that way.

Dennis' voice sounded weary. "Then tell me you weren't."

"This is asinine, Dennis. I've had a rough day. Okay? I've been gone since seven this morning."

"Whose fault is that?"

Men felt himself become angry. "What the hell's that supposed to mean?"

"You have a roving eye. I know how you operate. I stole you away myself. Remember that kid, the one who wanted to be a Presbyterian minister?"

Men stood up. "So what?" He sighed. "I'm tired, Dennis. I want to go to bed." He started toward the stairs. Dennis words stopped him.

to ride a wild pony

"So are you going to drop me too?"

Men turned, shocked. My God, did Dennis really think ... "I wouldn't do that." His voice broke. "You know, I wouldn't do that."

Dennis' voice had a pleading quality. "So where were you, Men?"

He turned and came back to the room and stood looking down at Dennis. He felt totally drained. "Okay, Denny. I *was* out with someone. Is that what you want to hear?"

"God, Men. My God."

"Oh, Denny." He knelt down and reached for Dennis' hands. "He means nothing to me. Nothing. Can you believe that?"

Dennis refused to allow them to touch. "Then why? Why did you do it?"

Men got up, walked to the couch and turned. "I don't know. I don't understand."

Dennis' words were forced, barely understandable. "If you want me to leave, I will. Do you want me to leave?"

The ironic thing was, Men thought, he'd spent the evening talking mostly about Dennis. Why, he asked, himself, did he have such a talent for messing things up?

He was jolted from his thoughts as he heard Dennis come up on the porch.

CHAPTER 5

Dennis looked tired and sweaty when he came through the door. Men felt he understood what Dennis had told him, maybe even better than Dennis himself. It wasn't that he wished Men dead. Rather, it was allowing himself to face the worst that could happen. Men knew Dennis too well to think otherwise. And he had this compulsion to be totally open. He never seemed to accept that sometimes it was best to keep things to yourself.

He watched him come into the room before he spoke.

"Look, Denny," he said, "I can understand your feelings. And it's okay. I was shocked at first ... and upset. But people can't help what they think."

Dennis frowned as if in bewilderment. "I love you so much. I can't understand what made me have such a thought."

"Human nature, I suppose. It's not worth worrying about."

Dennis smiled as he walked toward the steps. "I'm tired. I'm going to take a nice long shower."

"I'd like to talk to you."

Dennis turned. "Right now?"

"If you don't mind."

"I suppose not." He came back into the room. "What is it?"

"Sit down for a minute, will you?" He waited as Dennis sat in the rattan chair. "I told you before, I've been doing a lot of thinking. Not just now, but in the hospital." He looked at Dennis; he wanted to say this right. "I don't mean to be melodramatic, but when I lay staring up at the cracks in the ceiling, I imagined I could see all the facets of my life there between the walls." He tilted his head. "There wasn't a great deal I'd change. I almost thought I wouldn't have married. But if I hadn't, I wouldn't have Boris."

"I'm sorry, Men, for what I said. I had no right to tell you that."

"Hell, Denny, nobody's perfect. Not even you or me." He paused for a moment, tension making him short of breath. "You know, I've never really told you about what happened with Lucinda."

"She found a photo or something. Of you and another guy?"

---

to ride a wild pony

"Of me and a friend, yes. An innocent photo, or so I'd believed."

They were in the hotel, the first morning of their marriage. They'd come to Leipzig for a few days before going on—to Paris, London and back to America, just for a visit.

Men stepped into the shower just as Lucinda called to him. "Darling, where are our tickets?"

"My suitcase," he said. "In one of the side pockets, I think."

She told him she wanted to check on their departure time. "Okay," he said, turning on the spray, waiting for the water to become warm.

He remembered every detail, the brown water stains, the porcelain handles of the faucet. He soaped his body, the thick mat of hair on his chest, the coarser hair further down. Turning around and around, he let the water play over him.

He stepped out to hear Lucinda screaming. At first he couldn't understand the words. "That man; that man in the photo. I recognize that man."

He didn't know what she meant. He stood, dripping water, trying to make sense of her words. Then he felt a jolt of fear. He'd left a photo in the flap of his suitcase. He'd meant to remove it, but then he'd forgotten. It was a photo of two people kissing, the wrong two people.

She yanked open the bathroom door, her face distorted in fury. "How dare you," she screamed. "How dare you taunt me with such a thing." She ripped the photo in half. "Everyone knows what he is!"

"Calm down," Men answered, taking a step toward her.

"Don't you touch me. Don't come near me." He stopped, slipping, almost losing his balance on the tile floor. "I want you to get out. Do you understand what I say?"

He felt sick; it couldn't be happening. He'd tried; he'd tried so hard. Not seeing any of his male friends, cutting them off, except for those he knew to be wholly heterosexual.

The photo really was innocent. He and the other man, Paul, had simply been friends. They'd met at a gallery and started to talk. Paul was an expatriate from Nebraska. His parents had given him a sum of money and told him never to show his face again. He wandered to Europe, picked up odd jobs here and there, before settling down.

Often after that first meeting they found they'd been invited to the same parties, attended the opera or the theatre on the same nights. There was nothing sexual between Men and Paul. They'd never been attracted to each other.

The photo was taken at Paul's friends house, his lover's house, an older man, very wealthy. They'd been together four years. Men become good friends with them both.

At the wedding Paul had given Men a copy of the photo. "Since you're leaving," he said, "I might not get to see you soon again. I want you to have this. Think of me and Nils when you look at it."

Men had slipped it into the inside pocket of his coat. "I envy you, in a way," Paul had said, "that you're able to do this. To have this marriage. Nils and I, we're happy, I suppose. But it's hard to live as we do. Others don't understand."

Touched by what the other man said, Men threw his arms around his shoulders and drew him close. "Take care of yourself, and take care of Nils," he said and hurried away.

"Lucinda, please, please listen to me," Men had pleaded. "He's a friend. Nothing more than a friend."

"And, of course, you deny you are anything like him."

"No, Lucinda, I don't." He started to shiver, and wrapped the bath towel around his body. "I admit I've had those kinds of feelings."

"I suspected as much," she said. "But you tricked me."

He dropped the towel and stepped into the bedroom. "I didn't mean to trick you," he said, taking a step toward her.

She picked up a glass and threw it, barely missing his head. "I want you to get out. You … you fucking homosexual."

"Please, please, Lucy …"

"The Countess Lucinda," she said. "To you I'm the Countess Lucinda."

Like a cornered animal striking back, she picked up a tray, a desk set, her purse and threw them each as hard as she could, sobbing, gasping, screaming. She pulled off her wedding ring, her engagement ring, and slammed them into the wall.

---

to ride a wild pony

"Get out. Get dressed and get out. I never want to see you again. I never want to hear your name again. I never want to think of you again." She sobbed hysterically.

He grabbed some clothes, not caring what he wore. She sat in a chair by the bed, her face puffed and blotchy. "My friends tried to tell me," she said. "They tried to tell me what you are like. I refused to believe the stories."

"He's nothing but a fucking queer," they said. "But no, I told them, not my Melvin. Not my love. Oh, yes, they said, we saw him on the Boulevard. He was with a man called Robert. A man called Sidney. A man called Raymond. I ignored them because I couldn't make myself believe … But it's true. It's true." She looked up at him, and he'd never seen such hate before, such disgust. "Leave me alone," she cried. "Get out! Get out!" Again she seemed to go wild. She grabbed a cut glass bottle, expensive perfume. It hit him above the eye; he felt blood run down his face.

As soon as he could, he struggled into his clothes and hurried to the door, abandoning his belongings. Out in the hall, he heard the glass in the bureau shatter.

Men focused on Dennis. He shrugged. "She gave birth to Boris and five months later was dead.

"Jesus, Men, I never knew. I'm so sorry."

"Oh, no, I was asking for it. What right did I have to think I could lead that kind of life?"

"You didn't deserve that. You didn't deserve what happened."

"And Lucinda? What do you think she deserved?"

"It wasn't intentional."

"So I've told myself. It doesn't do any good. I've lived with it every minute since then. I'll live with it till …"

"How would you like some lunch?" Dennis asked. "I came home to get you lunch." He stood up. "Let me take my shower first, okay?."

"I'm not hungry."

"You have to eat," Dennis said

Men sighed. "Whatever you say, but we need to talk some more."

"I'll take a quick shower, then heat up some soup and fix toast."

He climbed the steps.

Men thought then of Boris and his intention of leaving everything to him. Boris didn't need it. He was a successful neurosurgeon, making far more per year now than Men did in his best years.

In a short while Dennis came through on his way to the kitchen. Men heard him opening a can, setting a pot on the burner. He called Men to the table.

They ate in silence, the only sounds the pounding surf and the muffled voices of people passing by. "Is there anything I can get you?" Dennis asked when they finished.

"We need to talk, if you don't mind. There's more that needs to be said."

"What is it?" Dennis asked. He cleared the table and held the dishes under the running tap before sticking them into the dishwasher.

"Come and sit down for a minute, will you, please?" Dennis frowned; Men supposed he wondered what this was all about.

"Okay," he said.

The kitchen was bright, with yellow curtains at the window. Dennis poured himself a second cup of hot water for tea. "Another cup of coffee?" he asked Men.

"No, Thank you," Men answered.

Dennis came over and sat at the tiny table, across from Men. "What is it?" he asked.

Men laughed mirthlessly. "I loved Lucinda or thought I did. It was very hard for me." He looked up. "She was a beautiful person, Denny. You'd have liked her. So I got her pregnant, and she had my child. And I killed her as surely as if I'd run her down myself."

Dennis had trouble believing this. He'd known about Lucinda's accident. But that's all it was, an accident.

"She was killed crossing the street, wasn't she?"

"Yes. She stayed on at the hotel, the same hotel. God knows why, as some sort of self-punishment, I suppose. The baby was five months old. Until then I didn't know I had a child. I never knew I was a father."

Dennis reached across the table for Men's hand.

"Ah, Denny, what a tangled mess our lives become." Men was getting short of breath again. "She left the child in the care of a maid at the hotel. Apparently, she'd done that on several occasions. It was a woman she felt she could trust, I know, or she wouldn't have done it. She told the maid she was going across the street, to a beauty salon. She wanted to have her hair done."

"Men," Dennis said, "you don't have to tell me. You don't owe me an explanations."

Men looked into his eyes. "I think I do."

"All right." Dennis shrugged. "But you're getting so upset."

"Showing a little emotion; the strong, silent one actually feels." His tone was filled with self-deprecation. The truth was, Dennis thought, he always did think of him that way. Now he was being proved wrong. All these years, he thought, and the other person is so familiar, so predictable. Is it all an illusion?

"And now the worst part, Den. The part that proves I was responsible. Before she left, she told the maid that if anything happened, if she was killed or died, the maid should get in touch with Lucinda's parents. She knew, Denny. She planned it. Maybe she couldn't live with Boris as a reminder. I don't know. But she went out there and deliberately got herself killed. From what I gather, witnesses said she didn't even look before she crossed ..."

"Maybe she was just preoccupied, her mind on something else."

"No." It was a single syllable, but it shut out all other possibilities.

"You didn't need to tell me, Men. Don't you know I'd love you no matter what? I don't care what you've done in the past. I care about now, about today ... and tomorrow."

"You always believed me so self-sufficient, didn't you?" He quickly shook his head. "No, don't answer. I know you did. You always thought me so strong."

"I didn't know—"

"Let me tell you exactly how strong I am." He licked his lips. Dennis got up for a glass of water. He handed it to Men who nodded his Thanks.

He took a sip. "After Lucinda found that photo, I was filled with self-loathing. I felt I deserved whatever she said, whatever she did. After I left the hotel room, I stayed in Germany, and that's what I want to tell you about."

"I thought you came home," Dennis said, "and started to teach at State."

"Not right away. I couldn't face anyone here. What would my folks think?" He toyed with the glass of water. "Would it shock you to know I tried to kill myself?"

"Jesus!"

"I can see that it sort of ruins the image." That mirthless laugh again. "I took pills. I wasn't man enough to use a gun. Or even to step in front of a car like Lucinda did later. I'd rented a room in a cheap, little hotel, just for that purpose. A maid found me. She'd forgotten something, a towel maybe, I don't know. She came back to the room, knocked and figured I wasn't there." He reached across the table, took Dennis' hands, squeezed and let go. "They got me to a hospital, pumped my stomach. When I opened my eyes, finally regained a semblance of consciousness, the physician stood there in my room. 'Herr Aradopolos,' he said. 'No Fraulein is worth it.'

"Secrets, Denny. All of us have them. It's a front. We're afraid to show our true selves, afraid we won't be accepted or loved."

"I'm glad you told me."

"I told you about the cracks in the ceiling. That's one of the things I saw there. One of my two big shames. You want to know what my other is?"

He didn't like Men's color. He didn't like what was happening. "Don't overdo," he said. "You're sure you're all right?"

"I'm all right, believe me. I have to finish saying what I want to."

Dennis shrugged; later he'd try to get Men to lie down, take a nap. He looked exhausted.

"My other great shame?" He paused. "It was wanting you so much. I wanted to make you completely mine."

"What's wrong with that? You mean you loved me, so what? I never doubted it."

"Instead of giving you freedom to paint, I tied you down, kept

to ride a wild pony

you dependent."

"I told you before that I went into it with my eyes open. You said you believed in me, in my work."

"Of course, I did."

"Then what's the problem?"

"There's no problem at all. I've decided to give you your freedom."

"What do you mean?" He frowned; what the hell was Men getting at?

"Freedom, Dennis. Not just the illusion. No strings attached. Go where you want, and do what you want. I'll give you whatever you need."

Dennis felt as if the wind had been knocked out of him. "You're kicking me out?"

"Jesus God, that isn't what I meant. I don't want to kick you out."

"I don't know what you want me to do." He'd felt this kind of panic only once before, with Mattie. It was a repeat of something terrible.

"Do? Why do whatever you want. I've kept you prisoner all these years and now I'm setting you free."

"You haven't kept me a prisoner, damn it."

"What can you do, Dennis? Are you trained for anything? Have you ever had a job?"

"You know damned well I haven't."

"Hell, Denny. Don't you understand? I made a big mistake. I'm trying to rectify it; I hope it isn't too late."

It was like a dream, a nightmare. Maybe he didn't know Men at all, know anything about him.

"So think about it. Where you want to go, what you want to do, what you want to have. Anything. Anything within my power to give you."

"Why are you talking this way? I don't understand. Please, damn it, help me understand." His mouth felt so dry he could hardly speak.

"I told you a while ago that, in effect, I feel responsible for Boris. For bringing him into the world. That somehow I should provide for him and his family. While you were out, I decided differently."

"I'm not sure I want to hear this."

"I'm trying to tell you the savings are yours."

"Jesus, Men, I don't believe this."

"I'll keep what I think I'll need. But that's very little. With my pension and social security. And Boris doesn't need it."

Dennis felt weak. "You get used to the way things are, and suddenly everything's changed. All the rules are changed."

"Yes, well, you decide what you want to do. How much you think you'll need. When you've decided, just let me know."

"I don't want ..." If Men wanted him out, then Goddamn it, he wouldn't stay. "Whatever you say, Men." He stood, picked up Men's glass and placed it carefully in the sink.

He walked from the kitchen, through the living room and on upstairs. Nothing seemed real; it was as if he were separated from the world by invisible panes of glass.

to ride a wild pony

CHAPTER 6

So many emotions warred inside Dennis' head that he really didn't know how he felt.

He grabbed a suitcase from the closet and began to stuff it full of clothes, not bothering to figure out what he might need or want. How could he? He had no idea even where he'd go. He had maybe twenty or thirty dollars in his wallet. He had no credit, so he couldn't possibly charge anything.

He couldn't believe what had happened; it was as if he didn't know Men at all. At least, he didn't understand him. It was the second time in his life he'd been kicked out. And he admitted to himself that the first time, when he was thirteen, influenced many of his later actions.

Men had said he was to blame for Dennis' quitting school. But it wasn't true. Dennis had vowed back when he was thirteen that he'd try never to be without a place to live. At State, of course, he'd lived in a dorm. But he accepted that; it was temporary. Then he'd met Men.

When the subject of his moving in came up, he jumped at it. He saw it as maybe his best chance ever for security. Maybe he *had* been to eager to accept whatever terms Men set.

But he did love him, and the love had grown through the years.

He finished packing, snapped the suitcase shut and sat on the bed. He had to think. Where could he go? He'd have to get a job right away, that was certain. What would he do for immediate cash, for money to eat on, for renting a place to stay?

Jesus, his worst nightmare was coming true, the nightmare he'd carried with him all these years.

How different his and Men's pasts had been, yet how similar. With Men it was his wife who kicked him out. With Dennis it was his aunt.

There'd been a man in the next apartment, a guy who lived by himself. Looking back now, Dennis thought he must have been around thirty or so. To a kid of thirteen it was hard to tell.

Friendly, he always talked to Dennis, asked him about school. Dennis got up enough nerve to show him some of his drawings.

"They're fantastic," the man had said, looking at each one carefully, commenting about the composition and the lines.

"Would you sell me one?" he asked.

They were standing in the hallway outside the man's door. It was a short time after school, but already starting to get dark. Winter wind howled, carrying great shovelfuls of snow up against the side of the building.

"You really want to buy one?" Dennis asked.

"Sure, why not?" The man had dark brown hair and a droopy moustache. His voice was deep, and every time Dennis saw him he was smiling. He reminded Dennis a great deal of those knights on horses he used to draw.

"It's a deal," Dennis said, holding out his hand.

The man took it and laughed. "Come on in for a minute, and we'll haggle over the price." He winked to let Dennis know he was kidding about the haggling. "Then we'll celebrate your first sale with a cup of hot chocolate." The man looked at him in mock seriousness. "This is your first sale, isn't it? I wouldn't want to buy something from somebody whose sold a drawing to everyone who came around."

Dennis had laughed. "Nobody ever asked me to buy one before," he said.

"Come on in, then." The man unlocked the door. "By the way," he said. "My name's Rick. What's yours?"

"Dennis. Dennis Thompson."

"Well, hello, Dennis Thompson." He opened the door and held it for Dennis to enter first. The apartment was beautiful, nicer than anything Dennis had ever seen. The living room held a black sectional sofa with white throw pillows and a white shag rug. It looked like the window of a store. Aunt Mattie's furniture was old and frayed, spots worn nearly through on the cushions.

"Take off your coat," Rick said, "and sit down." Dennis wore a pea-coat, too big for him. It had belonged to Mattie's oldest son, now in the Army. A plaid, woolen scarf hung around his neck.

Rick held out his hand and Dennis gave him the coat and scarf.

to ride a wild pony

"Now what do you say?" the man asked. "How much do you want?"

Dennis had no idea what to answer. He shrugged. "I don't know."

"Ah, these artistic types," Rick kidded, striking a pose. "No business sense whatsoever."

Dennis laughed.

"What are you laughing about, young man?" he said, his voice gruff. "If you're going to get anywhere in this world, you have to know where you're going." Quickly, the man sat down beside him and again took the drawings Dennis was holding. "Really, Denny, tell me how much you think they're worth."

"I—I don't know."

Rick leafed through them again. There was a drawing of a garbage truck, a ship, two old women walking down the street. "These are damn good. Don't ever waste your talent." He looked at Dennis. "Are there any you especially don't want to sell?"

"No," Dennis answered. He knew that more than likely he'd just stick them away somewhere. He already had dozens hidden under his clothes in the dresser drawer at Aunt Mattie's. He almost never took them out.

"Then I'll tell you what," Rick said. He leafed quickly through them again, finally choosing the drawing of the two women. "This is the one I like, and I'll pay you five bucks. Take it or leave it."

"Five dollars!" Dennis had said. He'd never had that much money.

"Okay, six, and that's my final offer."

"I didn't mean that wasn't enough. I mean—"

"Uh uh. I said it was my final offer and I mean it. Is it a deal?"

Dennis nodded as Rick took out his wallet, found a five and a one and handed them over. "Now for the celebration," he said. "I have no champagne on hand, so hot chocolate will have to do."

Dennis sat at the kitchen table, while Rick heated a sauce pan full of milk.

That was the beginning of their friendship. The next day Rick invited him in to show him the drawing. It was matted and in an ornate wooden frame, just behind the television set in the living room.

After that Dennis took to stopping in every day. Rick worked nights; he was the designer and technical director for a theatre company, a little one horse outfit, as he called it. "Lots of glue and paper clips," he said once of the sets. So he was home most afternoons.

From the beginning Dennis felt himself drawn to the man. One night he even dreamed of him, and when he awoke, the sheets were wet. He'd heard some of the other kids talking about dreams like this one, so he wasn't frightened. But it was like he wanted to be with Rick more and more. All his fantasies now included him.

Dennis led him on; he knew that. Rick was reluctant. But Dennis took whatever opportunity he could to touch him, to accidentally brush his hand or his leg.

Rick finally said something about it. It was a couple of months later. "Are you sure you know what you're doing, Denny?" he asked.

"I—what—what do you mean?" Dennis stammered.

Rick smiled and chucked him under the chin. "Come on, Denny. No pretense. No dishonesty. We both know what you've been up to. I've been around, you know."

Dennis felt his face burn with embarrassment. "I like you," he managed to say. "I like you a lot." He felt like he wanted to turn and run.

"Hey, there, whoa. I know what you're feeling. I felt the same way too."

"Did you?" Dennis asked, his voice small.

"Uh huh. I know just what you're going through. I understand completely."

Dennis felt a great relief. Here was someone else, someone nice, who felt as he did. Guys who liked other guys weren't weirdos, as all the kids at school seemed to think.

Rick led him to the sofa and sat down beside him. He leaned over and gently kissed his lips.

That was the beginning. He began to spend more and more time with Rick, and to talk about him to his cousin and to Aunt Mattie.

His aunt became suspicious. "Who is this Rick? What kind of

to ride a wild pony

a man is he if he wants to spend hours with a kid, instead of people his own age?"

"He's just my friend," Dennis had answered, realizing that in his enthusiasm, he'd talked too much.

They sat at the table, just after a dinner of hot dogs in sauerkraut, with mashed potatoes. "I don't think it's healthy for you to spend so much time around this man. Do you understand?"

"Yes," Dennis said, beginning to panic. He didn't want to lose Rick. Not ever. He was the one person he really loved in the whole world. Rick cared about him, did things for him.

Then it happened; the worst thing imaginable. Dennis stopped in once after school. He and Rick had a cup of hot chocolate, as they usually did, and went on into the bedroom.

There was a pounding on the door. Rick grabbed an old flannel robe and went to answer. Aunt Mattie stormed inside and into the bedroom. "This is what I suspected," she snarled. "I'm going to call the police, Mr. Child Molester. And as for you, young man, I want you back home immediately."

Everything felt dirty; what had been so good had been made bad. Rick wasn't a child molester. Child molesters were dirty old men who preyed on young kids, kids not old enough to know any better. Dennis was old enough to know what he wanted.

"I won't come home," he shouted. "I won't."

"If you don't come with me now, don't ever bother to come." She went to the door. "I'm warning you, Mr. what-ever-you-call-yourself, I'm calling the police." She slammed the door and left.

"You better do as she says, Denny."

"I don't want to leave, Rick. I like you. I—I love you."

"I know, buddy. I like you too. But don't you understand? In the eyes of the law—"

"No," Dennis had shouted. "No."

"I think I'd better clear out," Rick said. "I never liked this neighborhood anyway."

"She won't call the police. I know she won't."

"Maybe not right away. But if we keep seeing each other, she will. You'd better go now."

Dennis hurried into his clothes, grabbed his coat and raced out into the hallway. Instead of crossing to his apartment, he ran down the steps and outside.

Rick was the only person he'd ever loved. He couldn't love Aunt Mattie, even though she'd arranged for drawing lessons, even though she'd kept him longer than any of his other aunts and uncles. Mostly, he knew, she thought of him as just another mouth to feed.

He ran to the corner and kept on running. His breath made puffs of steam in the air. He slowed down and started to walk. Fine-grained snow fell lightly, giving a halo effect to the street lights.

He wandered around for hours and finally headed back home. When he reached the doorway to the apartment, all his belongings were piled outside. He pounded and pounded on the door, but no one came. He went to Rick's apartment, but no answered there either. He sat down and cried, something he hadn't done in years.

He lifted his suitcase off the bed and carried it downstairs. He set it in the hallway and went into the living room.

Men sat at the desk writing. He looked up. "I'm writing a letter to Boris. I feel I owe him that much. An explanation at least."

"And what do you owe me?"

"I don't understand."

"I'm leaving, if that's what you want."

"I didn't mean for you to leave this instant. Make plans. Figure out where you want to go, what you want to do."

"Jesus, Men, I don't understand this. I'm not going to beg you, that's for sure. I've never begged for anything in my life. I never begged my Aunt Mattie. I won't beg you."

"This isn't the way I meant it to be. You're making me feel, I don't know, like the biggest shit of all time. You've got to see my viewpoint. I'm like a damn mother bird or something, shoving you out of the nest. Hoping—"

"It's fucking ridiculous. I don't want to go anywhere. Jesus Christ, I don't."

"I said I'd give you whatever you want."

"I don't want anything, Men. Do what you planned. Give it to Boris."

"What are you going to do?"

"Shit." He walked behind the couch, leaned over, pounded his fists sideways into the pillow. "I don't know. I really don't know. It's my problem now, not yours."

Men laid down his pen, let his hands drop into his lap. "You're going to walk out, and that's it?"

He straightened up. "You got it." He felt if he didn't leave he might disintegrate; all the emotions building inside would simply blow him away. "I packed a suitcase."

"Don't do this, Denny. You've no place to go." Men stood up and walked toward him.

"I'll find something." He came around the couch and walked toward the hallway. He didn't want to be near Men right now. He couldn't stand to be that close and feel the way he did.

"Won't you let me help?"

"Jesus Christ, Men, you're kicking me out."

"Oh, God." Men covered his face with his hands. "You're deliberately misinterpreting my words."

"Am I?" He picked up the suitcase.

"You know very well what I said."

"I'll pay for the suitcase and my clothes." He knew he was being petty; he knew he was striking out. Two parts of him warred. He wanted to take Men in his arms. At the same time he wanted to hurt him. "After all you bought them."

"Don't do this, Dennis. Please, don't do it."

"You can sell the rest of my stuff. I don't want it. I don't want anything here."

"That's it then." Men could hardly speak; tears ran down his cheeks. "We have nothing to say to each other. It ends like this."

"Lord, Men, how do you want it to end?"

"I want to help you."

"Don't be ridiculous."

"Don't leave like this." Men came toward him. "You said you wouldn't beg, but I will. Please don't leave."

"I'll see you around." He turned toward the door.

He heard Men running toward him. "Here, Goddamn it, at least take this." He held out a wad of money.

"I don't want your money."

For a moment, Men didn't speak. "Since when?"

"What?" Dennis couldn't believe it was happening. Thirty-five years, right down the drain. How could they hurt each other this way? God, he thought, please let this end.

Men's face was hard. "You heard me. I said since when. I've helped you all your life. Why not now?"

"God, Men, you didn't need to tell me that. I did some things in return." He opened the door.

"That's it, Denny. Find another sugar daddy. Except you're a little old."

Dennis turned once more. "Yeah? And what about you? How many students do you think you'll attract at your age? Of course, when you get your checkbook out, it's different."

"Get out, damn you." Men's face was purple with fury. "Just get out of my life."

"And I'm not looking back."

"Damn you, damn you, damn you." Suddenly, Men clutched his chest. "Uh— Uh— Get—"

"Oh, my God." Dennis threw down the suitcase and rushed toward his lover. Men collapsed against him, and he led him to the couch. Cradling the smaller man, Dennis eased down and reached for the phone. "Ambulance. Please hurry." He gave her the address and hung up the phone.

"So— Sorry, Denny," Men said. "I'm sorry."

"Shh. It's all right. It's okay. I'm here."

to ride a wild pony

CHAPTER 7

The first thing Dennis had to do, he decided, was to call Boris. He knew Men hadn't wanted him to know he'd been ill. But Boris had the right to know.

At the hospital Men was hurried on back to the emergency room while Dennis answered questions. He was certain the receptionist disapproved once she figured out that he and Men were lovers.

With a haughty air she told him to take a seat, that someone would let him know Men's condition as quickly as possible.

The room was crowded. Dennis sat in a hard plastic chair and tried to concentrate on a magazine. He leafed through from beginning to end before he even realized what it was: *Psychology Today*. He threw it down on an end table littered with candy and gum wrappers and half-empty styrofoam cups.

He stood up and walked to the entrance. Outside the day was still bright. He glanced at his watch. It was only a little after three. That didn't seem possible. It seemed days ago he'd run on the beach and then gone to see Bill Rizzo.

Oh, God, he thought, Men was going to die. And it was all his fault. He could never forgive himself. All the emotion he'd been holding inside suddenly burst forth in great racking sobs. He pushed open the glass door and reeled out into the parking lot.

Barely aware of other people, he staggered to the side of the hospital and sat on a park bench.

"Hey, buddy, are you all right?" someone said.

Dennis looked up to see a man about his own age, arms covered in tattoos, a baseball cap perched on his head. "Yeah," Dennis managed and tried to smile. "I'll be all right." But he wasn't sure of that. Men was the only one he loved, the only person in his life he'd ever really loved—except for Boris, and that was a different kind of feeling.

He leaned back and looked out over the parking lot. If Men died, he didn't think he could take it. Stevens had told him Men was to avoid conflict.

He stood up; he shouldn't be out here. He should be inside in case there was any news. He walked back to the entrance. He was almost afraid to open the door, to face what lay ahead.

In the ambulance Men had looked terrible, his face drawn and pale. The paramedics gave him oxygen, but they didn't do much else.

He pushed open the door and walked over to the desk. Fiftyish, overweight, doused in perfume, the receptionist looked up. "What is it?" she asked, her tone cold.

"I wondered if there was any word—"

"I told you we'd let you know. Now I suggest you go sit down and let me get back to work."

"I was outside; I thought maybe …"

The woman ignored him as she shuffled through a sheaf of papers.

He couldn't stand the waiting. Maybe he'd call Boris now. He thought to wait until he had some news, but that might take a long time.

He spied a couple of pay phones over against the wall, searched in his pocket for change, found only a quarter and some nickels, not nearly enough to make the call.

He pulled out his wallet and searched through the plastic windows. He found the card he needed to charge the call, and before he could change his mind, hurried to a phone.

Would Boris even want to hear from him? The past few years he'd been pleasant but distant. Well, there was no use worrying about that.

The phone rang several times, and he was about to hang up, when Melissa came on the line.

"Melissa," he said, his voice trembling. "Is Boris there?"

"Yes, he is. What is it Dennis? Is something wrong? Is it Dad?"

Dennis throat ached so he could barely talk. "He's in the hospital. We just got to the hospital. I don't know anything yet."

"I'll get Boris," she said. "Just hang on."

"Hello, Dennis," the voice answered, a mellow voice, but now with a tone of aloofness. "Is Dad ill?" he asked.

"He wouldn't want me to call. I know he wouldn't." He told

Boris about Men's hospitalization and what Stevens had said.

"Tomorrow's my day off," Boris said. "I've no surgery planned for the next couple of days. I'll see about a flight to San Diego. I can get someone to cover for me at the hospital."

"Let me know," Dennis said. "I'll try to pick you up."

"Yes. All right. I'll probably see you tomorrow then." Dennis gently replaced the receiver. What would Boris think if he knew about the argument? He'd have to tell him; he couldn't live with it.

He walked back across the room and sat down. A little girl, three or four, played with a ball, rolling it back and forth on the floor. She looked up at Dennis and smiled. "Hello," she said. "What's your name?"

"Dennis," he answered, speaking softly. "What's yours?" Over a blouse with puffy sleeves, she wore a jumper. Kittens chased butterflies up and down the light blue fabric.

"Don't bother the man," the girl's mother said. She looked to be in her mid-twenties.

"It's no bother," Dennis said, and was grateful for the diversion. "What's your name?" he asked the little girl again.

"Jilly," she said. "Do you want to play ball?" She rolled the rubber ball toward him, and he bent over and rolled it back.

"My daddy got hurt," she said. "He got hurt real bad."

Dennis looked questioningly at the girl's mother. "An accident at work," she said. "I was just on my way to the baby sitters. Something about a fork lift. I'm not—" She looked down and then up again. "Sorry."

"It's okay," Dennis answered. "I hope it's not serious."

Out of the corner of his eye she saw someone hurrying toward him. He saw it was Stevens, and he was smiling. Thank God, Dennis thought, he's smiling.

"Mr. Thompson. Dennis," he said, "let's step outside for a moment. All right."

Dennis nodded as he stood up. He looked at the little girl. "Goodbye, Jilly. I'm sure your daddy will be okay." He smiled at the woman, nodded and followed Stevens to the door.

"We'll just walk around the side here," he said, leading Dennis

---

to a grassy area, dotted with tall leafy trees.

"Let me tell you first off that it's nothing serious."

Dennis suddenly felt so weak he could hardly stand.

Stevens grabbed his arm. "Maybe we should sit down."

"I'm fine," Dennis said, "I'm really fine. I was so damned worried."

"Sure," Stevens said. "Anyhow, the best thing I can figure is that it was an anxiety attack. Did anything happen? Anything out of the ordinary? I mean, like a tense situation?"

Dennis expelled his breath sharply. "We had an argument," he said. "A damned argument." He hit his hand into the front of his thigh. "I know he's supposed to avoid excitement; he's not to get all worked up. Damn it—"

"Look, Dennis," Stevens said. "I've known you for a long, long time."

Dennis nodded. "I guess just about ever since Men and I moved to La Jolla."

"Okay, then." He put his arm around Dennis' shoulder. "And you know what? All of us lose our tempers, all of us argue. We wish we didn't, but we do. We're human—whatever the hell that means." He chuckled. "I'm a doctor, and I've never quite figured it out."

Dennis looked at him closely for the first time. A man in his sixties, slender, wearing a light brown suit. He smiled, a little sadly. "Anyhow, Denny," he said, "I think you're a damned good man. I can tell how devoted you are." He dropped his arm. "A hell of a lot of married couples I know could take lessons from you, from the two of you. Okay?"

Half laughing, half crying, Dennis sniffed. "Okay," he said.

"Now why don't you go in there and talk to that old reprobate. He should be settled in his room by now." He started to leave, then turned. "You know, his heart's not in good shape. But I'll bet even money that despite everything, he's going to be around for a long, long time."

Dennis grabbed Stevens hand in both of his. "Thank you," he said. "Thanks, especially for that."

"He's on the second floor; stop at the nurses' station. They'll be able to tell you his room number. We'll keep him overnight and

to ride a wild pony

send him home tomorrow."

Men was okay, Dennis thought. He was going to be okay. He felt like jumping and clicking his heels. Instead, he strode quickly into the hospital and up to the elevators.

Once again, Dennis was struck by how tiny Men looked. He lay on his back with his eyes closed, the sheet pulled up to his chin.

"Men?" He spoke softly in case Men was asleep. If he were, he decided, he'd sit by the bed till he awakened.

"Denny!" Men opened his eyes. "It turns out there's very little wrong. Nerves; anxiety. I feel a little silly, causing such a stir."

"Hush," Dennis said. "It certainly doesn't matter. You scared me." He took Men's hand, raised it and brushed it lightly with his lips. "I'm glad you're okay."

"Denny?" Men frowned.

"What is it?" Dennis pulled the chair closer to the bed.

"I had no right to say— to say all those things. I was controlling again, trying to. I didn't ask what you wanted. I was seeking a balm to my own conscience. 'This is what's best for Denny,' I was saying. 'I'll give him a chance to be out on his own.' But it would be the same thing, wouldn't it? We'd just be living apart."

"Why don't we talk about this later, Men? We can work things out."

"No, Denny. I need to say some things now. I was feeling guilty, and I tried to force the issue. I just want to say I'm sorry."

"Me too," Dennis answered. "I know what the doctor said, and still I argued. I baited you. I'm the one who should apologize."

"Apology accepted. Now that's enough of that." Men smiled, and it seemed to Dennis it was his old smile, the one he loved.

Then Dennis thought of Boris. "Oh, God," he said. "You're going to be angry." He picked roughly at a thumbnail. "I called Boris. I didn't know how serious it was. I didn't know what was wrong. I suspected—"

Men laughed. "So you called him, so what?"

"Ah, Men, he's coming to see you." Dennis laughed. "And now you're okay. I think I better call him back. Is there anything I can get you while I'm gone?"

"Nothing."

"See you in a while."

For the second time Dennis dug through his wallet for the long distance card. Melissa answered. "He's on his way to Boston," she said.

She told Dennis Boris had called immediately to arrange a flight and decided to drive to Boston, a couple of hours away. He'd just wait around then until time for departure. "There's no way I can reach him," she said. "But I'm glad Dad's okay."

She paused then for a moment. "Actually," she said, "I think it's about time for a visit. It's been a long, long time. And Boris regrets that, I know. We've talked about … about you and Dad and … Well, anyhow, there's a message on your answering machine about the flight. Bright and early tomorrow morning." She laughed. "But that shouldn't bother you. I remember how early you like to get up."

"Too bad we won't get to see you too. You and the kids? How are they?"

They chatted for a few more minutes and Dennis hung up. So, he thought, tomorrow he'd pick up Boris. He wondered how things would go. The thought of seeing him again caused a tightness in his stomach.

He'd stop in and see Men once more. Then he'd go home and hit the sack. It had been a terribly long day.

to ride a wild pony

CHAPTER 8

Boris' voice on the answering machine had been cool, devoid of emotion. He said he'd be arriving at Lindbergh Field just after seven. Since Men wouldn't be discharged until ten, Dennis decided he'd pick Boris up. Then they'd stop somewhere for breakfast.

He really wasn't up to facing him alone at home. There were too many uncertainties. A neutral place would be better.

Dennis was up by 4:30 and out on the beach running by a quarter to five. Rather than pacing himself as he had before, he felt that on this particular morning, he needed to run, as long as he could, as fast as he could. Maybe it would calm him down, settle his nerves.

Tiring quickly, he turned in a wide circle and slowed once more to a trot, enough to keep him from chilling, not fast enough to make him struggle for air.

Running lightly up the steps, he shucked his clothes on the bedroom floor, bent, picked them up and folded them before dropping them into the hamper. He glanced at the clock by the bed. Just after 5:30.

He showered, then dressed in light blue slacks and a knit shirt, leaving the top two buttons open. Downstairs again, he put on the tea kettle and called the hospital, only half expecting to be put through so early.

Men picked up the receiver on the first ring. "Yes?" he said.

"'Morning. Thought I'd give you a call before I go pick up Boris."

"He's arriving?"

Steam began to rise from the tea kettle; Dennis reached over and turned it off. "A little after seven." He opened the cupboard door and took out a mug, filled it and pulled out a tea bag, cranberry. "I thought maybe I could reach him to tell him you're okay— You are okay, aren't you?"

Men chuckled. "Of course, I'm all right. And wanting to get the hell home."

"A few more hours, think you can last?" Dennis dunked the tea bag up and down.

"If I know it's no longer than that, I can."

"Anyhow, Melissa told me Boris had driven to Boston, and there was no way she could reach him."

"Yeah, well, I guess he had to know about me sooner or later." He paused. "Listen, Denny, I know what I said. But in the ambulance last night, thinking this might be it, I really wished I could see him."

"Well, that's one wish we can make come true."

Dennis finished the tea, rinsed out the cup and grabbed a lightweight jacket from the hall closet. He'd take it along just in case. Men was the one who was always cold; Dennis enjoyed cool weather.

By the time he left it was a little after six. It took about twenty minutes to the airport. The fast run hadn't worked. The closer he came to Lindbergh Field, the more apprehensive he felt.

Maybe, Dennis thought, he was placing too much emphasis on what had happened so long ago.

He got off Route 5 and followed the signs to the airport. Not that he needed the signs; when Men was teaching, he flew to meetings and conventions a couple of times a month. Dennis always brought him to the airport and picked him up.

The parking lot was nearly empty. He pulled into a space, locked the doors and crossed to the terminal.

Too nervous to sit and wait, he walked through the airport, stopping now and then to look in the shops. Dennis checked the schedule and saw that Boris' plane was on time.

He walked toward the arrival area and leaned against the wall. Disembarking passengers streamed toward him. He wondered how Boris looked. Had he changed, put on weight, grown his hair, added a moustache?

Then he spied him, the same as always, a slender man, looking younger than his years. He was nearly thirty-eight. Dressed in slacks and a short-sleeved sport shirt, he carried a small canvas bag. He spied Dennis and hurried toward him.

"Dennis," he cried, holding out his hand—a little hesitantly?

---

to ride a wild pony

"Thanks for being here. I hoped it wouldn't be too much trouble to pick me up."

"Hello, Boris," Dennis said, grasping his hand. Boris returned the pressure. "Did you have a nice flight?"

"It was fine." They started up the corridor. "How's Dad?"

Dennis laughed. "I'm afraid it was rather a false alarm."

"What do you mean?" Boris asked.

Dennis decided to get it over with. If Boris was angry, so be it. "The collapse was caused by tension."

"Tension?"

"Your father didn't want me to tell you. Up till now, I mean." He held the door for Dennis. "He was in the hospital for nearly a month. A heart attack." They crossed the roadway to the parking lot. "He didn't want to worry you. But then yesterday, I took it upon myself—"

"Let's back up," Boris said. "You said Dad had a heart attack, and no one let me know?"

Dennis was on the defensive. "It was what he wanted."

"Hell, Dennis, he's my father. I think I have a right to know."

"Sorry," Dennis said.

"Forget it. I can't blame you." He chuckled. "I know how stubborn Dad can be."

"I suppose," Dennis said, not giving in before he knew the territory.

"Anyhow, it was time we saw each other. Had I known the situation—that he's pretty much okay—I'd have arranged things differently."

As they reached the car, Dennis unlocked the passenger door. "I forgot to ask if you had other luggage."

"No, just this." They climbed inside. "I started to say I'd have arranged things differently. Brought Melissa and the kids along." Boris shook his head and looked toward Dennis. "But you know what? I probably wouldn't have."

"Oh?"

"It's so easy to go along in a rut. Easy to accept the status quo. It's familiar and so damned comfortable."

Dennis wondered what the words implied. "I thought we'd stop for breakfast, okay?"

"If you like," Boris said. "I could do with another cup of coffee."
He chuckled. "I had several cups on the plane. I'm always telling
my patients to cut down, and here I'm having a caffeine fit." He
glanced at Dennis again. "You're still a tea drinker, I suppose."

"That's right," Dennis answered.

At the toll gate, Dennis reached into his pocket for change. Boris
held out a dollar bill.

"So how have you been?" Dennis asked, driving away from
the airport. "Not working too hard?"

"Okay, and yes," Boris replied. "How about you?"

"Minor aches and pains. But then I'm getting older, just like
everyone else." He pulled out into a stream of traffic. "Any place
you'd like to stop?"

Dennis still was unable to read Boris' mood or attitude. He
seemed responsive enough, but the stiffness still was there, and
Dennis regretted it.

Then it started to make him a little bit angry. He'd never done
anything to Boris to cause him to change his feelings. Dennis was
what he always had been, and he wouldn't apologize to anyone
for it.

They stopped at an Allie's. Dennis ordered an omelette, an
English muffin and tea. They didn't have herbal, so he settled for
Lipton's.

He thought fleetingly of coming right out and asking Boris why
he still seemed to hold a grudge. But then he decided against it. If
Boris was going to remain distant, that's how it would have to be.
And Dennis particularly didn't want to create more anxiety for
Men.

When they left the restaurant, it was still only 8:30. They had
an hour and a half to kill before they could pick up Men.

Boris asked if they could drive out to Torrey Pines. Dennis
wondered why. He hadn't been there in years, not since Boris was
in junior high.

They parked and walked to a picnic table. Dennis sat on one
side, Boris on the other. Dennis slipped into his jacket. Boris held
onto his shoulders, hunching over in the cold. Pine trees stretched

to ride a wild pony

to the sky; the earth showed brown where no grass grew.

"Old memories," Boris said. "I hadn't thought of this spot in years. Then all at once I remembered." He chuckled. "I just didn't remember its being this cold."

Dennis didn't reply; he sensed Boris was going to say more. He'd wait and see what it was.

"Dennis." he said, "I've been a shit. All these years I've been a shit. The whole way here on the plane, thinking Dad might be dying, I tried to think how to tell you that."

He rubbed a spot on the table. "At the airport when you told me Dad was okay, I thought I'd gotten a reprieve. I wouldn't have to tell you. I wouldn't have to face it." He looked up. "I love you, Dennis. I just wanted you to know that."

He got up quickly and strode back to the car, leaning over the top.

Jesus, Dennis thought, Sweet Jesus.

"You know how when you do something wrong," Boris said as Dennis came back to the car, "it gets harder and harder to fix it." He looked into Dennis' eyes. "I was a dumb kid. And then I couldn't admit it. I tried to tell myself it didn't matter, but I know damn well it did."

He opened the door and climbed in. Dennis slid behind the wheel. "Melissa knows how I feel. She's been trying to get me to say something for six or seven years. But I guess I'm stubborn like my old man." Looking straight ahead, he reached over and squeezed Dennis hand.

***

It was a long time from when the patients were awakened till Dennis and Boris would come pick Men up. They allowed him to take a shower, which he certainly appreciated, since he hated the damn sponge baths in bed.

He tried to dawdle over breakfast—dry cereal, toast without butter, orange juice and coffee—as long as he could to make the time pass more quickly. But still he had a couple of hours to wait.

Stevens came by, listened to his heart and said it sounded fine. "Call my office and make an appointment for a couple of weeks from now, just to make sure you're doing okay."

"What happened was just because of nerves?" Men asked.

"Because of tension, yes. But our emotions do funny things to our bodies. We're only beginning to investigate that thoroughly now." He shrugged. "I know realistically a person can't avoid tension and conflict. But we can try to do our best. The next time you might not be so lucky." He patted Men's shoulder. "This is the last time I want to see you here, at least for awhile."

"I'll do my best," Men said.

Stevens walked to the door and turned. "People care about you, you know. One person in particular cares a hell of a lot. You owe it to him."

Men smiled. "Thanks, Sam."

He wondered if Boris had made it. He hoped so. It had been much too long a time. He thought of his grandchildren; they'd been little more than babies when he'd last seen them. Now Jimmy was in first grade, Dawn in kindergarten.

He hoped Denny and Boris were getting along. Denny had never talked about the trouble between them, but Men knew it was there. He hoped it would be resolved, but didn't know if it could be. Feeling guilty about so many things, he might as well add his sexual preference to the list. Boris didn't approve; he knew that. Maybe it was an unnatural environment in which to rear a child, but that couldn't be helped.

A little before ten they came through the door, Boris first, and Men knew immediately. Everything was okay.

"Dad," Boris said, rushing to the bed. "You had me worried. You had us all worried."

"It's so good to see you."

"I know, Dad. I know." Boris grasped his hand and held it tightly, then leaned over and kissed his cheek.

"How's Melissa? How're the kids?" Men asked.

"Just fine. Melissa's back in school, working on her Ph.D. in art history." Boris laughed. "We'll have so many doctors in the family we'll never be able to keep track." He stepped back. "What's

to ride a wild pony

this about your not telling me you were in the hospital?"

Men didn't answer at first, then decided to be honest. "A couple of reasons, Boris. First, I didn't want to worry you. There was really nothing you could do. Then …"

"I know what you're going to say, Dad, and I'm sorry. It took me years to work things through. Too many years."

"But now everything's all right." It was half statement, half question, but he didn't expect an answer.

Dennis handed Men a small suitcase with clothes to wear home. "Want me to call a nurse?" he asked.

"I can manage. Just go make whatever arrangements you have to make to check me out. By that time I'll be dressed." He glanced toward Boris. "How long can you stay?"

"I should get back tomorrow. But I'll spend the night."

"That's good; I'm glad."

Despite Men's protests, an attendant insisted he ride a wheelchair to the exit. "Hospital policy," he said. Men finally gave in.

"How are you feeling now, Dad? Tired?"

"Not especially, no."

Boris sat in back, leaning forward to talk. "Then I thought I'd like to take you to lunch. I know you always liked La Valencia."

Men started to laugh. "I think this is where I came in."

CHAPTER 9

After lunch the three of them sat in the living room, talking. It was like old times, Dennis thought. Yet, it was different. Boris was an adult. Vestiges of the kid he'd been remained, yet he'd grown far beyond the kind of person he'd been fifteen or twenty years before.

Although there was a new respect and liking between them, Dennis sensed a continuing awkwardness, not the same as the stiffness that had existed for so many years. More like two strangers feeling each other out.

In fact, they were strangers. It was like the feeling Dennis had on his first trip back to Brooklyn. It was the same place, yet unfamiliar. It would have been impossible to pick up his interrupted life there.

They'd been talking about the past, Dennis asking about people he'd known.

"La Jolla has changed," Men said. "It's not the quiet village it was when we bought the house. Freeways, tourists. San Diego's growing like a cancer."

"That's progress, I guess," Boris said, leaning back. He and Men shared the couch; Dennis sat in the chair opposite them.

"I'm not complaining," Men said, "merely stating a fact. But a lot of people are concerned. There've been various moves to limit new construction."

Dennis chuckled. "And those damn bumper stickers that seemed to proliferate for a time. 'Welcome to San Diego; Now Go Home.'"

Boris had contributed little to the conversation. Now he stood, walked to the window and turned. "You may have gathered, Dad," he said, "that Dennis and I have made our peace. No, that's wrong. Dennis was never at war. Just me." He bit his lip, pulled out the chair near the desk and straddled it.

He seemed suddenly nervous, ill at ease. "Damn," he said. He stood once more, walked behind Dennis, squeezed his shoulder and went back to the window.

"Do you remember the Dempsey kids?" he asked.

"Ted and Carl," Dennis answered.

"Yeah," Boris blew out his breath. "Ted was older by a couple of years. Carl was about my age." He shook his head. "It's really hard—" He hit his fist against the top of the chair. "Remember when I was in first grade and all those kids were calling me names—" He looked from Dennis to Men.

"I remember," Dennis said.

"I wanted to go to their parents," Men said. "As a matter of fact, I did that later."

Dennis was surprised; he hadn't known that.

"Then Ted and Carl couldn't play with me anymore."

"I hadn't thought about that in years," Dennis said. "Then yesterday I did. Funny you'd bring it up."

"No, Dennis, not at all funny."

"I didn't mean—"

"I'm sorry." He wiped the side of his finger across his upper lip. "That was just the beginning. They never left me alone after that."

"Who do you mean?" Men asked.

"Those two kids—sons-of-bitches." Boris' face flushed with anger or maybe shame.

"What do you mean?"

Boris held up a hand. "Where in the hell they ever heard that kind of language I don't know. I didn't even know what they were talking about. Ted was the one. I doubt if Carl knew, either." He closed his eyes for a moment. "They kept it up and kept it up."

Dennis leaned forward. "After that first time, you mean?"

"It got so bad, I couldn't stand it." He shook his head. "Damned peer pressure. I think what my two kids have to face, and I feel—" He spread the curtain and looked out the window.

"Anyhow, I started to resent you two guys, started to take my feelings out on you."

"You don't have to tell us this," Men said. "I understand."

He let the curtains drop. "No, goddamnit, you don't!" He ran a hand hard through his hair. "I'm sorry. Dad? Dennis?"

Dennis shrugged, tried to smile. "Okay."

"And I'm sure you remember that time, Denny, when you tried to talk to me. I lashed out at you. That was the beginning—"

Dennis nodded and glanced at Men. He seemed intent on what Boris was saying. "It's over with now. Everything's okay."

"Maybe I shouldn't do this, Dad. But I feel I've just got to tell you.

"Tell me what, Boris?" His tone was quiet, soothing.

"Those goddamned, fucking kids." He shook his head. "I'm sorry. I thought I'd learned to live with what happened. I guess I didn't. I guess I never can.

"Shit!" He strode to the hallway and turned, framed in the archway. "Ted and Carl and a bunch of other kids. The Dempseys were the ringleaders; that's the ironic part. They're the ones whose parents forbade them to play with me anymore." He swallowed hard, walked to the window again and stared outside.

He began to speak in a monotone, without turning back toward the room. "It was after school one day. I was in the ninth grade. It was mid-September, about the same time of year as now. I was walking home with a couple of friends—Freddy and John. All at once Ted and Carl rushed toward me out of nowhere." His voice broke, and he took a moment before going on.

"They had three other kids with them, all a little older than Carl and me. They told Fred and John to get lost and said they wanted me to come with them. I told them no, I didn't want to. One of them punched me hard. I doubled over and couldn't breathe."

He turned back, his lips drawn tight. "They took me to the Dempseys, half pushing, half pulling. I was scared to death. I didn't know what they'd do."

"Jesus Christ!" Men said. "Why didn't you— why didn't you tell us?"

"Shame. So ashamed." Boris sobbed. "I couldn't tell you."

He looked straight at Dennis. "Mr. and Mrs. Dempsey were out of town. The house was empty. They took me in, made me go to the bedroom. They held me down and pulled off my clothes." He ran both hands down over his face.

"And then—they— they got undressed, too. And they told me

---

to ride a wild pony

they knew my old man was queer. And Dennis was queer. And so I must be too. And they—" His voice broke. "And they said you must have given me lessons on how to suck cocks. They said I had to suck their cocks." All at once he started to sob and ran from the room, into the hallway and on out front of the house.

Dennis was stunned. He glanced at Men, whose face was filled with anguish. Dennis stood, walked over to Men, bent down, squeezed his shoulder. Then he straightened up.

"Jesus, Denny, what did we do? What did we do?" Men sighed brokenly. "You think you're doing the right thing— My God, to live with that all these years."

"There was no way to know this would happen. Look at all the other guys we met who had kids. The Gay Fathers group; no one ever had trouble like this."

"How do you know that?" Men asked, and Dennis had to admit he was right.

"I'm going to go talk to him," Dennis said.

"You're better at it than I am …"

He didn't know what he'd say; maybe it wasn't important. Maybe just letting Boris know he was there, that he cared, was what mattered.

Boris stood on the top step looking out over the ocean. "It's warming up," Dennis said.

Boris turned to him. "Maybe … Maybe I shouldn't have said anything. I don't know." He looked back toward the water. "I've wrestled with it for years."

"If it were me," Dennis said, "I think I'd hate much more. If it were me, I don't think I could ever forgive."

Boris nodded, a sad smile on his face. "Thanks," he said.

* * *

When Boris was a baby, Men used to marvel at the miracle of him, not only in his very being, but in his ending up in Southern California. He hadn't, of course, even known Lucinda was pregnant. So it was a shock to learn he was a father.

Boris, he thought. Never a name he would have picked himself.

Boris Aradopolos, a real contradiction. Yet Lucinda had talked of a great-grandfather who'd come from Russia. Papa Boris, she called him, her favorite relative, who'd died when she was a little girl.

Through all this chain of circumstances, Men had been entrusted with the tiny life. And he'd been overwhelmed. He had no idea how to treat a child; he'd been frightened. The first couple of years he'd left him with baby sitters, older women who flocked to his house in answer to ads in the *Union Tribune*.

Then came Dennis, seemingly molded for the role of parent, of father. Men sighed. Both his lover and his son stood outside on the porch. He could hear them talking, a low murmur lacking distinguishable sound.

Poor kid, Men thought. To carry it inside him all those years. In contradiction to his slender build and sensitive eyes—weren't brooding eyes a Russian trait? —he had to be strong. He'd done well, gone far.

Men sighed. He couldn't understand the feelings he had. Shouldn't he be more upset? He was surprised at this reaction but welcomed it.

From now on, he decided, he had no need to control. Somehow he'd been released. He remembered the poem again and thought it ironic that twenty-four hours earlier, give or take a few hours, he'd been reminded of it. Then he wouldn't have believed he'd feel as he did now. There was an easing, an acceptance and everything was okay, at least for the time being. He smiled to himself; he doubted seriously if he could ever remain so serene.

He looked up as Boris and Denny came through the door.

The three of them spent late afternoon and evening playing Thirty-One. Dennis even rooted through drawers and found the old money bags in which they'd kept their nickels.

"When am I going to get to see my grandchildren?" Men asked as they sat around the kitchen table, arranging cards.

"When would you like to see them?" Boris asked.

"Tomorrow," Men answered.

Boris laughed. "That's perhaps a little too soon."

"Next week then, next month, what do you think, Dennis?" Dennis nodded.

to ride a wild pony

"I haven't taken a vacation this year," Boris said. "Over Christmas, when the kids are out of school and Melissa's on break, we'll come to California or you can come to see us."

"New England in the winter?" Men said. "I've already done New England in the winter. I'd rather stay right here."

"It's a deal." Boris played one of his cards. "I want those kids to know they have a grandpa—" He shook his head. "That they have *two* grandpas in Southern California."

They played till ten; then Dennis excused himself to make the bed in the extra room.

Boris stretched. "It's one o'clock by my time. Think I'll turn in."

"I'm so glad you came."

"It was long overdue." He reached across the table for Men's hand. "I'm proud that you're my father. That you and Dennis are my fathers."

CHAPTER 10

Dennis had been doing a lot of thinking. He'd opted for security, with good reason, but that really wasn't enough.

Funny, he thought, that you go along with your life, and there seem to be no real ups and downs. And suddenly all sorts of things occur.

It had been an incredible past couple of days. Things had happened that couldn't be changed. And there was no turning back.

He'd dropped Boris off at the airport and was on his way back to La Jolla. Since the plane left a little after seven, Men had decided not to go along. In a way Dennis was glad; it gave him time by himself. There were decisions that he had to make.

Generally, his thinking time was early morning while he jogged. But this morning Boris had come along. He was glad. There was a closeness now that had been missing for years. He knew that even though Boris would soon be a continent away, it would not seem as far as it had.

It was still hazy with morning mist as he drove north on Route 5. Men, he was glad to see, apparently had come to terms of a sort. He'd accepted what Boris had told him without frustration or anger.

He knew Men had always felt guilty, had always been a little ashamed of being gay. In many ways, Men was the far more mature of the two. But not in that respect. Long ago, Dennis had come to terms with what he was.

Not that he'd come to terms with every facet of his life. That was the problem. He knew himself well enough to understand why he hadn't really tried with his painting. He was scared. He'd rather go on thinking he had the potential to be good, rather than risk being proved wrong.

He really couldn't blame himself for the feeling. He'd had little in life he could hang on to. Of course, he had Men; but that was a kind of gift. He needed something of himself to believe in. Just like Men had held back on his time in Europe, his marriage to Lucinda, so Dennis had been vague about himself.

He'd be vague no longer. He'd come to another decision as well.

to ride a wild pony

He was going to talk to Bill Rizzo again, find out more about that job.

Men had joked about feeling like a mother bird, wanting to shove Dennis out of the nest. But now, Dennis concluded, it was time for him to see if he really could fly.

He pulled the Thunderbird into the garage in back and came around the side of the house. Through the window he saw Men sitting at the table drinking a cup of coffee as he read the paper. All in all, he decided, life was not so bad. He ran up the steps and inside.

"Did you get Boris sent off okay?" Men asked.

"At least, I got him to the airport. You know how I hate goodbyes. I just dropped him off."

"I suppose he'd call if there was any problem."

"Yeah," Dennis said, walking to the stove to heat water for tea. The clock on the wall said it was nearly eight. He thought Rizzo got to the gallery around nine. He'd give him a few extra minutes.

When the water heated, he chose a bag of almond tea, filled his cup with water, dunked the bag and sat at the table.

Men laid down the paper. "So what do you think?" Men asked.

The question surprised Dennis. "What do you mean?"

"Sorry." Men chuckled. "I guess you can't read my thoughts, though being together all these years I sometimes wonder. I was referring to Boris."

"I think he's one terrific kid. I've always thought so."

"That episode. He seems okay. Don't you think he's okay?"

"What about you?"

"It's funny, Denny, but years ago, maybe even days ago, I'd have been furious. But I'm not. It's like, well, it was unfortunate. But it's past."

"I thought I'd stop in at the gallery again," Dennis said.

"Rizzo's?" His voice was filled with surprise.

"Yeah, that's right."

"Care to tell me why?"

"You know, Men, each human being has secrets. After I see him, we'll talk. Right now, I thought I'd go look through some of my paintings. You don't mind, do you?"

"Of course not. Why would I?"

"Can I get you anything."

"I'm not an invalid, damn it."

Dennis laughed. "But you're getting pretty crotchety, in your old age."

"Maybe I am." Men chuckled. "Go on upstairs, do what you want."

Dennis threw the tea bag into the trash and carried his cup with him up the steps.

In making Boris' bed, Dennis had been forced to gather up his paintings. He found he was pleased with what he saw. He wanted to look through them again and see if he did indeed have enough so that he could try to persuade Rizzo to give him a showing.

He gathered great stacks of them and sat on the bed, spreading them around him. Some, he found, were from years before. They did show promise, but there were hundreds of other painters just as good.

These were the more realistic; California mountains, scenes from Old Town and dozens of other recognizable places in San Diego. His favorite, of course, was the tree in Scripps park.

Of all his realistic paintings, he'd done the best with the tree. He thought briefly that maybe it was because he felt a kinship with it. Like him the tree was far from perfect. He laughed at himself for thinking such fanciful thoughts.

He made a pile of discards on his left. Some of them really were pretty bad. He wouldn't even save them. He'd stack the acceptable paintings on his right. On second thought, he'd make a third pile of "maybes," those that were okay, but not up to his best.

Well, he decided, if he was going to use that as the basis, most of his earlier stuff would have to be tossed. Some of it he was attached to, particularly those landscapes that somehow were associated with Men, places they'd explored together, like the scenes at Point Loma. The lighthouse, downtown San Diego in the distance, tiny boats far below. He and Men had decided that the park was one of their favorite spots. There were things he'd change about those paintings now, but back then, just after he'd quit school, he'd done his best.

He didn't do many portraits. But there were several of Boris, some of Boris and Men together, Men pushing him on the swing set outside the school, the two of them riding a merry-go-round.

Some of the paintings he had a hard time judging; he couldn't be objective about pieces of his life.

Finally, he settled on a small stack, thirteen or fourteen, that he thought were pretty good. The others he piled in corners to be tossed out or stacked on closet shelves.

Of those remaining, he'd re-mat the ones that needed it, maybe frame a few of them to show them off at their best. Yeah, damn it, he was going to find out once and for all if he had it. Maybe he was fifty-five, he thought, then laughed. But look at Grandma Moses.

After straightening up the paintings, he pulled the sheets off the bed in the extra room, folded them and dropped them in the hamper.

He glanced at the clock. It was a little after nine. He trotted lightly down the steps, waved to Men and said he was leaving.

"Be back in a little while," he said.

Cars lined the street; swimmers, sunbathers, surfers filled the beach. Dennis hurried down the steps and around the corner.

The gallery didn't open till ten, but he knew Rizzo liked to go in early to set things up and do any book work that needed done.

He walked up onto the porch and tapped on the door. In a moment Rizzo appeared. He looked surprised.

"Dennis," he said, gesturing for him to come on. "How are you? How's Melvin?"

"He's all right. Had to go back to the hospital again, but they just kept him overnight. He's home."

"His heart?"

"Anxiety."

"It can do funny things, I guess." He closed the door. "Did you want anything special?"

Dennis shrugged. "First, I owe you an apology."

"Maybe you do." Rizzo's abruptness surprised Dennis. But then he might have guessed. "You did run out damn fast the other day."

"Well, the truth is, Bill, I was hoping you wanted to see me about my own work."

Bill laughed. "How about a cup of coffee?"

"You wouldn't have tea?"

"Sure, come one back. I have a hot plate; I can heat some water. I have Lipton's and a couple of types of herbal."

"Herbal. Whatever kind."

They walked into the office; Rizzo motioned for Dennis to sit down while he filled a sauce pan from the water cooler and set it on to boil. "So what were you saying about your work?"

Dennis stretched out his legs and leaned back. "I thought when you wanted to see me, it was because of my painting."

"Actually, it was. You didn't give me a chance to—"

"I thought you wanted me to help keep the gallery open."

"That too. But that's not the important part." He leaned back in the swivel chair, folding his hands across his chest. He wore a woolen sport coat, reddish brown, and rust-colored slacks. "Look, Dennis," he said, placing his feet flat on the floor, learning forward on the desk. "I've been thinking for a long time about this. Maybe because I've always wanted to try myself to paint."

"Oh?" Dennis would never have believed that. He saw Bill strictly as a businessman, with little or no creative side.

"What I'd like to do is start a kind of art school? Small, at first. One or two classes. It wouldn't be aimed toward a degree or a certificate or the like. But just for fun. And that's where you come in."

"I don't understand," Dennis said.

"I've known you a good many years now, haven't I? You and Melvin."

"I guess."

"And like I told you once before, you impressed me a great deal. I mean in how you treated Boris and all the other kids. Jesus, you were always helping them, teaching them. You're a natural born teacher, you know."

Dennis felt flattered. "Thanks." He nodded. "So what you're leading up to is asking me to conduct one of the classes."

"Yeah, so what do you think?"

"I—wow—I never even thought of such a thing."

"But it appeals to you, right?"

"To be honest … yeah, I guess so." The water had heated by this time; Rizzo pulled a styrofoam cup from an already opened package and a tea bag from a box of Sleepytime Tea and passed them both to Dennis, who pulled the outer wrapping from the bag and slipped it into the cup, gently dunking it up and down. He looked around for a waste basket, spied one by the cooler and dropped the bag inside. He took a sip as he sat back down. "I'd like to know more about it," he said.

"Well, my idea is to have class once a week, to begin with. In the evening. For two, three hours. We'll let anyone who's interested enroll. Doesn't matter if they've had experience or not."

"What kind of painting? I mean oils, acrylics, water color?"

"Up to you; whatever you'd like to start with. I'll pay you a percentage. I thought maybe we'd split it fifty/fifty. We can figure out the details later. So what do you say?"

"I'd like that— I'd really like that."

"Now about your own work, Dennis. I knew that was why you'd left so abruptly. It didn't enter my mind at first, I mean when I asked you to stop by. But you're not one of those guys who can hide their emotions very well."

Dennis shrugged. "You're right. What can I say?"

"I've thought your work is pretty fair. But you know what? I saw how good you are, and I saw you piddle around with it all these years."

Dennis nodded, took a sip of tea.

"But I'll tell you what. If you prove to me you can go on producing, I'll take you on. Handle your stuff. I think it has a good chance of catching the public eye. We'll see. Okay? And I'd still like you to help run the gallery."

"I'd like to do that," Dennis said. "I've done a lot of thinking lately; a lot has happened. And I've changed my mind about several things."

"So when would you like to start?"

"Any time."

"Tomorrow? Come in around two, or earlier if you like. We'll work things out. I can't afford to pay you a lot, but you'll get a

---

commission as well on any pieces you sell. So it's not starvation wages."

Dennis drained the cup and stood up. Jesus, he thought, fifty-five years old, and here he was with his first real job.

CHAPTER 11

Men sat on the front steps as Dennis came home from the gallery. "You doing okay?" he asked as he came up on the small porch.

"Why? Shouldn't I be?"

Dennis felt a flush of anger. "What the hell's that supposed to mean?"

"Nothing." He stood up. "I decided to get some air. Watching the waves." He brushed off the seat of his pants. "Mesmerizing."

"Like a mantra or something. Like the rhythm of our bodies."

"Not an original thought, Denny."

Again, he felt a nagging bit of anger. "I didn't mean it to be. It was just what was going through my head." He turned to the door. "I'm going inside, how about you?"

"I've had my bit of sun for the day—if you can call it that. It was out from behind the clouds for maybe five minutes. Oh, well, one of the disadvantages of living next to the ocean."

"There's something I need to talk about."

"The reason you went to see Rizzo?"

"Yeah ..." He spoke hesitantly.

"I suppose you decided to take the job after all. Am I right?" He sat on the couch, picked up the *Times*.

Dennis strode to the window. A young man and woman in bathing suits strolled down the sidewalk hand in hand. She continued to laugh at something he was telling her.

He turned to Men. "Remember the things you told me about ... about Lucinda."

"Of course, I remember. I may be getting old, but I'm not senile."

"Hell, Men, what is it with you today? I can't say anything but you misinterpret it or pick at me."

Men laid the paper across his lap. He sighed. "I don't know. Maybe I miss Boris. Maybe ... I wish I was back teaching, was able to teach. Hell, I don't even have the energy to work on my book. I hate being a goddamned invalid." He looked directly at Dennis.

"What about Lucinda?"

Dennis held up his hands, fingers spread, palms outward. "Look, the reason I brought it up is—I don't know. I suppose it was some kind of cathartic effect? Telling me about it."

"So?" Men asked; Dennis knew for some reason he still felt defensive.

"I'm just saying—" He licked his lips. "Everyone, I suppose, has things he'd rather not talk about." He walked to the rattan chair and sat down.

"You're implying that you do?"

"Men, what is it? Is this a bad time to try to talk?"

"Hell, Denny, I'm just feeling my age, I guess. I can't pretend any longer I'm not getting old."

"Is it so bad that you are?"

Men laughed. "Well, when you consider the alternative …" He leaned back and clasped his hands behind his head. "It's ironic, isn't it, that Dad was a surgeon in New England, and I wanted to get away. So I moved here. Now Boris is right back where I started out."

"Does that bother you for some reason?"

"No … Yes. I don't know. I guess I feel he wanted to get as far away as he could."

"Maybe," Dennis answered. "But I think things are different now."

"Not going to allow me to be crotchety, are you?" His tone was mocking. "Not going to let me wallow in self-pity?"

"Oh, I think everyone's entitled to a little self-pity. I never knew why it had such a bad name."

Men laughed. "I hope you're satisfied. You got me out of the mood." His tone became more serious. "What did you want to tell me, Denny?"

"I've decided something, something pretty important, so far as I'm concerned." He stretched out his legs, stared at the tips of his shoes. "Before I go into it, I'd like to tell you my reasons."

"I'm listening."

"I told you Aunt Mattie kicked me out, and I told you why."

"The neighbor?"

"Yes. And I also told you when I came back home, all my things were piled outside the door. Not even enough to fill a small overnight bag."

"Damn, Denny, so many things could have happened. So many bad things. Instead …"

"Yeah, well, that's another story." He pursed his lips, folded his hands, finally continued. "Can you imagine how shocked I was? I couldn't believe it. Sure, I knew what I was doing with Rick was wrong. At least, I felt kind of guilty, without really knowing why." He shrugged. "I really never thought that I was molested, that Rick was a pervert. Hell, I wanted it as much as he did. Probably even more."

"The idea is that kids that age don't know their own minds," Men answered. "Maybe don't even know what's right or wrong. They look to adults for guidance." He paused. "Look, I'm not arguing what was right or wrong in your case. But when I think of Boris at that age …"

"But don't you see it was different? I had no family, no one who really cared. I was seeking approval, most of all love."

"And that's what made you so vulnerable."

"Lord, Men, I knew I was queer from the time I was six years old. No, I take that back. I knew I liked guys, but I guess I thought everyone did. I didn't know at first I was different."

"I suppose."

"Well, I saw this pile of stuff, and I panicked. God, can you imagine? It was the middle of winter; I had nowhere to go, no one to turn to." He shook his head. "I gathered everything up, my clothes, even an old writing tablet that I'd stuck my drawings in. I tucked it inside my coat, and rolled everything else up, and tried to tie it. Like a bedroll, I guess. Like I'd seen cowboys do in Westerns. And the whole damn time I was crying. Thirteen years old and crying like a baby. I could hardly see through the tears.

"Where was I going to go? What was I going to do? I didn't know."

He shrugged. "The first thought I had was to try to get Rick to take me in. Maybe he was still there. I pounded on the door, but no one came. I pounded and pounded till my knuckles were bleeding and raw."

"Christ, this Aunt Mattie must have been some kind of monster."

"Maybe she thought she was doing right, I don't know."

"Doing right to kick a kid out into the streets? I hardly think so."

"Later I found out she never meant to do that."

"Why the hell did she?"

"To teach me a lesson, I guess." Men only shook his head. "Either Rick wasn't there or he didn't answer. I guess he was scared. Afraid of what the police might do. Everyone hates a child molester. You've heard the stories. They're the lowest sort of scum."

He sighed. "Anyhow, that was out. And I can see his point. If the police had found me there, it would have been that much worse." He stood, walked to the window, turned back. "Later, I found he wasn't there. He packed what he could in suitcases and went to stay with a friend. And so far as I know, the police never came. It was just a threat."

"Oh?"

"He gave a key to some friends, people from the theatre where he worked, and they came back and got the rest of his things, arranged to have his furniture moved."

"How do you know all this? I thought you never went back there."

"I didn't." He sat down again, elbows on the arm of the chair, his two index fingers under his chin. "God, can you imagine? Thirteen years old. I panicked. I'd even have gone back to Aunt Mattie. But I didn't think she'd have me.

"So I had all this crap with me, everything I owned, and I ran down the steps again, three flights. It was a lot colder; a driving kind of snow that hit and stung. I sat for a little while on the steps. Three cement steps leading into a red brick building. I have such a vivid picture. Some of the bricks chipped and cracked, paper and shit all up and down the street. I didn't know where to go; what to do. It was dark by now, almost no one on the streets.

"I was freezing sitting there. And I had to move, had to keep moving."

"That fucking aunt of yours. She must have been a bitch."

"It's funny, Men, but I really can't blame her. She had taken me in, and she was by no means rich. She had one kid at home already. Her husband, my uncle, had taken off and never come back. She was strict, that's all, trying to do what was best, I suppose."

"Kicking a kid out is best?" Men's tone was sarcastic.

"I won't pretend it wasn't awful. And I was scared. God, I was scared. Afraid I'd be kidnaped or killed. And that wasn't so fanciful. Someone was always being murdered in the neighborhood or a few streets this way and that."

"God, Denny, I wish I'd known all this."

"What good would it do? It's past. Sure, it's affected what I've done, just about everything I've done, but it can't be changed."

"I'd still like to string up that aunt of yours."

"Maybe I shouldn't be telling you all this. I don't want to get you upset. I just want to try to explain … me. It's important right now, I think, for you to understand."

Men nodded. Dennis could tell he was making an effort just to listen. He thought it odd that he'd heard what happened to Boris, and he'd been able to accept it, but he was having trouble with this. Maybe because of the circumstances. What Mattie did was an adult thing, but what was done to Boris wasn't.

"After a while I started to walk; I was so damned cold. Cold and hungry. I hadn't had anything since lunchtime, except the hot chocolate. I kept thinking of the people in all the apartments I passed, how warm they must be, as they ate their dinners."

He massaged his forehead. "This is the hard part, the part I thought I'd never tell anyone. I never have till now." He sighed and then went on. "In a little while a car pulled over to the curb, and the driver rolled down his window.

"'Pretty cold out there, isn't it?' he asked. I tried to ignore him. I was still afraid, so I kept on walking. He pulled up near the curb and followed me along. He wore a hat, brim snapped down in front. I could tell he was an old guy, but not much else. 'I'll take you where you want to go,' he said. 'No strings attached.'

"And I don't know, Men. I guess I thought anything was better than being so cold. I don't mean I wasn't still scared. I was. But I figured if I gave him some sort of story about where I was going, there was at least a chance to ride in a warm car. I couldn't think much beyond the minute." He shook his head.

"I got in the car, and the guy asked me where I was going. He seemed concerned. I could see him better now; a light had come on when I opened the door. Looking back, I suppose he was in his fifties or early sixties. He had a kind face. And all at once my mind went blank. He asked me if I was lost, and I lied and told him I was. 'You can come home with me,' he said. 'I'll bet you're hungry, and I know you're freezing. We'll fix you a hamburger, and you can have a nice hot bath. What do you say?'

"I would have agreed to just about anything. So, he took me home, and you can guess the rest. I never told you. I never told anybody." His voice broke. "I've kept it all inside, Men. And so what do you think of me now? A hustler, a goddamned little hustler."

"Jesus Christ, you poor kid."

"I thought I had a good thing going. It was easy. Most of the guys wanted to suck my cock. Sometimes they wanted me to suck theirs. And that was okay. For the most part they were nice guys, let me stay all night, fed me, gave me five or ten bucks. A fortune back then, to a kid like me who'd hardly ever had a dime.

"When I was flush, I'd invent some story and rent a room. I was careful; I never picked the best places. Not quite fleabags, but close to it." He ran his hands across his eyes. "This kept up for about a month. I never went to school, but nobody bothered about me. They figured it wasn't their business, I suppose. So that's it, Men? My damned, dark secret."

"What did you do? Obviously you went back to school."

"Yeah, I did. One of the guys who picked me up—if you believe this—was an art critic. Or at least he said he was. And he went on and on about how good my drawings were. Besides paying me ten bucks for the night, he bought three of my drawings—five bucks each. They were ratty as hell by this time, my lugging them all around. He encouraged me to go back to school. Maybe to salve his own conscience, I don't know. But he convinced me at least to go on with my drawings.

"I traced Rick too. I remembered the name of the theatre company over in Manhattan. I looked up the address and hired a cab to take me there." Dennis remembered that he'd hoped Rick would take him in.

When the cab had pulled up in front, Dennis wondered if it was the right place. It was a pawn shop. Then a noticed a small entryway. A sign above it listed the name of the theatre.

He prayed Rick was there; he'd be glad to see him. He hoped maybe they could even stay together.

He opened the door; the stairway was dark, but he could hear voices up above. He crept up the steps, into a large open room, like a big warehouse. Battered theatre seats, wooden and without any padding, stood in haphazard patterns. At the front of the room was a platform, a foot or so above the rest of the floor, unpainted.

Several people walked with books in their hands, reading lines to each other. A couple of others were putting up scenery. Suddenly, Dennis saw Rick. He came out carrying a couple of long pieces of lumber. He laid them down and went out a side door.

Dennis felt a great relief. He'd found him and wouldn't have to walk the streets anymore. It was nice to have all that money. But he'd rather be with Rick.

Staying close to the wall, he scooted toward the front, hoping no one would notice him. He came to the side door and peeked through. Rick and a couple of other guys stood smoking, drinking coffee from paper cups. He wanted to try to get Rick alone.

"Hey, you, what are you doing here?" He turned, and a man with a bushy beard came toward him. The action on the stage had stopped and everyone stared.

"I—I—"

"Yeah, what is it?" Close up, the man smelled strongly of tobacco and sawdust. "Why did you sneak in here?"

"I'm a friend of Rick's," Dennis stammered.

"I'll just bet you are." His voice was filled with mockery. "Well, now that you've managed to interrupt everything, we'll just call him out here."

"Richard," the man bellowed. "Come here a minute, would

you?"

Rick and the two other men came toward the door. Then Rick saw Dennis. "What in the hell are you doing here, you little shit?"

Dennis couldn't believe it. This couldn't be Rick, not treating him this way. "I came— I thought—"

"Get the hell in here," Rick said, taking hold of his upper arm and dragging him into the scene shop. "Excuse me," he said to the others. "This won't take more than a minute." He kicked the door with the side of his foot, slamming it shut.

"Now what in the fuck did you come here for?" he asked.

"I thought …"

"What did you think, you little prick? Haven't you caused me enough trouble? I had to sneak the fuck out and get friends to go back for my things and arrange to move my furniture. I had no place to go and had to stay with a friend."

Dennis wanted to tell him what had happened, that he had no place to go either. But not now he wouldn't. He'd never tell him now.

He stared at him for a minute. "I thought you were my friend," he said. "I thought you liked me; I thought you'd help me." He turned, yanked open the door and raced through the room and down the stairs. Outside, he leaned against the building, his heart pounding, his breath coming in gasps.

"After that, I didn't know what to do," he told Men. "I thought it was the end for me, that now I'd never get anywhere. I'd never be an artist. I … I really wished I was dead."

He'd walked down the street till he found a drug store. The night and the cold no longer terrified him. He realized, of course, that there was still a chance of his being badly hurt. But he'd learned to get along.

He had twenty-three dollars stuck in his pants pocket. More than enough for what he wanted. He went inside; it was brightly lighted, making him squint, hurting his eyes. He walked up and down the aisles, randomly picking up bottles of pills.

Going to pay for his purchases, he noticed a soda fountain. He went back and ordered the largest drink of seltzer water they could give him. They put it in a milk shake cup with a lid. He went outside, walked till he came to a bench, sat down, pulled out bottles of pills and opened them at random.

Without looking at what they were, he popped the pills into his mouth, took the lid from his drink, sipped and swallowed.

A cold wind swirled around his feet and up his pants' legs. It didn't matter. Soon he wouldn't have to care about getting cold. He took another pill and another and another. And they came back up, and he vomited on the street.

He got up then, leaving the pills and cup behind, and started to run. He raced as fast as he could, block after block, dodging through traffic, ignoring blasts of horns.

When he couldn't run anymore, he slowed to a walk. Pretty soon, a car came by as he knew it would, and he climbed inside.

"I might have been trapped right there," he said to Men. "But I was a hell of a determined kid. I don't know what made me that way." He stood up once more, crossed to the window and looked outside, seeing nothing.

"My dad was a drunk," he said. "I vowed never to be like him. Maybe that saved me." He sat in the desk chair. "I went back to the Y to see if I could still be in the class.

"'Dennis!' Mr Franks said when I walked in. He was the teacher. 'You're aunt's been frantic. She thought you were ... that you were dead.'

"'My aunt kicked me out, Mr. Franks,' I told him.

"He finally persuaded me to stay while he called her, and she hurried right over. She told me that she was just going to let me, in her words, 'stew for at time,' and then allow me to come back in.

"She was filled with contrition and God's punishment and all kinds of shit like that. The gist of it is, I refused to go back with her. Child Services placed me in a foster home. Not the best of places, but not the worst. Mr. and Mrs. Peoples were fair, though a lot was expected of me in helping them run their business—a shoe repair shop.

"But they let me continue my art lessons, and I worked like hell both at home and at school—and you know the rest."

"Jesus, Denny, there's nothing I can say. You think you know a person inside out. And then you find out things like this."

Dennis smiled. "I've had the same sort of thought."

"Now you're accusing me of not being original." Men chuckled. "I really admire you, Denny, even more than I did. You're quite a guy."

"A hustler, huh? You didn't know you were getting a hustler, did you? Someone who could have taught you all sorts of tricks, things you never even thought of."

"Don't, Denny. Please, don't. I love you. I won't have you say things like that. I won't have you feel that way."

"Sometimes … sometimes, I can't believe that was me back then." He looked at Men and suddenly felt sad. But he had to go on with what he intended. "There's a reason for telling you all this."

"What is it, Den?"

"I don't know how you'll take this, Men. I don't know how it will affect you. But I'm going to move out."

Dennis could see Men was frightened. "I don't know what all this means. What it has to do with your moving out?"

"Back then, Men, when I had nowhere to stay and nothing except what I could carry with me, I vowed I'd never be without a home again. I'd never be without the security of knowing all the necessities of life could be taken care of. That became more important than anything else." He sighed. "Hell, Men, I wanted to be an artist, sure. But not as much as I wanted security. And I saw my art as a way out." He looked into Men's eyes. "But how many people—beyond gallery owners or entrepreneurs—make a living at art?"

He shook his head. "You never had to worry about the necessities, Men. Let alone the extras. I did. I knew it was up to me to keep myself alive. I did what I had to. And most of the time I didn't like it. I sold myself to whoever wanted to use me."

He ran both hands through his hair. "Most of the time I tried not to think of who I was with, what was going on. Kids that age, hell, they can come five, ten, a dozen times a day. And it's easy; it doesn't mean very much, if you don't want it to. And most of the time I didn't.

"At first, I romanticized a lot." He chuckled. "You know I'm

to ride a wild pony

good at that. I love happy endings. But I found you really have to work at them."

"What does this have to do with your moving out?"

"It was so easy, so easy, Men. You said I could move in, and we'd share everything, half and half. I couldn't pass that by. It was too good to be true. All the security I'd ever want, and nothing else mattered." He looked at Men. "Ah, shit, you know I don't mean that, not entirely. You matter, you've always mattered. I love you."

"And yet you're going to leave?" Men shrugged. "I understand, as much as possible, for not being in the same set of circumstances."

"I've never flown. I've stayed in the nest and kept it clean and presentable. I took care of the baby bird. He's long gone, and I'm still here."

"What are you going to do?"

"I'll find a place to stay."

"You don't have to do this; you can still have freedom. Whatever freedom you want."

He smiled. "I appreciate that. But I've got something I need to prove."

Men sighed. "Long ago, I thought this had to happen. Then, as the years went by, I hoped maybe it wouldn't." He laughed. "You're feeling guilty about it, I can tell. Well, don't. If anyone should feel guilty, it's me. I knew what I was doing. But like you, I couldn't help it. My home, my childhood were different, granted. But my life wasn't all that idyllic either."

Men stood up. "Oh, yeah, I had all the material things I could want. But I had to earn them. I found that out at an early age. I had to be the best at whatever I tried, or I was no good at all. In my parents' eyes. I didn't measure up, to him or to her.

"I played the piano. It didn't matter; my mother was better. I got good grades. So what? I couldn't compete with my father. He was number one in his med school class.

"They controlled me, like actually pulling strings." He shrugged. "You said you made some vows back then. I did too. I vowed I'd never be controlled by anyone ever again." He reached out and Dennis came toward him, taking his hand.

"I controlled you; hell, I knew it. And I could see you weren't always happy. But just like you had an overpowering need, so did

I. I needed to be in control. Not a very envious trait, is it?"

Dennis sat beside him. "I didn't mean to imply I've been unhappy."

"I know." He squeezed Dennis' knee. "Before we met, I rented a little house in Ocean Beach. I've showed it to you, I think."

Dennis nodded.

"I had a neighbor there, a young woman, about my age. Late twenties. Her husband worked for Pacific Bell, installing phones. They had two kids, preschoolers. One day I was out in the yard, and we started to talk. She was complaining about her kids. How they got on her nerves. 'But I'll bet you wouldn't trade them for anything,' I said.

"She looked at me kind of funny. And she said, 'Well, sometimes I'd rather have a wild pony.'" He looked at Dennis. "God, Denny, I'm going to miss you. All these years and you've always been here."

Dennis laughed. "I'm not leaving the planet. I'll be around."

"I guess what I'm trying to say, Dennis, is that I understand. And I want you to go ride that pony. Everyone has a right to that chance."

CHAPTER 12

It was a small room with a tiny bath hidden behind long green curtains. Just inside the door stood a refrigerator, stove and sink, separated from the rest of the apartment by counter space and two bar stools. It even had a small balcony, big enough for the lawn chair Dennis bought at the Good Will Store. Best of all it was furnished and cost only $150 a month.

Dennis had been discouraged. Everything was more expensive than he figured. One-bedroom apartments ran as high as $500 or $550. Even efficiencies were $300 or $350. He'd stopped at an apartment complex, with a security gate and so many restrictions he couldn't remember them all.

Then walking down a side street on the way back to his car, he saw a for rent sign tacked up on a porch pillar. The building was old with peeling paint, the front porch sagging. He decided to give it a try.

A tiny woman with a shuffling step and rounded shoulders answered the door. Incredibly old with sparse grey hair, she wore fluffy blue slippers and a faded cotton dress, pinned with an ivory brooch.

"Yes, young man?" she asked, and Dennis was caught by surprise. It had been years since anyone had called him young.

Tall trees shaded the yard. Red and yellow roses bloomed at the front and sides of the porch. "I saw your sign," he said.

"Oh." It was as if she were taken completely off guard. "Won't you come in? I'll call my husband." He followed her through a wide hallway and into a living room filled with potted plants. "Sit down," she said. "Sit down. May I offer you a cup of tea?" Then she shook her head. "No, I don't suppose I can. Nobody drinks tea anymore. It's all coffee nowadays. And usually that grainy sort in jars."

Dennis sat in a French provincial chair, the wood gleaming, the seat and back covered in a velvety fabric the color of faded roses. "I'd love a cup of tea," he said.

"Well, goodness gracious." She peered at him closely. "You

aren't just trying to butter up an old woman, are you?"

Dennis threw back his head and laughed. "No," he said. "I really prefer tea. I rarely drink coffee."

"I already have the kettle on. My husband's out in back. Puttering in the garden. He always putters in the garden. But then I suppose it gives him something to do." She hurried toward the back of the house. "Ed, Ed, Ed," she called, a staccato punching of the word.

"For heaven's sake, Millie, what is it?" a voice called back.

"There's a young man here to see the room. Why don't you entertain him while I fix us all a nice cup of tea?"

Dennis heard the man's laughter. "Do you really think he wants to sit around drinking tea with two old fogies like us?"

"Now never you mind," she said. "He's a nice young man. I can tell."

The man chuckled. "All right then. A cup of tea *would* be nice." He entered the room, a man as old as the woman, his face wrinkled, his hair pure white, sticking up in a rooster tail in back. He wore baggy grey work pants with bright red suspenders and a white shirt with the sleeves pushed halfway up to his elbows.

Dennis stood up as the man walked briskly toward him. "So you're interested in renting a room?" He didn't wait for an answer. "My name's Ed Ramsey." He held out his hand.

"Dennis Thompson." The man's grip was firm.

"English, are you? Well, so am I. Not that all that matters. Here we're one great melting pot." He turned and strode toward a flowered sofa with rounded arms and back. "Well, Mr. Thompson," he said. "What makes you think you might want to live in this house? It's not a fancy place, you know. But worth a fortune now. Millie and I have lived here fifty-eight years. Got the place for a song. Wouldn't sell it for anything; it's home. But decided to rent a room. With the children gone these many years. I said to Millie: it's a shame this has all gone to waste. So we called in a carpenter, had him make some changes. Filled it with furniture we never use. Bathroom's down the hall, though you have a toilet and sink in the room."

They were priceless, Dennis thought. He was charmed by them

---

to ride a wild pony

and was certain he'd take the room, sight unseen.

"Retired teacher myself. Public schools here for forty years. From merry old England. Different thing than public schools in England. Quite the opposite, don't you know. Took me a time to learn the system. Taught ten years at the University. San Diego State, not the other one up in La Jolla. My work, you see, in social studies. Fancy name for history. What about you?"

"I'm a painter," he said and knew for once it was true. He really was painting. "And I work in a gallery."

"Don't know much about painting. Only know that some of the things that pass for art, I don't like. Always thought some of the so-called old masters were over-rated. Dark, gloomy. Give me something bright and cheery every time."

Millie carried two cups and saucers, delicate bone china. Dennis hurried toward her to take one of the cups. "Nothing but old fashioned tea," she said. "Brewed good and strong."

He noticed a few shreds of tea leaves on the bottom.

"This is the way we always brewed it at home. When I was a girl in London. To my way of thinking it isn't tea if it's not done this way." She handed the second cup to her husband and went back to the kitchen.

"Suppose I should ask you for references," Ramsey said. "Everything's references these days."

Millie returned with a cup of her own and sat at the opposite end of the sofa. "I don't hold with that sort of thing," she said. "I judge people by knowing them. Not by what pieces of paper tell me. Now just let this young man drink his tea, and then we'll go look at the room."

He couldn't have found a nicer place to live, he thought. It was cozy. The Ramseys never bothered him, except to invite him in for desserts and home-brewed tea. Often he and Ed sat on the porch in the evenings talking, usually about the old days.

Ed spoke often about growing up outside London and his decision to come to America. His family was poor, his father a clerk in an insurance office. They wanted more for their son. As a wedding present, they scraped enough money together for him and his bride to book passage to the New World.

For years they never saw home again, and that was hard on them both, especially Millie. "But when you're close to your people," he said, "the miles don't matter. They're always right here in your heart."

It was a quiet evening when Ed told him this, the breeze blowing in from the ocean, salty and smelling slightly of fish. "Mum and Dad were very proud," he said. "So were Millie's folks. We were able to bring them here, thought they might stay. No sir, they missed the damp and fog of the Isles. They missed their home, don't you see. But Millie and I made a new home. Never regretted it, Millie and me. Wouldn't trade our lives for anyone's."

Dennis sat in his own room now, in a chair by the window, gazing out toward the ocean. He couldn't quite see the water but closed his eyes and imagined he could.

He'd just come back from the gallery, his class there. He wished he'd stopped in to see Men. He didn't want to make a pest of himself. God, how he missed him.

* * *

Men's biggest fear was being alone. Being alone and having a coronary, unable to phone, unable to summon anyone.

But then he could always have a neighbor or friend check in each day if they didn't see him.

He and Dennis had talked things over; some time, if he really believed he could be financially independent, Dennis said, he'd move back. A month, two months, half a year at the most.

It was nearing the end of September, the days getting shorter. In a month they'd be on standard time, and that would be worse.

Men sat in the living room, the last rays of the sun casting long shadows, darkness coming in waves. He missed Dennis so much. A hundred times a day, he'd start to call to him and then remember.

Dennis had found an apartment, an efficiency unit, in Pacific Beach; La Jolla rent was high. When he'd become discouraged, Men had suggested once more that he stay where there was no rent.

Dennis had placed his hands on the sides of Men's face, bent, kissed him lightly. "I'd thought we'd gone all through this," he'd

to ride a wild pony

said.

"Yes," Men had answered. "Forgive an old man—"

"Now, I won't have that kind of talk," Dennis said. "I'm not running out on you. I'll drop in whenever I can, if you'll have me, that is."

"Don't be silly. Of course, I'll have you. It's your house—"

Dennis placed a finger to Men's lips. "Shhh. We agreed we wouldn't talk about such things. Not now."

Men sighed, thought to get up and turn on the light, decided it was too much effort. And the darkness was comforting. Before too long, he could go to bed, and then it would be another day. A day closer to the time when Dennis would come back.

It was strange, he thought, to depend on another person so much. He'd never have believed it of himself. He was the self-sufficient one, the strong one, the one in con—

Oh, Denny, he thought, I want you back home so much.

He got up, went outside, sat on the steps. If he closed his eyes, it was easy to imagine a stretch of beach in the wilderness. No one walked by; no cars rode past. If he strained, he could hear the gently lapping water, comforting.

"After I've proved what I have to prove," Dennis had said, "I'll move back in. On one condition."

"Oh? What is it?"

"That we go halves on everything."

"Now, Denny, there's no need," Men had answered.

"That we split expenses right down the middle. In fact, I'd like to draw up an agreement to that effect."

It hurt. To have so much more and not be able to share. A cat wandered up the step, looked up at Men and meowed.

"You lonely too?" he asked and bent down to pet it. Before he reached it, the cat ran away.

"Old man," he told himself, "we had this talk not long ago about self-pity."

"Well, no one's here to know," another part of him answered.

Aloud, he muttered, "Yes, that's right," and thought he must be crazy to carry on conversations with himself, speaking out loud as if otherwise he wouldn't know what he was thinking.

He thought of Boris and the kids, and of Melissa. He'd wanted to know her better. A nice girl. No, not girl. Woman.

When did a person become a woman, he wondered. Or a man. In his eyes, Dennis had always been a man. Now he had to prove his manhood.

Across the water, Men saw the lights of the Beach and Tennis Club. A few birds skimmed low, pelicans.

So many things go into making a life, he thought. Experiences others would never suspect. He wondered what his neighbors would think if they knew about Lucinda? If they knew about Denny's time in the streets?

Did it matter? he asked himself.

His knees creaked as he stood up. No matter what Dennis said, he was getting old. He went inside, snapped on the light, walked to the downstairs bathroom, took his medication from the cabinet, downed it with barely cool water.

Then he went up to bed, undressed, and climbed under the sheet. It was only eight p.m.

to ride a wild pony

CHAPTER 13

There were so many things Dennis had never considered about living on his own. He'd rarely paid bills; he hadn't tried to balance a check book in more than thirty years. But he loved the feelings of competence it gave him.

It was Tuesday evening just after his workshop at the gallery, and he was feeling good. He'd stopped to talk with a student, and it was later than usual. About 10:30. He was sleepy; before working at the gallery, he most often was in bed by this time.

Even so, as he locked up and climbed into his car, he decided he'd stop in and see Men. He'd come to a decision, worked out the details in his mind, and wanted to discuss it, the sooner the better.

On the way he thought about the class. It seemed to be a huge success, with twenty-two people enrolled, at all levels of experience from beginner to the professional who wanted a different viewpoint. It was a wonderful feeling to work with them, to know that they all viewed him as a serious artist. He'd even begun to look at himself as a professional.

He liked working at the gallery during the day as well, answering questions about technique, pointing out differences among artists' work.

Rizzo told him he was a born teacher; he began to feel that maybe he was. And that surprised him. When he thought about it, he regretted wasting all the years when he could have been working. But he couldn't dwell on that. And he had painted. Even after leaving State full-time, he took the occasional course there and at other places. But not till Boris was older.

He loved simply being at the gallery; he kept all his own supplies there, and during his off hours he often hung around, sometimes painting in the back room where the classes were held, at other times just puttering around, as his landlady would put it.

He felt he was developing well; his style was more distinctive. Three or four of the students already had asked what techniques he used to get certain results.

When he'd been at State full-time, he'd found that often the instructors didn't want to share their own methods. Rather, they guarded them fiercely, afraid someone would steal them, cheating the artists out of something they'd discovered on their own.

Dennis didn't feel that way. It was a joyful thing to develop his techniques and to create painting after painting. But it felt just as good to pass on his discoveries to someone else. One of the older members of the class, a man who had his work in a number of galleries across the country, couldn't believe he'd do that.

"Why not?" Dennis asked one day after class. "Nobody's execution will be just like anyone else's. You know that."

The man, Lenny Dodd, agreed. "Too bad everyone starting out couldn't have teachers like you."

Dennis appreciated comments such as this. All in all, he was happy. On most days, he was able to drop in and see Men, if not before going to the gallery, then on his way home.

He still kept up his schedule of running and walking, but now in Pacific Beach; his apartment was eight blocks from the ocean. All in all, he was happy. His salary wasn't fantastic, but it was enough to get along. He'd proved what he wanted to.

He pulled up in front of the house and stopped. It was early November; he'd been on his own for more than a month.

Through the window, he could see Men at the desk, he supposed working on his book. He quickened his steps, then knocked on the door.

"Who is it?" Men called.

"Just me." Dennis stood on the steps.

"Jesus, Dennis, come on in. You don't have to stand out there. It's still your house as much as it's mine."

As Dennis stepped inside, the two men embraced. "How are you, Men?" he asked.

"Good. I decided to get back to my book. It helps fill up the hours. How about you?"

"I'm doing okay." For some reason, he felt suddenly shy. "I'd like to move back, if it's all right?"

"What the fuck are you talking about?" Men snarled. "Why in the hell wouldn't it be all right?" They walked into the living

to ride a wild pony

room. "Ah, Denny ... it's been hell. I'm so used to your being here. I never realized how big this damn house is."

"Big?" Dennis kidded.

"You know what I mean. What can I get you? Can I get you anything?"

Dennis sat on the couch. "No, Men," he said. "I just want to see you, talk to you. I tried to get rid of the class as early as I could, but a student wanted to ask me about her painting. A watercolor. A landscape, really pretty good. I was hoping you'd still be up."

"So when are you coming back?" Men asked.

"We need to talk about that." He paused to figure out how to begin. "I miss you, a hell of a lot. But I needed to be gone. I proved what needed proving, I think. But ..."

"What?"

"Like I said before, when I move back, I want us to split everything down the middle, all the expenses, I mean."

"I— I suppose. There isn't that much."

"And I feel I should pay you rent."

"In your own goddamned house? Like hell. It's already paid for, and, no, I won't back down about this. What's past is past; the house is paid for, and that's it."

Dennis threw back his head and laughed. "Taxes then?"

"Okay, you can pay half the damn taxes. So when's it going to be?"

"My apartment's paid up till the fifteenth."

"Screw that," Men answered. "It doesn't matter. Since there's no rent here, it'd be the same whether you left or not. And I'm not trying to control anything, I'm just stating facts."

"Okay, okay, I give. You've persuaded me."

"So have you got your things in the car?"

"No, Men, I don't have my things in the car. And speaking of the car, my car, I'm going to pay you. And no arguments."

"We'll see."

"I love you, Men. Do you know that?"

"Damn it, Denny, I should; you've been telling me for thirty-five years. Ah, hell ... I love you too. I can't contemplate life without you."

Dennis stood up. "I better be getting back. I'm really sleepy; I can hardly keep my eyes open. I have to be at the gallery early, and I want to get up and run. How about this weekend?"

"I'm not hallucinating. You're really moving back?"

"I'm moving back."

"Thank God," Men said.

Dennis leaned over and kissed him on the cheek. "Goodnight. I'll stop in tomorrow. Maybe start carrying in some of my things. Jesus, it'll be good to be home."

Dennis felt like dancing down the street. It was a glorious night. Clear. A billion stars. He started the motor and pulled away from the curb. He was sleepy, really sleepy. But he felt so good.

When he pulled onto the freeway, he didn't see the other car.

* * *

After Dennis left, Men went back to the desk, tried to write a few more sentences and gave up. He leaned back, hands clasped behind his head, legs stretched out.

It would be good to have Dennis back. Realistically, he knew, that two people couldn't live together in perfect harmony. But they'd made it for thirty-five years. How was that for beating the statistics? he thought.

He gathered up his notes, piled them on the side of the desk and went to the kitchen for a glass of milk. He drank it, standing over the sink. It was Tuesday, he thought. Only three days till the weekend.

He walked to the bathroom for his medication, took it, rinsed out the glass and went on upstairs. Moonlight filtered through the sheer curtain across from the foot of the bed. For a time he lay on his back, then turned over and went easily to sleep.

* * *

A persistent ringing brought him awake. He looked at the luminous dial of the clock. Eleven twenty- three. He hadn't been

to ride a wild pony

asleep more than half an hour. He wondered who could be calling at this hour and considered ignoring it. Yet it might be important, he thought.

He struggled to sit up, the sheet binding around his legs. Freeing himself, he reached for the receiver.

"Mr. Aradopolos?" The voice sounded almost mechanical. He was sure he didn't recognize it.

"Yes."

"Mr. Melvin Aradopolos?"

All at once he was frightened; he wanted to hang up the phone, burrow back under the covers. It was a bad dream of some sort, and he didn't want to know the ending.

"This is Melvin Aradopolos," he answered.

"Mr. Aradopolos. Do you own an '89 Ford Thunderbird. California License 1BCS—"

Oh, my God, he thought, it's Dennis. Something had happened to Dennis. He was in an accident. He was hurt. His voice shook as he tried to answer. "Yes, yes, it's—it's my car. It's in my name."

"Sir, I'm afraid there's been an accident."

Not now, God, not now. Just when Dennis is coming back. Just when everything's going to be okay.

"I'm sorry, sir, did you hear me?"

"Dennis?" He tried to go on. "Dennis Thompson?" He felt his body trembling, shaking

.

CHAPTER 14

Late November, well into the rainy season. Such a contradiction. Winter and the greening of the hills. Back in New England the leaves would long ago have changed and fallen.

Men sat at the kitchen table, drinking a second cup of coffee. Sometimes he missed the hush of winter, pine trees heavy with snow. Boots squeaking on sidewalks. Everything pure and white.

God Almighty, he thought, are people destined to spend their last years in hospitals, as patients or ... damned spectators!

It had been weeks now, and nothing much had changed. Dennis lay in a hospital bed, unmoving except for the rolling of his eyes, as if he were dreaming. Or sometimes his lips moved a little, as if they were about to form words. They never did. In the first couple of weeks, Men had been there all day long, sitting outside ICU, unable to contain himself until he could get back inside for five minutes every hour on the hour.

Somehow his friends had heard, neighbors, co-workers Men hadn't seen in years. He hadn't even known they were aware that he and Dennis were ... Lovers? Partners? The fucking most important thing in the world to each other.

People invited him for dinners and lunches. He was polite but firm. He wanted to be alone. He didn't want to talk about Dennis to all these people.

Damn, it was so fucking unfair. Doctors had told him, Boris had told him there was very little hope anymore. But he couldn't accept that. He couldn't give up.

Somehow the days passed, the weeks. He arose at his usual time, fixed a little breakfast. Real coffee now. What did it matter? Usually two cups, sometimes three.

The bones in Dennis legs and hips and pelvis were healing nicely; he was mending in every way, except the most important way. Inside his brain.

In his time away from the hospital, Men had taken to sitting by the desk, the curtains spread looking out the window. At one of these times he remembered a conversation, as if a tape unwound

---

to ride a wild pony

in his head. That was happening increasingly now, bits and fragments of his life.

They were in the car, on the way to Los Angeles. Dennis suddenly turned to him and gripped his upper arm.

"If you'd ever die, Men, I don't know what I'd do. Promise me you never will. Will you promise me that?"

Men had laughed. "I won't die, Denny. I don't expect to die. I'm not even thirty-five."

Men glanced over and saw terror in Denny's eyes. It was the same night they agreed that Dennis would move in.

He stood up, walked to the kitchen, rinsed out his cup. He thought he'd work on the book. The rough draft was nearly finished. If he kept at it, he'd have it done in a couple of days.

He came back to the living room, opened the desk drawer, drew out paper and pens, lined them up at the left. He hadn't cried yet. His closest friends didn't understand that. Maybe they thought he didn't care. But sometimes concern is too deep for tears, he thought.

He picked up a stack of five by eight cards. References, notes on Greek government since World War II. Greek government of the present; projections for the future.

Suddenly, a sob escaped his throat. "Denny!" He thought of a novel he'd read years ago. A woman whose husband was in a coma. She sat by him carrying on constant dialogues as if he would answer.

"Jesus, Denny, it's hard," he said. "I was the one who was wearing out. My fucking heart was wearing out."

He became aware of the cards in his hand. There was no reason to finish. No one cared if he did or not, least of all himself.

He laid down the cards, walked to the closet and pulled out a sweater. "Think you'll get cold, old man?" he muttered. "Out in all that sunshine?"

He opened the door, walked outside, stood on the porch in the sunshine. Watched the youngsters across the street. It was a beautiful day, only wisps of mist left playing across the water.

Out on the sidewalk, he rounded the bend to Girard. Occasional strollers nodded or smiled.

He paused in front of the gallery, then went inside.

Rizzo stood at a table framing a painting. "Melvin!" he said. "How are you?"

"I'm all right. Shouldn't I be?" Rizzo frowned. "Sorry," Men said. "That wasn't very civil."

Rizzo shrugged. "How about a cup of coffee?"

"I'm just about all coffeed out."

"Tea then. There are all sorts since Dennis—" He broke off. "I'm sorry, I didn't mean to say that."

"He does exist. For fifty-five years he's existed. He's not dead yet."

"Come on back. There's no one here. If someone comes in, I'll hear them."

Men followed him back the hallway. Rizzo stood aside and mentioned him into the room that served as his office. It was stacked with mats, paintings, frames. "I'll heat the water."

Men sat in a black sling chair as Rizzo busied himself getting water from the cooler, turning on the hot plate. He spoke over his shoulder. "How is he? No change, I suppose."

"No change."

"The students ... Dennis' students. They want to establish a scholarship, for deserving artists. A scholarship in his name."

"What?" Men said.

"His class. The people he taught, they love him. And that's not empty talk." Rizzo laughed. "Like he's the damned Messiah or something. Or the patron saint of all unrecognized artists."

The sauce pan began to steam. "Cups, tea bags, instant coffee, creamer, sweetener. Help yourself."

"You want anything?" Men asked.

Rizzo shook his head. Men turned off the burner, chose a tea bag at random, opened a pack of sweetener, dumped it into the cup with the bag and covered them both with water. The water turned red. Cranberry.

Rizzo leaned back, hands clasped behind his head. "One guy in class is pretty well known." Rizzo chuckled. "Dodd's his name. Confessed he came here only for studio space; things were getting too crowded at home. Then he met Dennis and got himself all fired up."

"You were talking about the scholarship." Men dunked the tea bag up and down.

"There's going to be a showing. The best work from each of the students. Even Dodd agreed, and his stuff's priced way up there. Some of the pieces aren't great, but what the hell? We'll advertise in the *Light* and in the *Union Tribune*. Put out flyers, spots on KPBS. A big reception. We'd like you as guest of honor. I was going to call."

Rizzo leaned forward. "He's a hell of a man. I love him too. I always have. I know he suspected I had ulterior motives." He laughed. "Well, damn it, I did. But more important I've always loved him as a friend. I respected him." He leaned his arms on the desk. "Hell, I knew his work was good, but I never gave him a showing. I tried to explain why once ... Did you know that people were starting to collect his work?"

Men shook his head. Rizzo was talking as if Dennis were dead. Maybe Men was being too much of a pollyanna, and was ashamed at himself for the thought.

"I suppose by rights you should have the say over what's to be done with his work."

Years before they'd talked of giving each other power of attorney if the time ever came. "I hadn't given it any thought." And he wondered why he hadn't; the art was such a part of Dennis. "I haven't seen his recent work."

"Finish your tea, and I'll show you."

Men took the last few swallows and tossed the cup into the waste basket.

"We haven't worked out the details," Rizzo said as he stood up. "We'll set up a panel, I guess. Pick a deserving student. Pay him or her the yearly interest on the amount we raise. It won't be a lot. Of course, if Dennis recovers, he can administer it himself."

Men read in Rizzo's eyes that he didn't believe what he was saying.

***

The paintings overwhelmed him. Powerful, with bold strokes of color, they seemed to leap right out of the canvas. Was it because they were Dennis' that they affected him this way? He glanced toward Rizzo.

"You're wondering, aren't you, if it's just you?" Rizzo's eyes filled with moisture.

There were so many things Men didn't know about this man. "They're ... overpowering. I've never felt such force from a work of art."

"Everyone's affected that way. I love to watch the reactions. They come in, look in the front of the gallery, wander on back to this room. It's like they're kicked in the gut. What a terrible power and beauty."

Suddenly, the thought struck Men that he'd prevented Dennis from painting this way. He groped for a chair. "All those years," he said. "All those years, and I never knew."

"No one could have predicted it," Rizzo said.

"But you don't understand. My God, I made it so easy for him not to paint. I never knew. I never knew." He felt very small, guilty as he had only once before, the night of his marriage.

"You want to know something, Melvin? I've never seen a kid who could paint like that. It takes a certain maturity. It's not just a blending of color and texture. It's not just the composition. It's the knowledge of life. It's having lived. It's distilling our experiences, it's what we've become and what we've learned, gathering it up and translating it into art."

Men looked up. "You know what?" he said. "You're an eloquent son-of-a-bitch for being such a hard-assed businessman."

Rizzo laughed so hard Men thought he was in danger of collapsing.

For the first time in weeks, Men felt truly hopeful again. He patted Rizzo's shoulder. "Gotta get to Hillcrest to the hospital." He walked toward the door and then turned. "You know what, Rizzo? We're going to beat this thing. Dennis and I. We're not giving up."

"You know what, you little shit? I think you may just be right."

THE END

Sounding Brass

A Novella by

Marsh Cassady

"Though I speak with the tongues of men and of angels and have not love, I am become as sounding brass or a tinkling cymbal."
I Corinthians 13:1

Learning about Sex

It was June 10, 1948, Martin's twelfth birthday, when Aunt Sarah gave him a book called *Learning about Sex*. Lying in bed on Saturday afternoon he read it through. Much of what it said he already knew, except he was kind of mixed up. It didn't have any pictures or drawings, and when he tried to visualize what a girl or woman looked like naked, it was just sort of blank.

There was something else he didn't understand. The book said a person should never masturbate. Martin wasn't sure what that meant. He'd heard some older boys in the locker room at school talking about "beating off," and he knew this must be the same thing. Yet what was it?

For almost three years now he'd felt his penis grow stiff, sometimes at embarrassing times—like when he was sitting at his desk in school. Once it was stiff when the dismissal bell rang, and he didn't know what to do. He didn't want anyone to see. Yet he couldn't just sit in his seat. Finally, he tucked his books under his arm, and stuck both hands in his front pants pockets, making fists, trying to disguise what was happening.

Mostly at night he got what Donny called "a boner." No matter what he did, it throbbed and ached in a way he couldn't understand. He wondered if this was what "beating off" meant because with each beat of his heart his penis seemed to jerk or beat.

Just a couple of weeks after he read the book from Aunt Sarah he had a bad sore throat, and his mother took him to see Dr. Carruthers. As he sat in the waiting room, he glanced through an old copy of *Life Magazine*. There was an article about a man named Jenkins, almost the same as Martin's name which was O'Jenkins.

Martin turned the page and saw the man's picture. He felt a thrill in the pit of his stomach and felt his penis begin to grow stiff. He thought Mr. Jenkins was beautiful, his face filled with angles and planes. Just then the nurse popped her head through the doorway. "Martin," she said, "Doctor will see you now."

Martin stood, not wanting to let go of the magazine, holding it till the last possible second. He closed it then and laid it on the square coffee table in the center of the room.

Two nights later he dreamed of Mr. Jenkins, how they'd become friends. In the dream, something inside him exploded, something that gave him the most wonderful feeling he'd ever experienced. When he awoke and knew it all had been a dream, he felt a sense of loss, a yearning like he'd had as a little kid wanting to be around his friend Donny's father, who coached the town baseball team. Yet this was a thousand times more intense.

Suddenly, Martin realized his pajamas were wet, sticky. For an instant he didn't understand. Then he remembered the book Aunt Sarah had given him. There was a chapter on nocturnal emissions, wet dreams, "a natural occurrence for the adolescent boy." Even so, he was embarrassed; he didn't want his mother to know. Nor his father.

He couldn't stop thinking about it, thinking about Mr. Jenkins, who looked a little like Mr. Lang, his physical education teacher. The teacher's hair was darker, but he and Mr. Jenkins had the same kind eyes, the same caring manner. They liked Martin; they paid attention to him, something no one else did, except to bawl him out.

Every night after that when Martin went to bed, he hoped, almost prayed, that he'd have another dream about Mr. Jenkins.

One day Uncle Stanley stopped by and said a Boy Scout troop had been started at the Lutheran Church near where he lived. Ray had already joined. Uncle Stanley said he thought it might be nice for Martin to attend the meetings.

Dan said he could drop him off, and Uncle Stanley would bring him home. Martin didn't know if he wanted to join since he didn't know any of the other kids.

"You know Ray," Uncle Stanley said. "And you'll get to know the others."

"Okay," Martin said, though he didn't like the idea. He changed his mind right away when he saw the Scoutmaster, Sam Holden. He went early the first time so Sam could talk to him before the meeting. He lived right next to the church, and when Martin knocked on the door, he hurried down the steps from the second floor, wearing a pair of grey work pants, but carrying his shirt in his hand.

Martin, seeing him through the panes of glass in the door, felt the same thrill he had when he'd seen the picture of Mr. Jenkins. Only this person was real, not just a photo. Sam looked strong, tanned, even though it was wintertime. His chest was muscular, the nipples hard, a patch of dark blond hair between them, a thicker patch just above his belt.

Martin flushed and glanced away.

Struggling into his shirt, the sleeves and front dangling open, the Scoutmaster opened the door. "Hi," he said. "You must be Martin."

"Yes," Martin mumbled.

He held out his hand. "I'm glad to meet you."

At the same time he felt embarrassed, Martin felt good. He took Sam's hand. It was dry, the handshake firm. Martin followed him inside. They sat in the living room while the Scoutmaster talked about the troop and the meetings and what Martin would be required to do.

Martin bought a uniform and a Boy Scout ring, as well as a couple of books about Scouting. In one of them there was a section that said some of the same things he'd read in the book from Aunt Sarah.

It talked about something else, too. It said that sometimes boys were sexually attracted to other boys, and if they were, they should try to find new companions.

Martin sat in the living room at home, heat from the coal stove warming his left side, leaving the right side cool. He sighed as he laid the book on the arm of the chair. He was all mixed up. It must be wrong, he thought, to have the kind of feelings he had about certain men. But they were men and not boys. He wasn't attracted to other boys. Was it wrong to be near the men as well?

He moved to the piano stool, away from the baking heat of the stove. This book too warned against masturbating. Although the practice didn't seem to be particularly harmful, it could, the book said, stunt the natural development of an interest in the opposite sex. Martin still wasn't sure what masturbating meant. He was just beginning to be interested in girls, though no one in particular. But if he masturbated or spent time around boys—men—to whom he was attracted, would he never marry, never have kids of his own? He swallowed hard. He didn't know; he just didn't know, and there was no one he could talk to about it. Even if there were, it would be too embarrassing.

He became a Tenderfoot and began to work on his Second Class rank. He'd joined the troop just in time to be able to go to winter camp.

Their first night in the cabin, his cousin Ray refused to get undressed and crawl into bed. "I'm embarrassed," he said. Martin thought he was just being silly.

"Come on, Ray," Sam said. "Everyone else is getting undressed."

"I don't want anyone to see me," he said.

"Don't you take gym at school?" Sam asked. "You have to get undressed there, don't you?"

Ray just shrugged and sat on his bed.

"You have the same thing as everyone else," Sam said. He smiled and nodded. "So come on."

Ray pulled back his covers, crawled underneath them and struggled to pull off his pants.

Sam laughed. "Okay," he said. "That's one way to do it." Then he undressed as well. He pulled off his shoes and socks, his shirt and pants, his undershirt. Aware that he was staring, Martin glanced around the cabin to see if anyone noticed.

Sam wore only his underwear now, a pair of jockey shorts, bulging in the front. Martin breathed in sharply when he saw Sam's legs. One was muscular, the other scarred and thin. Martin wondered why, but then forgot about it as Sam stood up, facing toward where Martin lay in his cot and pulled off the underwear. Martin's heart began to pound. Sam's cock was long and thick, surrounded by bushy hair, light brown.

Sam stepped into his pajamas, folded his clothes and stuck them into a knapsack. "Get the light, will you, Eddy?" he asked as he crawled into bed.

It was dark then as Martin lay on his back, wide awake. He'd never seen a naked man before. His own cock wasn't nearly the same size as Sam's. He wondered if it ever would be. Martin's pubic hair was just beginning to grow. Would it ever look like Sam's? He thought he must be crazy then because all he wanted to do was bury his face in that hair. He felt ashamed and somehow guilty.

* * *

A few months after Martin joined the Boy Scout troop, another one was formed in the town where he lived. The Scoutmaster was Rev. Johnson from the Lutheran Church down on the corner of the street where Martin lived. One Saturday the members, all of whom Martin knew, planned to go swimming at the Y in Johnstown. His friend, Donny, asked Rev. Johnson if Martin could go with them.

Martin usually went swimming in the stream on Grandpa's farm or once in a while at the pool in Clivesville. But his mom didn't often let him go there because she thought he might get polio. But she said it was okay to go to the Y.

In the locker room, everyone got undressed. Martin looked up and saw Rev. Johnson standing just on the other side of the bench from him.

Although he'd liked him from the first time he'd met him, he didn't feel attracted to him as he had to Sam Holden or Mr. Lang. Not until now. Broad, without being the least bit fat, he was a few inches taller than Martin's dad, close to six feet. He had brown eyes and a craggy face, but what drew Martin's attention was his chest and stomach, covered thickly with a mat of dark brown hair.

More than anything in the world Martin wanted to reach across the bench and run his hands down the front of Rev. Johnson's body, hug the man against him. Never had he felt so attracted to anyone. He knew he should finish undressing, but he couldn't move.

Finally, everyone left to go to the pool, and Martin shucked off his clothes and hurried to join them. Most of the kids already were in the water, as was Rev. Johnson. Trying not to make it obvious, Martin stayed as close to the Scoutmaster as he could, watching as the water slicked down the hair on his arms and legs and chest. Martin thought of the man's penis, long and thick like Sam's, buried in bushy hair, and his own penis hardened. He hoped the water would distort its appearance, and no one would notice.

On the way home he made sure he rode in the Scoutmaster's car, sat next to him in the front seat, squeezed over so that their legs often touched. He tried to keep hidden the fact that his penis once more had stiffened.

At home he went up to his room, undressed and climbed into bed. He'd never felt so excited in his life. He couldn't stop thinking about Rev. Johnson. As he thought of him, he stroked his cock.

His body grew tense, drawing back almost in a bow. Martin wondered if he were going to burst wide open, explode into a million pieces. But he couldn't stop. His hand in a fist, he began a rhythmic motion, thinking of Rev. Johnson's chest and broad back, his thighs, his body hair, his cock.

A chill began at the top of Martin's head, spread down his body as white liquid erupted, spurt after spurt after spurt across his stomach, onto the sheet. When it was over, he lay back, closed his eyes.

What if Mom came into his room? he thought. Quickly, he jumped up, grabbed a handkerchief from his drawer, wiped himself and the sheet. He remade the bed, dressed, wadded up the handkerchief and sneaked downstairs. No one saw him go into the living room where he opened the door to the coal stove and threw the handkerchief inside. He watched as it blazed up, destroying the evidence. He knew now he didn't have to wait for the occasional dream; being awake when it happened was so much better. He knew he'd discovered what the word "masturbation" meant.

After that it became almost a nightly ritual. He thought about Rev. Johnson, about Sam, about Mr. Lang, about neighbors up and down the street. He thought of them naked, holding him, caring about him.

Martin had been taking trumpet lessons for about a year. At his next lesson his teacher, Mr. Carlson, said he was going to retire. Tim, over on First Street and also in the band, told Martin about a musician named Tom Thatcher who was supposed to be a good trumpet player. He'd recently moved to the area, and had started to give a few lessons. Martin called and the man agreed to see him. Because he lived just beyond Sixth Street, Martin could walk to his house. Right away he realized the man was good, as good as Mr. Carlson or maybe even better. He also seemed to realize how serious Martin was about his music.

Because it was warm when Martin started lessons, Mr. Thatcher sometimes wore only an undershirt and pants. He sat in a chair beside Martin, who sometimes could barely concentrate on his playing. Mr. Thatcher was in his sixties, completely bald, with greying blond hair on his arms and sticking out the top of the undershirt.

They sat in the dining room, Mrs. Thatcher most often in the kitchen doing the dinner dishes. Out the window Martin could see a pasture stretching down over a hill.

Sometimes when Mr. Thatcher wanted to explain something important, he reached out and squeezed Martin's leg. Martin longed for him to do more; he didn't know quite what. But he tried to play his best to please this man, to make him proud.

Often at night now, he thought of hugging and being hugged by Tom Thatcher.

One Friday evening just before school was out, Martin's mom and dad decided to go to Uncle Stanley's. Once there, Ray and Martin went outside on the porch. Ray's brother, Garth, now five, followed them.

"Go back in, we don't want you," Ray said. He pushed Garth toward the door.

"Don't want to go in," Garth said.

"But I want you to, and you'll go." Ray shoved him toward the door. Garth stumbled and fell. He started to cry as he picked himself up. "I'm telling," he said. "I'm telling."

"So go ahead and tell," Ray said.

Martin was shocked. He'd always wanted a brother. If he had one, he'd never treat him like Ray treated Garth.

"Come on," Ray said, "let's go around to the pond." Uncle Stanley had scooped out dirt at the side of the house and poured in cement. That was a couple of years ago. Now the pond was filled with big goldfish. In the summer lilies covered the surface.

"Let's sit down," Ray said. There was a tarp by the pool.

"What for?" Martin asked.

"So we can talk."

Martin shrugged. Ray could be weird sometimes. "Okay," he said.

He sat down, Ray right beside him. "I'm going to camp out here tonight. That's why the tarp's here. I'm going to put up my pup tent. I'd like you to stay. I asked my mom and dad and they said it's all right. We'll take you home in the morning."

Martin wasn't sure he wanted to stay. "I don't know."

"Oh, come on," Ray said, "it'll be fun."

Martin sighed. He guessed it would be all right. But he thought he might be getting a little old to sleep out in the yard. But even though Ray was kind of funny, they had been friends, as well as cousins, ever since Martin could remember.

"Okay," Martin said. "But I'll have to ask my mom and dad."

Suddenly, Ray reached over and felt between Martin's legs. Martin was startled.

"You don't mind, do you?" Ray asked.

Martin didn't answer; he knew he shouldn't let Ray do it. He spread his legs apart. Ray unbuttoned his pants and reached inside. Martin felt himself get suddenly hard. Then he jerked away.

"What's the matter?"

"We'd better go ask Mom and Dad if I can stay." Martin stood quickly and buttoned his pants. What if Ray tried to feel him like that again?

Uncle Stanley and Aunt Rose already had talked to Martin's mom and dad about spending the night, so he had no choice.

Martin helped Ray put up the tent. Then the boys went inside the house to go to the bathroom. Aunt Rose gave Martin an extra toothbrush. "You two be sure to get some sleep," she said. "I don't want you staying awake all night talking."

"We won't," Ray said.

They lay on a sheet on top of the tarp, two blankets covering them. Ray wore pajamas, Martin only his underwear. He scooted over to the side as far from Ray as possible. In a little while Ray said he was going to sleep. He rolled to his side facing away from Martin.

Later Martin woke up, Ray's hand between his legs, underneath his underwear. "It feels good, doesn't it?" Ray asked.

We shouldn't be doing this, Martin thought, but he couldn't help it. He pulled down his underwear till his penis struck straight up. "Yours is big," Ray said, "a lot fatter than mine."

"Is it?" Martin asked, trying not to think about what was happening, yet wanting it to happen.

"Feel it," Ray said, "you'll see." Ray pulled off his pajama top and then the bottom. He grabbed Martin's hand and drew it between his legs. "See," he said.

Martin had never before seen anyone's penis hard except his own. "Stroke it for me," Ray said. He reached out and grasped Martin's cock and gently ran his fingers up and down.

Feeling a kind of release he didn't understand, Martin reached out and took Ray's cock in his hand, wishing it could be Rev. Johnson's, or Sam Holden's or Tom Thatcher's.

Later, when Ray was asleep, Martin got up and went inside to the bathroom. He hoped he wouldn't wake Uncle Stanley and Aunt Rose. He washed himself off. Then he sat on the front porch until he saw the sun come up.

Love Thy Brother

Sam thought he probably was on a fool's errand or he might be walking into a booby trap, though he doubted the latter. Ambushes or murders happened in the big cities, Pittsburgh or Philly, not in places like Johnstown.

He sat in his car, a Nash beetle, along the road to Hagevo, well outside any jurisdiction he might have.

He turned on the overhead light, though the sun hadn't entirely left the sky, pulled the note out of his pocket and read it once more, despite the fact that he knew it by heart.

> If you want to know who robbed the bank, meet me at 8:30 p.m. this coming Thursday. Just off Route 160, on the road to Hagevo is a strip mine. The old Park Miller farm. There's an overgrown road that leads to the strip cut. Follow it to the end. I'll be waiting.

Cheap tablet paper, block printing. There was no way to trace where it came from, though he hadn't showed it to anyone, except his partner.

"You're not going out there, are you?" Barry had asked. "Probably a wild goose chase, someone playing games."

They'd sat in Sam's office, a glare through the opened venetian blinds, the first real spring day after a slushy month of snow. Sam sat behind the desk, Barry in front, his feet propped up, looking more like a college prof than a cop.

"You know the old theory as well as I do, Barry," Sam said, taking a bite from a peanut and jelly sandwich.

"What theory?" Barry asked.

"That there's this guy who commits the perfect crime, and he keeps it all to himself. But then he starts thinking how smart he is, how much sharper he is than the cops. So he wants to brag about it."

"Jesus, Sam, how can you stand that kind of thing?"

"What?"

"The fucking sandwich. Christ, I stopped eating that kind of shit when I was ten years old." Barry said, his speech, contradicting his cultured looks.

Sam threw back his head and laughed, though it still startled him to hear profanity. He rarely swore, probably the result of being a son of the Sunday School superintendent in Jerome, PA. "To each his own," he said.

Barry chuckled. "Anyhow, you were saying something about this high-falutin' theory."

"Who knows, Barry?" Sam shoved the last bite into his mouth and crumpled the waxed paper he'd packed it in and tossed it into the waste basket. "I'm just thinking out loud. Now this guy who stole the money had his plan worked out pretty well. Got inside the bank, despite the alarm, knew exactly where he was going and got away clean with 18,000 smackeroos."

"Yeah. So what are you saying?"

"Like I mentioned, he was pretty darned smart. Buffaloed us, all right. Left no clues, no trail, no nothing."

"So you think he's the one who sent the note?"

"Could be."

"Or a neighbor, a family member, looking for some kind of reward."

"There's that too," Sam said. "I hear the bank is willing to pay five hundred or more for information."

Barry lowered his feet, picked up a cold cup of coffee, drained it. "At least let me go along with you, Sam. It could be dangerous."

"Can't. The note said come alone. We'd be liable to scare him off."

"Yeah, well, I'm against it. But knowing how stubborn you are, I'm sure that won't do any good. At least, tell the chief. All right?"

"And have him call it off? No, Thanks."

"You think he'd do that?"

"Or else send out a whole squad."

Barry shrugged. "Maybe you're right. But at least can I tell him after you're gone?"

"If you like."

Sam glanced at his wristwatch, an old Elgin that had belonged to his dad. It read twenty-six after eight. Sam turned off the light, pocketed the keys and got out.

He still wore his suit, brown gabardine, the seat of the pants shiny. He should have taken time to change to dungarees and a sport shirt. But he'd left the station, had liver and onions at a diner downtown and come straight to the mine.

The darkness came now in waves. He had a penlight that he flashed on the path. The narrow beam barely helped. As the note indicated, the trail was overgrown with grass and weeds, even the tire tracks pretty well hidden. It ran through woods which gradually changed into briars and blackberry bushes near the strip cut itself. Sam thought of when he and his brother used to go to the strip mines around Jerome to pick blackberries or in summer to swim in the water-filled hole, stagnant, covered with scum. They'd never told his mother.

He heard a noise, stones rolling down a bank. He stopped. The only sounds were a mockingbird off in the distance and cars passing by out on Route 160.

Was anyone here? he wondered. Maybe it had been stupid to come alone. He walked to the edge of the pit.

"Down here," a voice called.

He peered over the edge, saw a kind of path and gingerly started to feel his way down.

Suddenly, a sound slammed into his eardrums. His body jerked; blood spurted from his leg, and the darkness became complete.

***

He heard someone moaning. He felt lethargic, light-headed, dizzy.

"Take it easy," a voice said. "I'll get you to the hospital."

Sam opened his eyes, realized he was the one who was moaning. A man knelt beside him, doing something to his leg. A big man. Again the darkness descended.

Then he was riding in the passenger seat of a car. It was his own car. How could that be? "How ... how ..." It was too much of an effort to speak.

Before he closed his eyes again, he glanced at the driver. The same big man. Why was he riding in his own car with this person?

"We'll soon be there," the man said.

Sam suddenly realized they were traveling fast, squealing around corners. He wanted to tell the man to slow down, not to wreck his car.

He was being loaded onto a stretcher, being wheeled inside ... a hospital. Why was he at a hospital?

"You've done a good job. A damned good job," someone said. "But you'll have to leave him now."

Sam was wheeled inside, into a cubicle. Gentle hands lifted him, cut away the leg of his pants. He didn't want them to do that. It was his suit, one of his two suits. He couldn't afford—

He felt a pinprick and soon he was floating.

He awoke in a bed, stiff with white sheets. He glanced around.

"Hi," someone said.

He remembered the man because he was so big. He sat in a wooden chair by the side of the bed, a chair that looked much too small.

"Hi," Sam answered. "What ... what happened?"

The man stood up. "It's going to be okay. The doctors told me you'll be okay."

Sam felt tired, like he could sleep for a week. He started to close his eyes. Then he jerked them open.

"The strip mine," he said, his voice like a croak.

The man reached for a glass and pitcher, poured water, stuck in a glass straw, held it to Sam's mouth.

Sam took a sip. He hadn't realized how parched he was. He sipped the water, then pushed the straw out with his tongue. "Thanks."

"It's all right," the man said. He set the glass on the tray by the bed and held out his hand. Big, the back covered in red fur. "I'm Claude Frazier," he said. "And you're Sam Holden." He had a thick head of hair, tumbling in all directions, and a moustache.

"How did you know—"

"Your name?" The man smiled. "I know a lot about you. You're a cop, from Johnstown. In your thirties. Live in Southmont. Never been married."

"What?"

"You apparently were after someone."

"How did I ... what happened?"

"Oh, Jesus," Claude said, making it sound like a prayer. "Someone was playing rough."

Sam licked his lips. "What do you mean?"

"From what I can figure out, you were lured there by someone. Right?"

He tried to nod, and immediately regretted it. His head ached; his neck was stiff.

"A mean son-of-a-bitch, if you'll pardon the language." Claude shook his head.

"What ... what did he do?"

"I'm not sure I should be telling you this. It has to be pretty much of a shock."

"My partner ... he tried to tell me ..."

"Maybe I better leave. Give you time to rest."

"No!" The sound ricocheted off the walls. "It was a setup. He tried to kill me, didn't he? I know damned well he did."

Claude sat down, a stiffness leaving his body. "Yeah, he tried to kill you."

"What did he do?"

"It was an explosion. Dynamite. You're a lucky man."

"Lucky? I don't feel lucky. I've never hurt so bad in my life."

"But you're alive." Claude stood up. "Look, I don't want to tire you. They let me in with the understanding I stay only a minute or two. I'll be back this afternoon, I promise. Okay?"

Sam tried to smile. "You're the one who brought me in. Maybe you saved ... saved my life." Sam looked at the other man and saw moisture in his eyes.

"I'm glad you're doing okay," he said. "You rest now, take care of yourself."

"Thanks," Sam said, but the man had already left.

***

Dr. Rosenberg confirmed that Mr. Frazier's quick action had certainly saved Sam's leg, as well as his life.

Sam didn't hurt so much now, except for his leg, and that was hell. He'd demanded to know the extent of the injury.

"In blunt terms, Mr. Holden," Rosenberg said, "you're a hell of a fortunate man. Frazier knew what he was doing. Had first aid training." The doctor smiled. "You owe him a hell of a lot, I'd say."

"I know," Sam answered.

"You lost quite a bit of blood. You'd have lost more if Mr. Frazier hadn't used his belt as a tourniquet."

His leg had been blown to hell. He could tell that when the dressings were changed. Hacked up meat. Two-thirds of the flesh blown away. The doctor said he'd regain some use of his leg, but he didn't know how much. It would take a lot of work. Sam was determined to do whatever he needed and then do some more.

Barry visited, and the chief. Barry was angry as hell, the chief more philosophical.

"There's no use saying you shouldn't have taken it upon yourself to go there alone," Chief Robinson said. "So I'm not going to say it. It certainly won't undo anything." He was an older man, near retirement.

"So what was it all about?" Sam asked. It was his fourth day in the hospital. He'd begun to regain his strength.

"A warning," Barry said. He stood at the foot of the bed, the chief at the side, leaning on the railing.

"That's putting it mildly," Robinson commented. He looked at Sam, anger and frustration playing across his face. "There was a note, Sam. Pinned to your coat." He looked intently into Sam's eyes. "Are you sure you want to hear this?"

"Your damned right I do."

"It was the man who broke into the bank. Who knows why he went after you? Maybe he thought we were getting close. Ready to figure out who he was."

"Were we?" Sam asked. If so, he hadn't been in on it.

"Not in the least," Barry said.

Robinson nodded. "I don't understand his motives. But the note warned that if the investigation continued, we could expect more

---

men to die."

"To die!" Sam said.

"For all intents and purposes, you were dead, Sam. You were extremely lucky someone heard the explosion and came to investigate."

"What did the note say, exactly?"

"I've got it memorized, Sam," Barry said. "'This is an example of what will happen if you continue.'"

"So what are we going to do?" Sam asked.

Barry and the chief exchanged glances.

"God, Sam, if there was any other way—" The chief broke off, swallowed hard then seemed to make up his mind. "There's no 'we' involved anymore."

"What the hell is that supposed to mean?" Sam asked.

"You'll be retired. Medical reasons. A nice disability pension." The words contained a hint of sarcasm.

"Now wait just a minute," Sam said. "You don't know how well I'll be able—"

"I'm sorry," the chief said. "But that's the way it is." He paused, then resumed in a softer voice. "I didn't want to do this, Sam, but I have to. Sure, you'll have limited use of your leg. Maybe ... probably, be able to lead a fairly normal existence. But suppose you get in a tight spot. Suppose you have to rely on your ability to run, to chase someone. To get somewhere ... I'm sorry."

Sam turned his head away and the two men left.

My God, he thought, he was only in his thirties, and on a pension. Pensions were for people at the other end of the scale. He couldn't accept it, he wouldn't. He'd show them.

* * *

The only constants were the visits from Claude and the pain. When the pain became worst, Claude was there to hang on to, emotionally, physically. Sam learned he operated a sawmill, just over the rise from the strip mine. He'd been working late when he'd heard the explosion. He was Sam's only visitor, his parents long since retired to Florida.

Claude visited every evening, twice a day on weekends. When Sam began to improve, he wheeled him down to the cafeteria for coffee or an evening snack. He walked with him, supporting his weight. He brought him books and newspapers and bags of candy and nuts.

His visits highlighted each day. The rest was dross, something to get through till Claude appeared. And then Sam started to worry. What would happen when he left the hospital? Claude would no longer be there. He didn't think he could stand that.

Sam had always known what he was, though he'd pretty much kept it hidden. He'd had a few encounters, the first in the bus station in Johnstown when he was in his late teens. But nothing had ever continued. He'd never considered that it could.

Now, he knew, he was headed for a fall. Never through any sign at all had Claude shown he was aware of Sam's feelings. For that matter, Sam had done his best to keep those feelings hidden. He was sure a man like Claude would be disgusted to know of his proclivities.

Dr. Rosenberg came in one day and told Sam he could go home. The following day, just after breakfast. He didn't know what he was going to do. He didn't want to face the future alone. He began to feel terribly sorry for himself.

He was not the best of company when Claude came to visit. For some reason, Claude seemed ill-at-ease, as well. He sat down, got up and strode to the door, came back to the chair. Sam had never seen him this way before.

"Met the doc downstairs. He tells me you're going home."

"Tomorrow. Eight weeks in this place is long enough."

"I guess you know what's best."

"What ... what are you talking about?" Sam asked.

"Damn!" Sam had never seen Claude so ill at ease. "I'll say it, and get it over with. Then if you want me to leave ... I'll understand."

"Understand what, Claude?"

"I don't know how you feel—" He looked over his shoulder, turned and closed the door to the hallway. It was a semi-private room, the second bed empty. I'm trying to tell you ... Hell!"

Sam frowned, puzzled.

"You must know I like you, Sam."

"You've been awfully damned good."

"Look, being a policeman, seeing all sides of life, you must have encountered—" He closed his eyes for a moment, then opened them. "People like me."

Sam felt bewildered. "People like you?" And then the realization hit. "Oh, Jesus, Claude."

"I'll leave."

"Claude!"

"Yes?"

"Please don't. I don't want you to leave."

Claude stared at Sam. "You sure?

Sam nodded.

For a second, Claude seemed frozen, the moment itself frozen. Then he rushed to the bed and grabbed Sam in a bear hug.

The Potter and the Clay

Winter, 1940

John raced down East Beckert Avenue, shoes pounding the uneven cobblestone, suitcase banging the side of his leg. He ran blindly, dodging parked cars. He reached Troy Hill Road just as the downtown bus pulled up. He leaped aboard, gasping for air, sweat streaming down his face as he stumbled to a seat.

He couldn't believe it. His bitch whore of a mother, maybe. His dad had accused her often enough of cheating on him. But not Father Quillin. He was the one after whom John had patterned his life, the man responsible for John's own vision of a life in the church.

He pulled out his wallet. Not much money. But he couldn't go home to face his mother. And certainly not Father Quillin.

How could he go back to seminary? It was all a sham. He'd leave the damn church with all its Father Quillins. "No!" It wasn't the church; it was the people in it. John sobbed; most of all it was Father Quillin.

He leaned back against the seat. Where in the hell was he headed anyway? Impulsively, he jumped from the city bus downtown and ran to the Greyhound terminal. He pulled out his money and slapped it down on the counter. "I want a ticket," he said. He'd arrived home early; one of his instructors had been ill. That's how he'd come to see what he'd seen.

The clerk looked up. A man in his fifties, attractive like Father Quillin. "A ticket to where?"

Oh, God, Father Quillin, John thought. Don't you know that— he reached into his pocket for the ever safety present pin. He'd become good at opening it with one hand and then using it. His breathing quickened. He grasped the pin tightly between index finger and thumb.

"What do you say, buddy?" the ticket clerk asked.

"As far as this will take me. I don't care where."

The man glanced at a wall clock. "We got a bus going East in

... fourteen minutes." He counted the money. "This will take you about sixty miles, to Reels Corner. A crossroads. Not much of anything there."

John sat near the front of the bus. Dimly aware of the rhythm of humming wheels, he thought of his mother, a fucking whore of Babylon. And of Father Quillin giving in to demands he should overcome. Quickly, maliciously, he grabbed the pin and jabbed. He hit the slit in the head of his cock, penetrating moist, tender tissue. He could barely keep from screaming.

John had never gotten along with either of his parents. He'd entered minor seminary at the age of sixteen and felt he had truly found his home. He'd finished near the top of his class and had gone on, working for his B.A. and Bachelor of Divinity. In a little over two years, he'd be finished.

A sob escaped his throat. It wasn't God's will.

"Say, buddy," his seat mate said, "are you—" John turned toward the window.

Sunlight glared on the hard-crusted snow. A world of purity, John thought. No, he was wrong; the world wasn't pure. Father Quillin, his dick hanging out, scrambling into his pants, his hairy chest naked. The vision excited him till he thought of his mother with her sagging tits, looking defiant, almost proud, a pillow covering her snatch. It was enough to make him vomit.

John's thoughts flashed back to when he was twelve, when his sinfulness had started. Father Quillin was coaching a basketball team at St. Ignatius. After the second practice when everyone was all sweaty, Father Quillin came into the locker room, went into a corner and started to get undressed to take a shower. John moved as close as he could as Father Quillin pulled off his T-shirt and shorts.

John couldn't stop staring at the muscular body, the chest covered in a mat of brown hair, the long, thick cock. John's head filled with sinful thoughts of touching that cock, of kissing it. He tried to force himself to look away but couldn't. He hoped nobody noticed. Father Quillin folded his gym clothes and headed toward the shower. Only then did John take off his own T-shirt and shorts.

At home he felt sweat break out on his forehead. He'd committed a terrible sin thinking thoughts like that about a priest. He promised God he wouldn't think things like that about anyone ever again. If they came to his mind unbidden, he'd punish himself. He went to his mother's sewing box in the closet and took out an oversized safety pin. Breathing hard, he stuck it into his pocket. Every time he had a bad thought, he told God, he'd jab the safety pin unmercifully into his dick.

He was a terrible sinner, having to jab himself at least once a day. He tried to do it in the bathroom where he could blot up the blood with toilet tissue. But sometimes the thoughts came at awkward times, in school, playing ball with friends, and he had to do it then. He remembered his mother's questions about the occasional blood in his underwear, and the time he leaked pus for days.

It was nearing twilight when the driver pulled to the side of Route 30. "Reels Corner," he said.

Spring, 1940

John knelt on the dewy lawn of his cottage. Out of the corner of his eye, he saw Mrs. Kowalski next door looking at him and frowning. Screw you, he thought. It's right that a man should pray when he deems it necessary.

He bowed his head and squeezed shut his eyes. "I need your guidance, Papa Yahweh. I admit to Thy ultimate wisdom. But lately my soul is suffering strife, and I am becoming discouraged. I have no mission, at least that I can discern. Show me the way. Help me to learn and accept your will. Help me to find my purpose in life."

He'd wanted so badly to be a priest. He'd known that upon his ordination, his soul would be washed clean as snow.

But now he wouldn't be ordained.

He stood and brushed off the knees of his slacks. Why wasn't he given his mission? Why? Sometimes he'd hear Papa Yahweh speak, his voice deep as thunder. At other times it was the childlike voice of Lord Baby or the eerie keening of the Holy Spook. He called them these names because he was so close to them. They in turn called him Philos, meaning love. Teachers at seminary had told him the voices weren't real.

Well, fuck them too, praise Papa's holy name. Yahweh cared for his children and gently led them on the paths of righteousness. How else could He do that but by speaking to them?

John trudged up the steps to the porch. He'd wanted too much to preach Papa's word. But here he was in Cranston, eight miles from Reels Corner, working in a coal mine.

Reels Corner was a crossroads with a restaurant, a garage and a few houses. John had used all his remaining money, seventy-three cents, to buy a hamburger, fries and coffee, plus tip, when he'd arrived there on the Greyhound bus.

At the opposite end of the counter sat the only other customer, a man about ten years older than John. "Saw you get off the bus," he said, when John glanced his way. "Name's Dan Reynolds."

The waitress set coffee and a glass of water in front of John. He lifted the cup, blew the steam away and glanced toward the other man.

"You visiting in these parts?"

John turned away, tears in his eyes. It was all right to cry; he shouldn't be ashamed. Yet, he kept his back turned until the waitress plopped down his order.

"Say." The other man stood and walked toward him. "Are you— I mean—

John turned toward him. Young as he was, the man had greying hair, reminding John of a very wise person, like Father Quillin, a kind of father confessor.

John glanced now at his watch and saw it was 8 a.m. He decided to walk to church early. He'd given up on Catholicism and joined the United Brethren Church because that's where Dan and his family went. Dan had brought John home and had helped him get a job as a miner.

The church was a mile away, a pleasant walk amid budding trees and new grass. Once inside, John felt Yahweh's perfect stillness, the peace that passeth understanding deep inside his soul.

A ray of sunlight, diffused by stained glass, reflected in glorious colors on the holy of holies. John fell to his knees, touched his forehead to the deep pile carpet, his eyes full of tears.

He decided to take catechism classes and become a preacher. He thought how proud Father Quillin would be of him. Then he remembered the priest and his mother going at it like animals on a blanket in the middle of the living room floor.

Fall, 1941

It was 0600 and already hot, heat and air pollution lying trapped in the bowl of the San Joaquin valley, smoke inside a bottle. Yet John felt like whistling or praising God on his way to morning formation for he'd found his holy purpose at last. He was going to become an airplane pilot.

Suddenly, Major Reynolds stood before them, a pudgy man with red hair and freckles. Looking from face to face, the major told them they were all washed out, "at the convenience of the government."

John's face grew hot, his throat become thick. He felt like screaming his rage to the heavens. Again, his holy mission had been taken away. Was Yahweh a prankster, a joker? He loved Lord Baby and Holy Spook and Papa too—loved them with all his heart and soul. And now were they forsaking him?

Suddenly, John thought of Job. And then he knew! Instead of rejecting John, Papa Yahweh was making him one of the chosen.

Laughing and crying, his face flooding with tears, he could barely keep in formation on the way back to the barracks. He endured the other men's stares. He paid little attention; it wasn't important. All John cared about was that Yahweh was preparing him for whatever came next.

* * *

Kingman, Arizona, was the worst place he'd ever been, much worse than Minter Field where he should have earned his pilot's wings. John was to be a ball turret gunner, stuck for hours at a time in a bubble of plexiglass and steel under the belly of a B-17, unable to flex his legs, pissing through a tube.

The trials still continued. John had accepted not becoming a priest, a preacher or a pilot. But a ball turret gunner? Then when the war was over, would he go back to the coal mine, lungs filling with black dust, joints stiff with the dampness, hacking and spitting his way through life?

He had to trust Papa, Lord Baby and the Holy Spook. They had a plan for his life.

March 3, 1943

A Zero appeared out of nowhere, spitting fire. John rotated the turret, fired back, missed and felt a tremendous impact. The B-17 righted itself for an instant, then screamed toward earth. John rotated the turret and fumbled at the hatch. He had no parachute; there wasn't enough room. He had to get inside the plane. Papa Yahweh wouldn't let him end like this, body smashed and broken on an island off Asia. Papa Yahweh would save him, Lord Baby be praised.

He pushed and clawed through the hatch, reached for a parachute. The plane gave a lurch. He saw men jumping. He strapped on the chute, checked to make sure it was okay and crawled out into space. He felt urine soaking his leg.

John threw off his thin blanket and stumbled to the *benjo*. He tried to squat over the stinking hole. He felt dizzy, disoriented. He'd been at Omori twenty-nine days, and it seemed like half a lifetime. He couldn't dispel the doubt that crept into his mind—doubt of the omnipotence of the Three-in-One. Or perhaps he was still being punished.

John's head spun, and he feared he'd fall into the shit and white worms. He tried to wipe, found nothing to use and reeled back to his *tatami* mat, his stomach growling in hunger.

Lord Baby appeared in a dream to tell John that he was blessed. All the citizens of Nippon loved him, and he was to love them back. Lord Baby was suffused in light, pure, white heavenly light. John lay in a manger of golden straw, and around him flew angels with fine-feathered wings.

John's strength returned, and like most men in camp, he helped to load and unload cargo of nearby ships.

The Nipponese laborers who worked alongside the prisoners were good men, just as his dream had told him. And so he began to love them. It was harder to love the guards, but he managed that too. One guard often helped lift the heaviest crates and daily shared his cigarettes with the prisoners. Because of this John grew to love him most of all.

Each day, as John carried cargo back and forth, he talked quietly about forgiveness and love. Lord Baby had told him that the Nipponese were direct emissaries from Yahweh, but that they were forced to pretend. The occasional beatings they still gave the prisoners were a sham; a necessary evil.

Along with the knowledge that the captors were worthy of love came the knowledge that John had the task of working with them to spread their goodness. This is what Father Quillin told him one night in a dream as he lay curled against the priest's naked chest. Papa, Holy Spook and Lord Baby looked on in agreement.

Two days later, as captors and prisoners ate bowls of rice on the dock, John stood up. "I have a message from Yahweh," he said. "It came to me through the holy Lord Baby. The message is one of love."

He paused to smile upon the kindly guard, a stubby man, heavily muscled. "I love you," John said in Nipponese; he'd searched out the words he needed to convey this important message.

He stepped toward the man, opened his arms and embraced him. "I love you," he repeated. "I love you as much as one man ever could love another!"

The man broke free, kicked out and caught John in the groin. He doubled over and the man slammed a fist to his face. John sat down abruptly, gasping for breath, struggling to speak, his nose streaming blood.

He turned over, pushed himself to his knees, raised himself up and smiled. "Revile me," he said, "persecute me, piss on me, shit on me, and still I will love you. For you are of God and so you are

---

of love."

In a rumbling voice that shook the dock, Yahweh declared to John that he could bring peace to the world. Lord Baby had tried this once, and now John could pick up the yoke and succeed. Yahweh explained exactly how this could be accomplished.

John looked at each of the Nipponese men, tears of joy streaming down his face. "Not only am I a direct emissary of Yahweh," he said, "an emissary like yourselves, but I am in command of the Pacific Theatre of Operations. I will tell you what we must do to end these struggles. How we can stop this war. How we can work together for peace everlasting from this time forth."

John leaped up on the post again and yelled so all would be sure to hear. "Peace and love are the way to salvation. The way to paradise here on earth."

"Jesus Christ," someone yelled, "he's gone completely nuts."

Something hit hard against his back. He fell from the post and landed face first on the dock.

John pushed against rough wood on hands and knees and reached for his beloved guard. He hardly felt the toe of the boot as it smashed into his chin, breaking his jaw, for in that instant, he saw Lord Baby, drool dripping from his lips, reach down a tiny hand. Behind him stood the Holy Spook, dressed in white sheets, and Papa Yahweh with a face like Father Quillin's. Filled with joy and rapture, John put his hand in Lord Baby's. "John O'Shaughnessy is my beloved son," Yahweh thundered. "And in him, I am well pleased."

And there was with the guards and prisoners alike a host of heavenly angels singing and praising John in the highest.

And Have Not Love

Leaves of a maple tree brushed gently against the window screen; a breeze billowed the curtain by Martin's desk. He wished that life could be different. He wished that Sam could be his father or even Claude.

Martin wondered how the metal of his trumpet could feel so cold. It was June, the beginning of summer. He pulled out his *Arban's* and set it on the music stand. He held the mouthpiece for a moment buried in his fist to warm it, stuck it into the horn and blew gently through the tubing. He opened the music book to "Carnival of Venice." Someday ... someday he'd be able to play it like his teacher Mr. Thatcher did. With all the changes, the fast tempo, the triple tonguing from note to note.

Someday he'd be able to do anything he wanted, go anywhere in the universe. In the galaxy. All he'd have to do was hit the right notes and fly.

He opened the spit valve and blew the moisture onto the floor, not holding a tissue under it like Helen wanted. He turned to the exercises Mr. Thatcher had assigned, scales and slurs and staccato notes.

He closed the book and started to make up songs that fit his mood. He thought back to a time he'd been sitting in the chair by the kitchen window, Helen at the stove, stirring a pot of oatmeal. It was wintertime, the house warmed by the heat from the cooking. Bubbles plopped, spurts of steam shooting out of each, disappearing high above the pot.

Grandma was in the living room, playing the piano.

"Just listen to her," Helen said. "She would never give me lessons. No matter how badly I wanted to learn." She scraped the sides of the pot to keep the oatmeal from burning. "Then when I met your dad, he taught me to play the guitar."

"I know," Martin said, "you used to teach together."

"But I had to stop," Helen said. She picked up two pot holders from the shelf behind the stove and set the pot on the table. "Do you know why? You came along." She pushed a strand of hair from her forehead and began to dish out the cereal. "You want to know the worst thing?" she continued. "I didn't expect to teach after you were born, but neither did I expect to give up my music altogether. Every time I tried to play, you cried. You were a selfish little boy."

Babies always cried, Martin thought. Anyhow, why didn't she go back to her music now? She could practice; she could play with Dan's orchestra.

The song Martin created changed from sounds of sorrow to sounds of anger, sharp and blaring. Why did she blame him for everything. They'd gone on a picnic to Grandpa O'Jenkins farm the summer Martin was seven. While Dan helped Grandpa put up a stove pipe in the kitchen, Martin and Helen spread newspapers over the picnic table in the front yard. They set out the food, and Helen spread a blanket across one seat of the table and sat down.

Martin sat opposite her, looking down at the newspaper, the comics section. Dumb Orphan Annie with holes for eyes was talking to her dog, Sandy, who looked like he was made with a cookie cutter. The palms of Martin's hands felt clammy. "Helen?" he said.

"What is it?"

He felt his heart beating hard. He'd been talking to Billy and Tim about wanting a brother. Billy said he should ask his mom. So even though he would probably make Helen mad, he decided to ask.

"For heaven's sake why? I almost died when I had you. Do you want that to happen again?"

Martin watched an ant crawl across the edge of the paper and over Fearless Fosdick's nose.

"Look at me, Martin."

He looked at two deep lines above her nose.

"You almost killed me."

"I don't want a brother." His voice was only a whisper as he watched the ant crawl down the leg of the table.

"If you'd rather have a brother than me, okay. But remember

that I'll be dead. Of course, if that's what you want ..."

The notes became slower, quieter, sad. Once when he was three or four, Helen bawled him out for being bad. He couldn't remember what he'd done. He was in the kitchen playing with his toy kitty that clapped its hands. Helen went upstairs and came down a little while later carrying a suitcase.

"I'm leaving Martin," she said, "because boys who are bad do not deserve a mother."

"No!" he screamed. "No, no, no."

"Maybe some day I'll come back when you become the kind of boy who deserves a mother." She went outside, the screen door banging behind her.

"Nooooo!" Martin screamed, throwing himself on the floor. Later when he could cry no more, she came back. Because he knew he was such a bad boy, Martin went outside and beat his head against the side of the house. "Puh-puh-puh-puh-puh-puh-puh." A step higher.

Sam had asked Martin last night what was wrong with his head, why he had a big bruise. "Puh-puh-puh-puh-puh-puh-puh." Back down and up. "Puh-puh-*pu*-puh-puuh; puh-pu-pu-pu." Faster and faster, angrier and angrier.

He should have told Sam! He should have told what Dan had done.

"Puh-pu-pu-puh-puh; puh-pu-pu-puh." He'd forgotten to practice his damned magic tricks. Hadn't remembered that soon he'd have to perform at the Plumton Picnic. Dan grabbed his arm. "Pu-pu-pu-pu-puh-puh; puh-puh-puh." Shoved him hard; he stumbled, fell, hit his head on the metal frame of his bed.

Puh-pu-pu-puh-puh; puuuh, puuuh, puuuh.

Goddamn magic tricks. Son-of-a-bitching tricks. He hated having to do them.

He thought of Bobbie. How she'd always said she wanted to see him perform. He liked her a lot, which made him all mixed up. How could he like her when—

Maybe everyone felt like he did. Were all boys attracted to men? He didn't think so. Well, when he grew up and got married, when he had kids, he'd never hurt them. He wouldn't tell them how bad they were.

The bell of his trumpet stuck straight out, just the way it should. The fingers of his right hand were arched, the little finger free. Mr. Thatcher had told about someone who suspended his trumpet on a rope and didn't hold it, just steadied it and fingered the valves so he could be sure he wasn't producing the high notes through pressure, but through lip work alone.

Martin didn't have to hold his trumpet tight; it was a part of him. It wouldn't get away. He took a deep breath. Okay, Harry James, he thought, you'd better look out, 'cause here comes Martin O'Jenkins.

Suffer the Children

May, 1949

Dan O'Jenkins always dropped Martin off at the Lutheran church for Scout meetings on his way to teach. He had a little space he rented, the sun porch of a house, where he gave lessons and sold music books and supplies. He picked Martin up when he finished. Sometimes he was a few minutes late, so Sam often invited Martin to the house afterwards for a cup of hot chocolate or a soft drink.

Today Dan was later than usual; the meeting had been over for half an hour.

Sam and Martin sat at the kitchen table. Sam didn't mind, actually was glad for the chance to talk with the boy. Martin was shy around the other kids, yet Sam could see he was bright. He wished he didn't seem so sad all the time, as if he had to carry burdens far beyond his years.

He was glad Martin's uncle had suggested the boy join the scout troop, but Sam wished he'd know how to give Martin self-confidence.

Claude was at the sawmill, catching up on paper work. He refused to bring it home. He said that sort of thing should never intrude on the hours he and Sam spent together.

That was okay since Claude usually worked Tuesday evenings, the days of the Scout meeting, so Sam didn't have much of a chance to miss him. They'd been together more than two years now and still Sam hated to see him leave the house every morning. He wanted to hang onto him, not let him out of sight. Maybe, Sam thought, it was because of what had happened to him, when he'd been injured. Something like that made a person realize that life is tenuous; you should make the best use of it.

He'd heard people complain, husbands and wives, about how they couldn't stand each other for more than a few hours at a time. He hoped it never reached that stage with Claude. He didn't see how it could. He sensed that Claude felt pretty much the same way

---

he did, that each morning he left with reluctance.

Sam couldn't quite believe his good fortune. Obviously, there were many others like him, men who liked men; he'd met quite a few over the years but realized he didn't know much about their personal affairs. He'd always visualized them as lonely, visualized himself the same way—spending his life by himself, dying by himself. He was sure that would have occurred if he hadn't met Claude.

He wondered what gods had decreed him so fortunate and others less so. Other homosexuals. How did they seek out those like themselves, except for one-night stands? That part was easy; all you had to do was pay attention, find the right locations.

Maybe those who lived in big cities had an easier time of it because there were bound to be so many more of them.

The mug of hot chocolate warmed Sam's hands as he glanced across the table at Martin. "A penny for your thoughts." The boy looked vulnerable, contemplative, a million miles away.

"I was just thinking about what Ray told me before I joined the troop."

"About what?" Sam asked, hooking his index finger through the mug, his hands encircling it.

Martin flushed. "About you?"

Sam laughed. "What about me?"

"How you used to be a policeman." Martin looked away, over at a Clivesville Bank calendar on the wall. Sam knew the scene for the month of May showed a deer drinking from a mountain spring, a buck with a large rack of antlers. Martin looked back. "Uncle Stanley said ... well, he said I probably shouldn't say anything about it."

"About my ... injury? My leg?"

"Uh huh. He said you might get upset."

Sam was surprised that Martin even brought it up. No one else did, even though he was sure they wondered about it. "It happened, Martin. It's part of my life. I don't like to think about it, about someone who set out to— It's difficult to talk about. But someone did try to kill me."

"You were a policeman. A detective."

Sam smiled. "For almost four years. On the force altogether for nine years."

"Wow," Martin said.

"Not so long really. Yet it seems a long time." Sam glanced into Martin's eyes, worried about the boy. He thought he saw signs of physical abuse, but how could he be sure? "That looks like a nasty bruise, Martin. And a pretty bad bump on your head." The boy had seemed especially quiet tonight.

Martin flushed even redder. "Yeah," he said, but so soft Sam couldn't be sure he'd actually spoken.

Maybe he should mind his own business, Sam thought. But if what he suspected were true, wasn't it everyone's business? "Did you fall?"

Martin continued to look down at his mug.

"Was that it?" Sam insisted.

"Something like that," Martin said.

"Oh?"

"My head hit the bed frame." He looked up then, his gaze defiant. "I'm okay," he said.

Sam nodded, willing to change the subject, wanting to ignore the evidence he saw in front of him, at least for the time being. "So I hear you're a pretty good trumpet player, huh?" Suddenly, Martin's face lighted up. Stan O'Jenkins, Martin's uncle, had said something about Martin's being accepted into senior band, and only going into eighth grade. "Ray's dad told me you're doing pretty well."

"If you mean I'm in senior band, yeah, I am." Sam could see the excitement, almost as if Martin had come to life. "Only one other person got chosen. Bobbie Thomas; she goes to my church and plays clarinet. We're going to do a duet this Sunday for morning service."

"It sounds like your music's pretty important."

"I want to play in the Marine Band. Someday. They're the best. I want to play with them or else have a dance band, like Harry James. Except ..."

"Except what?"

"My dad thinks it's wrong. My mom too. Like once there was

a parade here in Clivesville. Senior and Junior Bands marched for Armistice Day. The VFW invited us all in for pop and ice cream. I wasn't allowed to go. Because they serve beer and stuff. One of the kids who plays sax—he's in eleventh grade and has a dance band—asked me if I'd like to sit in sometimes. But Helen and Dan won't let me."

"I guess they have to do what they think is right."

Martin shrugged.

"I used to be a musician too," Sam said.

"You did?" Martin sounded surprised.

"I played the organ. I started fooling around with the one in the church we went to when I was a kid. The organist there gave me lessons. When she quit, I took over."

"Do you still play?" Martin asked.

Sam shook his head. "No," he said and realized he missed it a great deal. After his injury he hadn't gotten back to it. Partly, it was his leg. His left foot really wasn't too nimble anymore, and he had trouble with the pedals. Claude kept trying to talk him into it. But even during the last couple of years on the force, he hadn't played much. He often worked Sundays and so had stopped attending church.

Occasionally, he'd gone back to keep up with his playing, but after the explosion it hadn't seemed worth it. Besides, Sam wasn't sure he ever wanted to attend church again. Almost getting killed could sour a person on a lot of things.

"Why not?" Martin asked.

"It's a long story." Sam shrugged. He raised the cup to his lips and drank; it was getting cold, a scum across the top. He looked at Martin's face and saw withdrawal. "The accident, Martin. That's mostly it. But you know, it's really a temptation. Every time I come in for a Scout meeting, it's like I'm almost drawn to it. Like there's a magnet trying to pull me on into the sanctuary and up to the organ. I've resisted so far, but maybe I'll talk to the preacher."

"Why did you become a policeman?" Martin asked.

The quick change of subject made Sam laugh. It pleased him that when they were together, just the two of them or sometimes with Claude, Martin often seemed to lose his shyness.

"I don't know. I guess where I grew up— Jerome, you know where that is?"

"Kind of," Martin said.

"Near Davidsville, Holsopple. A few miles southwest of Johnstown." Martin nodded. "Okay, we had this policeman, a nice man, and I decided I wanted to be like him." He chuckled. "I guess all kids at one time or another want to be policemen or fireman. Most of them outgrow it."

Martin laughed. "I guess you didn't."

Sam chuckled. "No, I had this idea because of Mr. Lamb—that was the cop's name—this idea that I wanted to help people, too." He shook his head. "If only I'd known." Martin looked puzzled. "It wasn't like I imagined. In a way I suppose it is helping people. But you lose sight of that. It's the corner cop, the one who directs traffic, who helps. The rest is learning a lot of things maybe better not learned."

Martin picked up his spoon and stirred his hot chocolate.

"It makes me sound pretty cynical," Sam continued. "Do you know what that means?"

Martin nodded. "Like distrustful or something."

"Right." Sam stood and took his mug to the sink. He ran the tap to rinse it out. Martin drained the last of his drink and Sam reached for his mug too. "A lot of the people you meet aren't very nice."

"Criminals, you mean?"

Sam sighed. "Yes, but probably not what you think. Petty thieves, the lower stratum of society. The malcontents." He glanced at Martin and saw that he'd lost him. "But it was okay, even if not as glamorous as I thought."

He came back to the table. "But now that's all in the past. I haven't worked in going on three years, and I became a Scoutmaster."

It was funny, Sam thought, but maybe that's what he should have done to begin with. Somehow he'd gotten the wrong idea. Ed Lamb was more like a Scoutmaster, not a cop, except in name. It wasn't that Sam hadn't liked his job; he had. He'd been very bitter for a time at losing it. And he'd been going stir crazy too, till he helped start the troop. Now even that wasn't enough. Sooner or later he'd have to look for a job.

"Wonder where my dad is?" Martin asked. "It's getting late."

"You don't have to go to school though, right?"

Martin rolled his eyes. "Not for the next three months, except for band practice a couple of nights a week."

"But you enjoy that."

"Yes. And then I practice one night a week with Dan."

"Your father?"

"I play with his orchestra. It's okay. Particularly when we do popular songs."

"Oh?"

"Yeah, we play some places—like we'll be at the Plumton Picnic Band but we won't play religious stuff much there."

"I'll have to remember. I'll try to go hear you."

Martin appeared embarrassed. "You don't have to."

Sam chuckled. "I know I don't have to, Marty. I want to."

"Nobody calls me Marty."

"Would you rather I didn't?"

"Except my Grandpa Schmidt." He looked into Sam's face. "You can call me Marty," he said.

August, 1949

No matter how hard he tried, he couldn't run. His legs were heavy; he couldn't keep up. Martin streaked ahead of him. He tried to catch him. He tried to yell, but no sound came.

Blackberry bushes grabbed at his clothes, slapped his face, scratched his arms. Already Martin was down the side of the strip cut, sliding over stones that splashed into the water. It was the old abandoned strip mine. The same mine!

"M-M-M-M!" He tried to yell the boy's name, but he couldn't get it out. Martin was headed for the place where they'd put the explosives. He had to save him. He had to save Martin.

"M-M-M-Martinnnnnn!"

The sound still echoed through the room as Sam sat bolt upright in bed. The sheet was wrapped around his legs. He was covered in sweat. The dream again. The same dream, except this time it was Martin, not Sam himself.

He untangled the sheet and swung his legs over the side of the bed. He glanced at Claude, still sound asleep opposite him. He smiled to himself. He used to sleep that well, too. But after a few years on the force—

He stood, stomped circulation into his withered leg, rubbed the remaining sleep from his eyes and struggled to the bathroom.

He hadn't had the dream in weeks; he thought maybe it had ended. Instead, it had only changed form. He turned on the light, lifted the lid of the toilet and sat down.

What was he going to do about Martin? Should he do anything?

Of course, he thought. He had to do something. He couldn't let the situation go on. He could see all the signs; he'd seen them many times in his work. Kids taken to the emergency room with broken bones, bruises, imprints of belts and hands burned into their flesh.

"Billy fell down." "Sally burned herself." "Ricky bumped his head." The excuses seemed endless; no one admitted the truth. He wondered how they could live with themselves.

Other than this one idiosyncrasy, they seemed like decent people, good people for the most part. Some idiosyncrasy. He knew the theory; an abused child becomes an abusing parent. He wondered about Martin's parents. Had they been abused?

And the physical signs, the broken bones, the abrasions, the contusions often weren't the worst part. It was what was done to the kids' emotions, their feelings, their perceptions.

Psychological abuse. How, by law, could you define it, let alone prove it? Yet in Martin's case that seemed to be worse than the physical side of it.

He pulled up his jockey shorts, flushed the toilet, washed his hands. It was the one thing he'd had a hard time stomaching. If adults wanted to beat each other, that was one thing. But when they did it to kids, he had no sympathy.

He didn't often lose his temper, but those times he'd been summoned to Mercy or Memorial and the abuse was so apparent, it was fair to say he became the least little bit perturbed.

It was unjust, the big guy picking on the little guy, the adult picking on the kid.

Sam glanced at his wristwatch. A little after 5:30. There wasn't much point in going back to bed. He'd go downstairs, have a piece of toast, a cup of coffee—enough to tide him over till Claude got up.

He limped down the steps, turned on the kitchen light, stuck a piece of bread in the toaster, turned on the burner for coffee. As he was measuring it out, Claude appeared in the doorway.

"What's the matter, babe?" Claude asked. "The dream again?"

"Did I wake you? I'm sorry."

"It's okay. I'd be up in another hour." He pulled a chair out from the wooden table, leaned on the back of it.

"Like toast?" Sam asked. "Eggs, cereal?"

Claude laughed. "I didn't come down to have you make me breakfast."

"I know. Just thought since I was in the business of fixing things ..."

"Appreciate it," Claude said. "Maybe just a cup of coffee."

The toaster popped. "Sure you don't want some toast?"

"I'm sure."

"Okay." Sam laid the toast on a plate from the cupboard, grabbed a knife and the butter dish, and brought them to the table.

"Hey, Sam," Claude said. "I asked if you had the dream again?"

"Yeah, but different."

Claude, wearing a pair of pajama bottoms, his chest and shoulders thick with red hair that reflected the light from the ceiling fixture, threw his arms around Sam. "I'm sorry."

Sam kissed Claude's neck as they held each other. He sighed then as he sat at the table across from Claude.

"You said it was different."

Sam broke the toast into halves, slowly buttered one half, then laid down the knife. "It wasn't me this time. It was Martin O'Jenkins."

"What do you mean?"

"He's the one they were after. He's the one they were trying to blow up—" His voice broke in a half sob. "Sorry. I thought I was over this. It's been a long time."

"Two-and-a-half years is not a long time, Sam. The hospital, the operations. You have a right."

"A big, tough police detective like me."

"A big, tough *ex*-police detective like you." Claude reached over, broke one of the halves of toast in two, shrugged and stuck it into his mouth. "You know, I'm glad you're not on the force anymore."

"Is that right?"

"God, Sam, don't misunderstand. I wouldn't want you hurt like you were—not for anything. But I'd worry, you know."

"Johnstown is not the big city. There was little to worry about. No gang wars, no street slayings. A murder was pretty rare."

"Sure, I know." Claude chuckled. "And what's the old argument? You could have been hurt just as easily crossing the street."

Sam laughed. "I could have. Crazy drivers."

"So," Claude said, "you're concerned about Martin O'Jenkins."

The coffee started to burble. Sam got up, went to the cupboard, took cups out, looked questioningly at Claude.

"Yeah," his partner answered. "I'll take a cup. The first of many."

"I don't want to nag, Claude. But do you think you drink too much coffee? It can't be all that good for you. Keeping you stimulated, eating up your stomach lining."

Claude winked. "It's not coffee that stimulates me, Sammy."

Sam laughed as he filled the two cups. "Anyhow, Martin is so unhappy, so intense. I wish he could just let go."

"Can't he?"

"No, and I understand." He shook his head. "He's been beaten down. A weaker kid would have caved in long ago. He doesn't realize how strong he is. He has low self-esteem."

"Because of his mother and father."

"Before I came downstairs I was thinking about it. I'm at fault too. I've just ignored it."

"What do you mean?"

"Jesus, Claude, the kid's a classic case of an abused child. And there's not a damn thing I can do about it besides threatening to beat the shit out of his father." He sighed. "And reporting it. But that's a hell of a big step, you know." He shrugged. "When I was called out on cases like this, I always wondered how things were allowed to progress as far as they did. Many times you could see all the scars—physical and emotional. I wondered why no one reported it."

"You're blaming yourself?"

"I'd like to just give him a hug. Throw my arms around him and hold him tight."

"Why don't you?"

"Lord, Claude, what would people would say? I often wonder if there's talk even now. I can't imagine there isn't."

"About us?" Claude shook sugar into his coffee.

"You're damned right, about us."

Claude grinned. "We're just roommates, aren't we?"

Sam spread his hands. "Besides all the other things the kid has to deal with, I'm pretty sure he's going to be ... just like us."

Claude tasted his coffee. "How do you know that?"

"Intuition. By the kind of kid he is."

"So you're afraid."

"Yeah."

"Look, Sam, I think you have to consider which is more important. Martin, or what you feel people might think."

"It's not that simple. It's our lives too."

"I can't argue that. You're right."

"But as you said, I also have to think of Martin."

"What are you so concerned about?"

"The black and blue marks. His parents pushing him so damned hard. He's supposed to be perfect. And I know he thinks if he makes any mistakes, he's failed. Isn't that a hell of a thing?"

Faint rays of sunlight appeared through the kitchen window. "I wanted something to do, now that I can't be a cop anymore. And I like working with kids. So I thought of the Boy Scouts. Be a leader, a Scoutmaster. It'll take up some of your time, give you something to do, I told myself." He took the last sip of coffee, stood, took the cup and saucer to the sink. "Hell, I didn't know what I was getting into."

"That's one of the reasons I love you, Sam. For being the kind of man you are. I doubt that most policemen—"

Sam rinsed the cup and placed it in the sink, then turned back to Claude. "Most policemen what?"

"I'd think, maybe like a doctor, that a policeman has to divorce himself from his work. That's why they often become so cynical. It's a way of standing apart."

Sam smiled. "So you're an expert on police mentality?" His voice was soft, gentle. Sam walked over behind Claude's chair and began to massage his shoulders.

August, 1951

Martin looked hot, his T-shirt soaked with sweat.

Sam met him at the door, barefooted, wearing a pair of levis and a dark blue shirt, the top two buttons open, the sleeves folded back.

"Martin!" he said, "I'm surprised to see you."

"Can I talk to you?"

"Come on in." Sam held the screen door, wondering what was wrong. He looked outside; there weren't any cars. "You didn't walk, did you?"

"Yeah."

It had to be at least eight or nine miles. "Sit down." He pointed toward the living room. "I'll get you a glass of lemonade."

"Thank you," Martin said.

Sam returned in a minute with a full pitcher in one hand and two glasses in the other. "Here we are," he said, handing Martin a glass. "Now, what can I do for you?" he asked as he poured lemonade for the two of them.

Martin took the glass and downed half of it.

"Pretty hot out, huh?" Sam asked.

"It sure is."

"So?" Sam said, sitting down beside Martin, hoping to draw him out. "If something's bothering you, I'll be glad to listen."

"I don't know if I can—if I should—"

"That bad, huh?" Sam smiled trying to put Martin at ease.

"I've never talked to anyone, except John. You know John?"

"O'Shaughnessy?" He shrugged. "I know who he is. I know he's disabled. I know the story of how your father took him in."

"Yeah, my father," Martin said.

"Is he the problem?"

"My mom and my dad. Helen and Dan, you know?"

"Martin, I really don't know what to tell you. I think I understand. I mean I know some of the problems. Okay?"

"You do?"

Sam shook his head. "I feel so damned helpless."

Martin looked into Sam's eyes. "I sneaked away."

"From home?"

"Yeah, my dad said I have to stay in the rest of the summer."

"You mean till school starts?" Sam couldn't believe it. What the hell could have been so bad as to warrant that?

"Except for band practice. And the Scout meeting; he did finally tell me I could come to that. And I have to stay in my room. I can't come out except to eat or go to the bathroom."

"Pretty stiff punishment."

"It was because he wanted me to do a magic show at Plumton."

"The picnic. The community thing."

Martin nodded

"Okay. But I don't follow. What's this about magic?"

Martin sighed. He looked up. Sam looked back, smiling encouragement.

"Okay," Martin said and began to tell him all about the tricks and having to practice and give shows. And how he hated it, and how he hated all kinds of things like that he was forced to do. About how Dan and Helen made him do things so he'd have a better life.

"And because you didn't want to perform ..."

"That was part of it, I guess. But then I got mad and said something."

"Like what?"

"I swore." Martin reached for his glass.

"So you lost your temper and swore," Sam said. "That doesn't make you a terrible person. All of us lose our tempers."

Martin shrugged.

Sounding Brass

"More lemonade?" Sam asked. Martin nodded. Sam refilled both glasses. "Martin?"

"Yes?"

"I think you're too hard on yourself. I think you're a good kid. I like you, a great deal."

"Oh? I ..."

"What, Martin?"

The boy flushed even redder than he'd been from the heat. "I always ..." He shook his head. "Always thought I was just pretty much there. That I wasn't important somehow."

"Oh, God, Martin." Sam clasped his hands between his legs. He didn't really know what to say.

"It's like— like I'm not important, like I've never been important."

"That's not right, Martin." He felt tears not far below the surface. "Look, Marty, it's hard. I realize that. And maybe I shouldn't say it, but I know you have it rough. Your parents are ... strict." He saw surprise on the boy's face. Not only surprise but a kind of relief, as if he knew someone finally realized what his home life was like.

"I wish I could help you," Sam said, feeling he somehow was failing the boy, "but I don't know what to do. I will think about it. Okay?"

Martin bit down hard on his lower lip. "There's something else." He looked toward the front window, as if not acknowledging Sam's presence. "Something I read about in the Scouting book a couple of years ago. Just after I joined the troop. I've been thinking about it ever since."

"What is it?"

Martin looked back but didn't answer.

"I won't bite," Sam kidded. "I won't even hate you. No matter what you say."

"It said ..."

"What did it say?"

"If— if you were around other guys—" He turned away.

"If you're around other guys," Sam prompted.

"And they give you— Oh, man, Sam. If you feel like, like you're attracted to them."

"Sexually attracted?"

Martin closed his eyes and nodded.

Sam reached out, squeezed Martin's arm. "It's natural, Martin. It happens to everyone. Don't you know what psychologists say?"

"What?" Martin asked, his voice a croak.

"That it's a stage. Everyone goes through it. Almost everyone."

"But it isn't—" Martin sobbed. He grabbed for his glass and quickly drank down the rest of the lemonade. "I have to go. My mom'll be home, and I'll be in trouble."

"Would you like a ride?"

"What?"

"I'll take you, Martin. I wasn't doing anything important. I'll take you home."

September, 1951

Dan was late again, so they'd gone back to the house. Sam went to the refrigerator for orange Nehis, opened them and placed one in front of Martin who sat at the table.

"Do you want to talk about it?" Sam asked.

Martin shrugged.

Sam slid into the chair opposite him.

"It's something Dan—my dad said."

"What is it?" Sam asked.

"He called me a ... a sissy." Martin's voice broke.

Sam smiled reassuringly. "Don't you think it's his problem, Martin? Not yours."

"But maybe it's because of the way I feel. The way I am."

"You asked me before about this feeling you had for other boys."

Martin flushed. "Not boys," he said. He was clearly embarrassed.

Sam hesitated. "But I thought—"

"It's men. That's why I was so mixed up. The Scouting book, not the manual but the other one..."

"Yes," Sam answered.

Just then Claude walked in.

Martin glanced up, and Sam thought he might not want to go on. It was probably difficult enough to talk about in front of one other person. But he underestimated the boy.

"There's a place in the book where it says it's wrong to be attracted to other boys. But I'm not. It's always to people I think would be ..."

"What, Martin?" Claude asked sitting down with them. "It's okay."

"People who'd like me." Martin spoke soft and fast. "People who'd care about me." He looked down at his clenched hands. "Take the place of my father, I guess."

"Jesus," Claude said.

"Remember what I told you, Martin? That being attracted to people of your own sex is a stage."

"I remember."

Sam took a deep breath. "Martin, that's not always the case." He stood and went over to Claude. "I'm taking a big chance, Martin. But you said you've always been attracted to people who are males."

"Yes."

"And not to girls?"

"I — not like that. You know? I have a friend, Bobbie. Maybe a girlfriend. But not really."

Sam stood behind Claude's chair. "Martin, Claude and I are the way you think you are."

"What!" It seemed to Sam that Martin's jaw actually dropped.

"It's true," Claude said.

Martin looked from one to the other, as if he couldn't believe it. "I'm scared," he said. His voice shook. "I'm really scared. I know what I'm like. I didn't think anyone else was. Except I read about it sometimes, in magazines my mother gets. About people like that."

Sam expelled a big breath of air. "You shouldn't be scared, Martin. It's not a frightening thing."

Tears formed in Martin's eyes.

"What is it?" Claude asked.

"I wish—" Martin jumped up and ran outside.

For a moment, Sam just sat there. "Why do you think he did that?" he asked. "Maybe I shouldn't have said anything."

"It's good for him to know," Claude said. "To know there are decent people who just happen to like people of their own sex."

"Why did he run away?"

Martin didn't stay away long, just a few days. Sam opened the door, saw the boy was in a terrible state, grabbed him and held him against his chest. "Whatever it is, you're safe here," he said, releasing his hold. "Claude and I were just having a cup of tea. Come on out to the kitchen."

Claude rose from the table. "Hi, Martin."

"Hi." Martin's voice shook.

"Sit down," Sam said, pulling out a chair between his and Claude's. "Did something happen?"

Claude grabbed a cup from a hook above the drainboard. "Would you like some tea?"

"Just ... just a glass of water first, please?"

Claude filled a glass and set it on the table. Martin grabbed it and gulped half of it down.

"Now some tea?" Claude asked.

Martin tried to smile but couldn't quite do it. "Yes, please."

"Do you want to talk about it?" Sam asked.

Martin sighed, then took another sip of water. He set the glass back down and slowly moved it back and forth. Then he looked up just as Claude brought a cup of tea. Martin glanced at both of them then back down at the table. "He tried to kill me."

"Oh, Jesus. Your father, you mean."

"My father. Dan." He raised the cup, took a small sip.

"He choked me, tried to strangle me." He raised his head so they could see his neck.

"That son-of-a-bitch!" Claude said. He paused. "Sorry, Martin. I shouldn't have said that."

Martin shrugged.

"How did it happen?" Sam asked.

"My Grandma and Grandpa are visiting. Staying with us for awhile. Grandpa and I were talking, about religion. About Billy

Graham. I said I thought he should use his money to help people. It was just a discussion; Grandpa and I weren't arguing. Dan got mad and told me to stop. Then Grandpa said something, and I answered him. It was like Dan went crazy." Martin shook his head, tears flowing from his eyes. "It's like he hates me; like I'm garbage or something."

Claude handed him a box of tissues. He pulled one out and blew his nose. "I don't know what I'm going to do. I hate them. I hate them both."

"How about staying here tonight?" Sam asked. "I'll call them. It'll be okay."

Martin leaned back in the chair "I'd like to stay."

"It's the same damn pattern I used to see," Sam said, his voice filled with anger, outrage. Martin was in the extra bedroom, sound asleep. It was just past ten. "The thing is I blame myself. Shit! I knew I should have reported it."

"What good would it have done?" Claude asked.

The two men sat at the table, cups in front of them, Claude's empty, Sam's half-full, the tea long cold.

"How the hell should I know?" He rose and walked to the window. It was a starry night, a few scattered clouds so near he felt he could reach out and touch them.

"Didn't you tell me that usually abused kids were back with their parents almost before they were taken away?"

"Sure, Claude. It's hard to prove; hard to make it stick. But that doesn't mean— oh, hell."

"Want to take him in?" Claude smiled. "Do you think that would work?"

"Take him in? You mean have him live with us?"

"Why not?"

"Oh, man, I don't know. I like him. I love him. But you and me, what would people say? If they found out about us?"

"Doesn't that have something to do with crossing bridges?" Claude went to stand behind Sam, nuzzled his face against his neck.

Sam turned to face Claude. "I'm not so sure we're not up to the bridge right now." He tightened his lips. "Sure, I'd like to take

Martin in."

"'But?' I can hear that silent 'but.'"

"There's so much to consider. Would it be best for him, first of all living with a couple of ... a couple of inverts?"

Claude shrugged. "The boy's homosexual."

Sam walked to the table, sat back down. "I suppose. But he's so young, fourteen ... no fifteen now, I think. How can you tell such a thing about him at his age?"

"Hell, Sam, I knew long before that, didn't you?"

Sam shrugged. "I did."

"But you want to be sure—"

"I am ... almost."

"You really take this seriously, that it could just be a stage, don't you? Even after we talked to him."

"If there's even a chance of steering him wrong—"

"I don't think it's wrong; I'll never think it's wrong. I had this friend." He played with his cup, batting it back and forth between his two hands. "He said he'd give anything to be heterosexual. To like women. His homosexuality was a monkey on his back." He looked up. "I don't feel that way. I never did; I never will. I'm glad I'm the way I am, despite the problems. It's the middle of the century. Things are going to change. It won't be so hard for people like Martin. And he's what he is. Believe me, I know the signs."

Sam chuckled. "Me too, I guess. I never thought of myself as a cautious person, but maybe I am." He spread his hands. "But there are his folks. Would they give him up? Would they even consider it?"

"His mother certainly didn't have any hesitation about letting him stay," Claude replied.

"She was probably frightened. According to Martin, it's the first time she's ever really opposed Dan. Yelling at him, trying to get him to stop."

"Maybe," Claude said. "But that still doesn't prove much of anything."

"You mean it will continue."

"Of course it will."

"From what I've seen, I agree."

Sounding Brass

"So if we report this, Sam, tell everything we know. If we get other witnesses—"

"But my God, do you want to open that whole can of worms?"

"You said you love him."

"And I do. You're damned right I do. I'd do anything I could to help that kid."

"I hear the words, Sam." He sighed. "I had a good home. Parents who loved me, did for me what they could. But when it came to what I am and their having to face it, it got rough. Martin has it rough already."

"Maybe because his father sees what he is. Maybe he's always seen the signs."

Claude nodded. "Could be. And once it's a proven fact, that will only make it worse."

"Don't get me wrong. I want to do what's best for the boy. Unselfishly, I'd hope that things would work out with Dan and Helen. But it doesn't seem likely."

"What about 'selfishly?'"

"I always wanted a son. Knew I could never have one. Now maybe I can."

Claude reached across the table for Sam's hands. "I love you."

Sam stood. "It's a hell of a lot to consider." He smiled. "You're one hell of a man."

"What brought that on?"

"All the responsibility we'd be assuming. And you're willing to do it." He walked to the hall. "I'm bushed. How about you?" Without waiting for an answer he walked up the steps to the bedroom.

* * *

Sam went in to wake Martin just after 6:30. Claude was downstairs fixing flapjacks and sausage.

The boy still slept, his face filled with peace. "Martin," he said. "Marty."

The boy opened his eyes.

"How about some breakfast?"

Martin sat up. He wore a pair of Sam's old pajamas. "What?" he said.

Sam chuckled. "Breakfast. Claude's downstairs fixing it. You want to wash up and get dressed?"

"Okay," Martin said.

"All right then." Sam ruffled Martin's hair and left.

"Is he coming?" Claude asked.

"In a few minutes, I guess."

"So what happens now?"

Sam poured himself a cup of coffee and sat down. "I wish I knew."

"Did you talk to Martin about it?"

Sam shook his head.

Claude flipped the flapjack from the skillet onto a stack beside him on the counter. He added butter to the frying pan and poured in more batter.

Sam turned to see Martin trotting down the steps.

"Hi, Sam," he said. "Hi, Claude."

Claude turned. "How are you feeling?"

"Okay," Martin said, coming to sit at the table.

Claude brought the platter of flapjacks over and started piling them on Martin's plate. "How many?" he asked.

"Two or three," Martin answered.

"There are plenty," Claude said, "so when you want more, let me know? Sam?"

"I'll start with a couple." While Claude dished them out, he took the paper towel off a dish in the center of the table. It was filled with link sausage. He passed them to Martin.

For a few minutes they ate in silence.

"Sam," Martin said, "Claude?"

"Yeah?" Sam answered.

"I suppose I better go home."

"You sure?" Claude asked.

"What else can I do?"

Sam looked at Claude then back toward Martin. "I'm going to have a long talk with Dan and Helen. And then…"

"It won't do any good," Martin said. "Dan'll just get mad."

"I'm willing to take the chance."

"You can't get them to stop. You can't."

For a moment nobody spoke. "Martin," Sam said, "Claude and I were talking about how much we'd like you to stay with us."

"Permanently," Claude said.

Martin stood abruptly. "I better get home."

Sam was surprised at the lack of reaction. But then maybe Martin thought it was a false hope, that he'd simply ignore it. He stood and gave Martin a hug. "Any time. I mean that."

"Would you like me to drop you off, Martin?" Claude asked. "It's on my way to the sawmill."

"Okay. Thank you."

Claude stood, hugged Sam and grabbed the car keys from the hook by the door. "Car's out back," he told Martin.

"'Bye, you two," Sam said.

"Goodbye," Martin answered, his voice sounding flat.

Sam sat back down at the table. He'd try to go talk to Helen and Dan.

October, 1951

Sam was on the phone to Dan O'Jenkins. Martin had disappeared and so had John. There'd been a note to Dan and Helen telling them not to worry.

"Pretty unnatural, don't you think," Dan said. "A stranger paying that much attention to a teenage boy."

"He's hardly a stranger," Sam said, "at least from what I understand. He's known Martin for years."

"You know what I mean, Sam," Dan said. "The thing is I want him back."

"I guess."

"What's that supposed to mean?" Dan asked.

"Maybe this isn't the time nor the occasion to say this. But—"

"What?" Dan sounded belligerent.

Sam sighed. "Okay," he said, glancing at Claude who sat at the table, drinking a cup of morning coffee. It was just past 6:30. For a moment he held a hand over the mouthpiece. "It's Martin," he told Claude. "John O'Shaughnessy's kidnaped him. At least that's Dan's story. I wouldn't bet on it though."

Claude looked puzzled.

"Sure, according to the letter of the law it's a kidnaping—the boy's underage. But I'll bet anything ..." He shrugged, took his hand off the phone. "Martin was here a few days ago, telling me something about being strangled."

"Oh, he was, was he?"

"Yes, Mr. O'Jenkins. I saw the marks myself. Bruises around his neck."

"A father has a right to discipline—"

"Not in that way he doesn't, Mr. O'Jenkins," Sam said, surprised at how easy it was for him to slip back into the role of policeman.

"That's neither here nor there, Sam. I want you to find my boy."

Sam was mad. "And then what?" He glanced again at Claude, whose face held compassion.

"I don't think I understand what you're getting at," Dan said.

"Mr. O'Jenkins, I've been remiss in my duties. I've known for months what's been happening—"

"Now see here."

"No, you see here, O'Jenkins. As I started to say, I've seen what's been happening, and I did nothing about it. Well, now it's about time."

"Are you trying to threaten me, Sam? Because if you are—"

"Take it however you want, Mr. O'Jenkins. But I'll do my best to see that Martin doesn't go back into that sort of environment."

"All right, Sam." His voice sounded only tired. "All right. But now the boy's missing. Whether you believe it or not, I love him."

Maybe he did, Sam thought. Maybe he did. "Why are you telling me this?"

"I understand you were a police detective."

So here it comes, Sam thought. Well, maybe it was time. He'd sat on his fat butt long enough. "That's right, Mr. O'Jenkins."

"Can't we drop the damned formality? Don't you understand, my kid's off somewhere with that damned crazy man?"

"I thought O'Shaughnessy was a friend of yours."

"Yeah," Dan said. "I thought so, too."

"What do you want me to do?"

"Find them. Bring them back. At least Martin."

"What if he doesn't want to come back?" Sam asked. "What then?"

"He's a kid."

From the beginning of the call, Sam had known he had to do it. Not for Dan. For Martin, and maybe for himself. Maybe as a kind of redemption for letting things go on. "Okay. Do you know anything about O'Shaughnessy? His background. Where he's from. Where he went to school."

"Pittsburgh," Dan said.

"That's a pretty big place. Can you tell me any more?"

"I'm afraid I can't. No, wait a minute. He was in seminary, studying to be a priest."

Sam was surprised. "You're sure about this?"

"That's what he always claimed. With John ..."

"And this was in Pittsburgh?" That should make it easier, Sam thought. There couldn't be more than one Catholic seminary.

"Yes. I'm sure of it."

"Okay, Dan," Sam said. "I'll do it on one condition."

"Oh, and what is that?"

He looked at Claude, took a deep breath. It was taking a hell of a big chance. Particularly if people knew about him and Claude. "We talked once—Claude and I—" He looked at his lover, who nodded. "We talked to Martin about ... about staying with us."

"What right have you—"

"Mr. O'Jenkins. Dan. The condition is that Martin decides. Martin decides what he wants to do." And God help him if he goes back with you, he thought.

There was a pause. "You've got yourself a deal."

* * *

It was easy. Sam called the priest at the Catholic church in Clivesville, asked him if he knew of a seminary in Pittsburgh. He did and told Sam the name. John's records were still there.

Sam figured the most likely thing was for John to go back to his old neighborhood.

In two hours time, Sam was in Pittsburgh. A map he bought showed him how to get to Mount Troy. Then he called the police, told them what had happened, told them his own background. He said he'd like to look around on his own.

Until they could get someone up there, that was fine, the lieutenant told him. But after that he'd have to play it by their rules.

He went to John's old address, not expecting anything. A woman in her thirties opened the door. "What is it?" she said.

"I'm looking for the O'Shaughnessys."

"You're the second person—"

"Is this where they live? It's very important."

"I told the other man that I know nothing about them. He seemed upset, said he was their son. Like I told him, maybe some of the neighbors would know. I'd try Mrs. Phillipi two houses up."

He did as the woman said. When he knocked, an ancient creature opened the door.

"Mrs. Phillipi?" he asked.

"Who is it wants to know?" she asked, her voice as thin as her wrinkled face.

"My name is Sam Holden," he said. "It's very important. We think John O'Shaughnessy may have come back here with a missing boy."

"A missing boy. My oh my, what next. Patrick does himself in. Blanche gets herself in a family way with the parish priest—and now ..." She peered into his face. "Kidnaped him, you think? Kidnaped a boy?"

"I wouldn't put it in exactly those terms. Most likely the boy wanted to come."

"Dear me," she said. "Why do you suppose he'd want to do something like that?"

"Mrs. Phillipi, can you tell me anything about John that might help. Where he used to spend his time. If there's anyone he might go to here."

"Crazy as a loon, that boy. Always a little tetched, if you know what I mean."

Sounding Brass

"Mrs. Phillipi?"

"Of course," she said, "you want me to try to help you."

"Can you?" Sam asked, standing on the doorstep, the sun hot against his back.

"Almost never went out. Almost never went anywhere. Then when he was just a kid, you know, he went off to seminary. Wanted to be a priest. Now isn't that a laugh?"

"You don't have any idea—"

"Used to hang around the deli, but that's been closed for years."

"The deli?" Sam asked.

"Down at the end of the block. Building's still there. Guess nobody wants it."

"Thank you, Mrs. Phillipi, Thank you very much."

Honor Thy Father and Thy Mother

March, 1949

The houses were surrounded by board fences, unpainted, splintering, a dull grey, except where a new board was nailed up or a new post replaced one that had rotted out. Rent was $24 a month, electricity included.

The alleys were cleared of rotten food, trash and coal ashes once each summer so that the "honey dippers" could empty the outside toilets.

Most back yards had vegetable gardens. Sweet williams, hollyhocks and flags grew along walls and porches. Each house had tar paper shingles, green or raspberry red. Each contained a living room, a kitchen and two upstairs bedrooms. In winter, inside temperatures often dropped below freezing after the fire in the living room stove was banked for the night.

Sidewalks and streets were dirt, except for a cement road which edged the town from east to west. Chickens scattered at the sound of approaching cars.

Below Second Street stood the grade school, yellow brick, two-stories, surrounded by a cinder playground. Since coming home from the war, John spent much of his time there, watching.

Beside the schoolyard, where the cement road started gradually up the hill, stood the old boarding house, now Millers' Restaurant. John passed by here every day on his wanderings.

Next to the restaurant squatted the company store, made of brick, tomato-puke red, as ugly inside as out, with its baby-shit walls and unfinished floors, stinking of oil to keep down the dust. Here the coal miners and their families could buy groceries, hardware, clothing, gasoline—all at exorbitant prices. Business boomed since everyone was in hock to the store, i.e., the Coal Company, up to their nose hairs, and had no cash to buy elsewhere.

The movie theatre next door cost eighteen cents for kids, thirty-six for adults. Most families could scrape that together every week or two to buy a couple hours' escape.

On past the theatre at the top of the hill stood the high school, red brick like the company store and a block long.

The town, two blocks wide, stretched six blocks from hilltop to valley. To the south stood an area, two-blocks square, and attached at an angle to the town proper. Its official name was Cottage Town, most often called Shanty Town by the locals. Cottage because the houses were smaller. Shanty because they lacked shingles, their unpainted slats an insult to any intelligent man's sensibilities. This is where John had lived since he'd first come to town.

John liked to walk. When he'd exhausted the possibilities of the "Village Proper," he'd continue on down to the tracks that led to the mine. The mine where the air was so thick you could hardly breathe. The mine where men lost arms and legs and died in cave-ins. The mine, where water dripped down back and neck every minute of every day.

John once told Dan that he figured that working in the mine was a little like going to hell and being redeemed anew each afternoon through the mercy of the Royal Bituminous Coal Company, the paternalistic entity which like Papa Yahweh, kept itself from sight. Only the bosses on First Street, like the preachers of the Word, were visible.

He stood now at the west edge of Cranston watching sunlight sparkle on the rushing water of the sulphur creek. He felt he knew almost everything worth knowing about the town and its people. He had plenty of time to observe. He hadn't worked since coming home from the P.O.W. camp four years earlier. Back to the U. S. of A., if not at first to the hills of Western Pennsylvania. First came a six-month stop at the nut house at Fort Sam Houston, released finally with enough money coming in each month to scrape by.

Nobody had lived in his house in Cottage Town all the time he was gone. Now the Company let him keep the place because he'd helped save his country from little yellow men. They gave him a house, but not a job. So he mostly walked.

After his daily outing John headed home—to play the guitar or putter. There was little else to do except attend church.

Maybe indeed he was disabled, John thought. He wouldn't

debate the fact. Still, he did exist; he had talents and capabilities and so his life should have purpose, a purpose he still hadn't found.

Such thoughts burned like a fever on this Sunday morning late in March as he shifted his gaze to the smoke curling upward from the ever-burning slag heap. He rolled up the sleeves of his dress shirt—white with tiny slashes of brown like miniature pine cones. He had a dozen such shirts and never wore anything different, except on occasion a T-shirt or no shirt at all in the hot months of summer.

At times John wondered at the workings of Papa Yahweh's mind in bringing him to this spot on the ass-end of civilization, giving him his disability and leaving him.

Still, he wasn't as bad off as many, he thought, watching a distant coal car dumping its load at the tipple. Had John's pattern for his life and Papa Yahweh's matched, by this time John would be bringing God's word to the faithful.

Yet his holy call to a vocation had been untrue, delivered by a false god speaking with the tones of the Three in One.

John turned and started north to First Street, past a block of boiled-egg-yellow garages, for rent to any who wanted them, and on to Shanty Town.

Papa Yahweh obviously hadn't wanted John to become a priest. Rather a miner? Apparently so, though he'd never asked the question directly. When he did ask questions, Papa most often failed to answer. Or worse, the false god answered.

Reaching his house, John hurried through the gate to his patch of front yard and knelt in the new grass. Hands clasped in front of his chest, he spoke. "Papa Yahweh, you know my heart is filled with love. I've striven to do your will. Yet lately, Papa, I cannot help but become a little disheartened. Where is the pattern for my life, dear Yahweh? Since you saw fit to send me to foreign soils, away from the mining of coal, saw fit that I return to this humble home without mission, I have begun to wonder."

He bowed his head and squeezed his eyes shut. "I need your guidance, oh, Papa Yahweh. I'm the first to admit to Thy ultimate wisdom. Help me to accept your will, amen."

He opened his eyes, stood and brushed off the knees of his

gabardine slacks. Rarely now did he hear the voices of the three-in-one. According to Dr. Smythe at Fort Sam, the voices had never been real.

Fuck you, Dr. Smythe, John thought. I do believe in Papa's love, praise his holy name. And a loving father cares for his children and gently leads them on the paths of righteousness. How the hell else could He do that but by speaking to them, damn it all to shitting hell?

John sighed as he trudged up the steps to the porch. He'd wanted too much to preach Papa Yahweh's word. He thought he'd known from the time of his first confession that this was to be his life's work.

John washed his hands at the kitchen sink, dried on a threadbare towel on a hook by the stove. He decided to have a cup of tea.

The taste was warm and homey. When he finished, he glanced at the kitchen clock, its dial the face of a cat. It was 8:30 Sunday morning. Maybe he'd leave for church now, get there early. The building was never locked. Often John went there to be alone with God. He loved to slip into one of the pews and run his hands over the polished oak, to watch sunlight gleam through the blues and reds of the stained glass windows.

The church was God's house, and although John knew that God existed everywhere, even in beer gardens and dens of iniquity, he felt somehow closer here to heaven. He was a child of God and so felt the almost palpable presence in this home of theirs to the Three-in-One.

Although John preferred to worship by himself, he knew what the Bible said: "Where two or three are gathered together in my name, there shall I be also." And that, of course, was only right. John had to share Their love.

He especially liked the Easter season with lilies and ferns and bright new clothing. Of course, John had no new clothes. He barely got by. He parked his car on the dirt strip beside the rutted road, stuck the keys in his pocket and trotted lightly up the cement steps. Inside, he felt at peace, the stillness that passeth understanding deep inside his soul. He climbed the steps to the sanctuary. A ray of sunlight, diffused by stained glass, refracted, reflected in glorious color on the altar. John fell to his knees, his eyes filled with tears. It was so good to be home, he thought, so very good to be home.

John focused his attention on Rev. Milliken.

"On Wednesday evening we will join with our Christian brothers and sisters in this holiest of weeks for community services at the Pentecostal Church on Elm. Thursday we'll journey to the Lutheran Church in Cranston ..."

Rev. Milliken announced Hymn 153, and old Mrs. Lundquist began to bang away at the yellowed keys of the upright. The choir stood, and John's attention switched to Martin O'Jenkins who had changed so much in the time John had known him. He was a good boy. Tall with blond hair that stuck up in a rooster tail at the crown of his head, he was very musical, the youngest member of the choir, though John knew he cared far more about his trumpet than about singing.

John felt his being suffused with love for Martin. In ways he and the boy were twins, even though John was twenty-eight, and Martin wouldn't be thirteen till June. Maybe soul mates was a better term, John thought, because their childhoods were similar. Helen and Dan treated Martin like shit; John's mother and father had treated him like shit.

Martin seemed like a little lost boy, and John had felt the same way. He could never be the kind of man that Dan was, a person who always took charge, who seemed to have no doubts.

He didn't want to hurt Dan or Helen, but he knew that sooner or later Yahweh would insist that he take action to save the boy. The thought had been in the back of his mind for years; only recently had he dared bring it into the light.

In the meantime what could he do? He knew Martin was hurting more than ever now since his grandparents had moved when Mr. Schmidt retired from his job at the mine.

John loved Martin with a fiery intensity, but he couldn't show his love in front of others, and he couldn't see Martin every day after school or people would start to talk. There was enough talk about him already.

At the end of the hymn he sat down. He so much wished he could help Martin endure. And then he felt guilty because despite what he'd seen in those early years in Cranston, he had abandoned the boy when he'd joined the Army, maybe even abandoned God's plan.

It wasn't entirely John's fault for leaving; there was the war. Yet he'd run away from Cranston, hoping to become a hero. Hoping somehow to redeem himself in the eyes of ... whom? The mother and father he hadn't seen in years? The community who even then judged him harshly for being different, for being filled with love? Helen and Dan?

After the benediction he hurried toward the back of the sanctuary and on downstairs to the vestibule.

Damn, if it weren't for everything Dan had done to help him—

If he had a son, he thought, he'd be the most important thing in the world. Next to Papa Yahweh and Lord Baby and the Spook. Maybe he'd ask Dan and Helen if he could buy Martin dinner. It would be doing himself a favor as well. The one thing he disliked about living alone was eating by himself. Yet even if he'd finished seminary and been ordained, he'd probably still be eating alone. Maybe he should have gotten married and had kids. They would be his purpose in life.

Suddenly, he began to sob and rushed outside. What the hell was the matter? he wondered. Why would he do a thing like that? The whole congregation had stared. Maybe he really was loony.

He remembered how holy the seminary had been, how safe. His life had been filled with such serenity.

He stopped for a moment and lifted his face to the sky, feeling the warmth of the sun.

He rushed down the steps and out to the sidewalk. He thought his chest might burst with the love he felt for Martin. And the sorrow. Yet that would someday be at an end. For just as Papa Yahweh in heaven saved the goodly of the earth from hellfire, John would save Martin O'Jenkins from the boy's own living hell. He didn't know how; he didn't know when. He knew only that it would come to pass.

April, 1949

Slushy snow still lay on the ground, but across the street from the school, trees in the yard by the Lutheran Church were beginning to bud. John held the door for Helen and Dan. The auditorium was nearly filled for the PTA meeting and concert. The junior band would play, and Martin had a couple of solos.

As the three of them took a seat near the back, the band came in from the back of the hall. The girls wore white blouses and dark skirts, the boys white shirts and dark pants. John watched as the kids took their seats, and the director came to the front, his back to the audience as if giving last minute instructions.

When everyone was settled, Mrs. Adamchek, the PTA president, came to the front of the gym. "As a special treat," she said, "the PTA is proud to present the Fairfield Township Junior Band, under the direction of Mr. Robinson Zweiler."

Mr. Zweiler turned to face the audience. He said that the first number would be the "El Capitan" march, "an arduous undertaking for a group such as this. But if anyone is capable, these kids are. I hope you enjoy the evening." He bowed and then turned toward the band. He tapped the baton on the podium and raised his arms.

Martin's solos were in the next to the last piece, a medley of old standards and recent popular songs. He blew moisture from his horn and ran the mouthpiece in and out of his mouth.

John watched intently, barely taking a breath, as Martin stood, raising his trumpet so that the bell stuck straight out. He began to play. The song was "The Merry Widow Waltz," and John felt chills run down his back. The boy was totally in command.

After a few measures' rest he and the other trumpets joined in with the woodwinds. Then it was Martin's turn again. His tone was light and filled with the humor of "Pistol Packin' Mama."

During the applause Mr. Zweiler motioned for Martin to rise. John saw almost a secret smile on his face. In a moment he sat down, and the band went into the concert finale.

Afterward, John raced up and met Martin at the door. "It was good, Martin," he said, grabbing his hand and shaking it. "Your solos were great."

"Thanks," Martin said, a vulnerability reflected in his face.

Dan and Helen and came toward them. "Ready, Martin?" Helen asked.

They went down the short flight of steps and out through the double doors. "You forgot to straighten your collar," Helen said. "It was turned under in back the whole way through the concert."

"Did you like it?" Martin asked.

John caught up with them. "Wasn't it wonderful?"

"It was all right," Dan answered, "for a school band." They had to wait for a car before they crossed the street. "I never heard a school band that was really any good."

Tears sprang to Martin's eyes as he took off running up the sidewalk. John sped after him, reaching the boy as he unlatched the gate.

"Let's go for a walk," John said. He took Martin's arm.

"I don't want to go."

"They don't have to be that way. You did a good job."

"So what?" Martin said.

"Please yourself, Martin, don't please them. Do it for you. Come on, I'll get you a banana split. We'll celebrate." Why couldn't Dan and Helen ever give him encouragement? He'd heard Helen tell Martin once that no matter how much he practiced, no matter how good he was at music, he'd never be as good as Dan.

Martin swung open the gate. "They won't let me go."

"I'll ask them," John said. He faced Martin's parents, just now coming close. "I'd like to take Martin to celebrate, is that all right? I won't keep him late." He pulled out his pocket watch. "It's not even eight yet. We'll be back by nine."

Waiting for them to answer, he thought how his own grandma and grandpa used to take him out to celebrate his achievements, a recitation at a school program, his scoring the most baskets in a game against Sacred Heart, Saint Ignatius' biggest rival. They went to a little delicatessen at the bottom of East Beckert.

For an instant then another scene flashed through his mind. The ice on the hill. The street slick and frozen. Grandma and Grandpa and Johnny headed down toward town to look at the Christmas decorations.

The car began to slide and Grandpa couldn't stop. Faster and faster they skidded, jumping the curb, hitting into trees, fences, cars.

Grandma, a little woman, grabbed Johnny and threw him over the seat and onto the floor in back.

"Mama, I'm sorry," Grandpa cried. Then the crash, and Johnny slamming into the back of the seat and the strong taste of metal. He lay there stunned. A man wearing a cap with ear flaps jerked on the door of the old LaSalle. With a wrenching sound it gave way. Someone pulled Johnny out and wrapped him in a blanket. But not before he saw the shattered windshield, Grandma and Grandpa covered with blood, eyes open, not moving.

John realized Helen was speaking. "What?" he asked.

She frowned. "It is a school night."

"I'll have him back." He glanced at Martin and smiled. "If it were me," John said, turning back to Helen and Dan, "I'd be too keyed up to sleep for a while yet anyhow."

"Be sure you do have him home by nine."

"See you at practice tomorrow," Dan said. The gospel orchestra met every Friday at Dan and Helen's.

John winked at Martin and put his hand on the boy's shoulder, turning him, pointing him toward the crossroads.

It was a clear night. "Were you pleased with the concert?" John asked as their feet crunched on the cinder sidewalk.

"Yeah," Martin said.

The boy was so fragile, John thought, as if he could crack and shatter. Yet there was a shell, harder, often impenetrable, that allowed him to survive. He deserved so much better.

Someone's dog howled, like a coyote, John thought, though he couldn't ever remember hearing a coyote even when he'd been stationed out west.

"John?" Martin said, his voice barely audible.

"Yes?"

"Nothing." He half shrugged and turned away.

"You were going to say something."

"I want them to feel proud, but I can't please them." Moonlight or a streetlight picked up the track of a tear on his cheek.

"I know you try."

"It's not just to please them, to make them proud or anything. That isn't even most important. I love my trumpet; I love it more than ... more than God or—"

"No, Martin! Yahweh is—"

"You know what I mean. I play it for me. But I keep hoping that they'll care."

"Someday, Martin, we'll go away. You and me?" He squeezed the boy's shoulder. "I haven't thought where. Maybe to Pittsburgh. I know Pittsburgh well."

They crossed Sixth Street, the lights of The Grill a kind of haven, John thought. Like "a beam across the waves. Some poor fainting, struggling seaman ..."

"Take a trip together?" Martin asked.

"It would be a haven."

Martin looked at him funny. John laughed. "Just to get away. You know what I mean?"

They crossed the road and climbed the steps. John held the door, then led Martin to the booth by the jukebox.

"When I was a little kid," Martin said. "I wanted to live somewhere else."

"Did you?" John asked. He knew it would work out—what he wanted, what he'd decided. Martin wanted it too.

Martin sighed brokenly, like he'd had a hard cry. "They tell me all this stuff. Like I can't— Like no matter how hard I try I can't be good at anything, and I keep thinking maybe they're right."

"No! Don't think it. Not ever."

"You heard what he said. What Dan said. That it was good for a school band ..."

"I heard," John said, "and that was a shitty thing— Sorry; I shouldn't use language like that. Shouldn't use it anywhere. I love you, Martin. Know that someone loves you. Your grandparents love you too."

"They moved away, to Philadelphia."

"Look, Martin, why are you the one playing solos?"

"Because I take private lessons. If the others took private lessons, they'd be as good or better."

"That's not true. You have ability."

"Tell that to Dan."

Mrs. Stanislaw came to the booth. "What would you two gentlemen like?" she asked.

John raised an eyebrow. "Martin?"

"I don't know."

"A banana split then. Two banana splits. And two large Cokes. We're celebrating."

"What's the occasion?" she asked, scribbling on her pad.

"Martin's debut as a trumpet soloist. With the Fairfield Township Junior Band."

"Really?" Mrs. Stanislaw said. "In that case, the Cokes are on the house."

She went back to the counter. "No matter what you think, Martin, you're good. I know you are. You should know it."

"When he says things like that, I want to run and hide. Helen didn't say anything either, except about my collar."

"I'd be devastated, Martin. To be so enthused about the concert, feeling so good about my solos, and then have that happen. That's why I want us to go away." He reached across the table and squeezed Martin's hand. "We'd find a place to live, a room maybe or a small apartment till I got a job. Then we'd get a bigger place with big rooms and hallways and fireplaces. You'd go to school and take trumpet lessons, just like now."

"I used to visit Aunt Sarah for two weeks each summer. I got homesick, John."

"We'd come back every week if you wanted to. Every weekend."

"I don't know why you're talking like this. It's dumb to think about something like that."

June, 1949

They sat in Dan's living room, eight of them, practicing. There were Tom and David Polski from Saint Michaels, Sara Komitsky and Bill Fedowski from Clivesville, Jenny Stein from up on the Lincoln Highway and, of course, Dan, Martin and John. Suddenly, Yahweh spoke to John in a thunderous voice, startling him so badly he jerked back in his kitchen chair kicking over the music stand.

He glanced around the circle. The others gave him quick looks but seemed totally unaware of the rumbling voice. Yet it often happened that the Lord God Yahweh spoke to him alone, though seldom had it occurred in a crowd but more often in the stillness of his room or on his walks.

"My son," the voice said, "know you not the commandment that you should honor your father and mother? For nine years, less than a facial tic in eternity, but long in earthly time, you have ignored the existence of Blanche and Patrick O'Shaughnessy, have failed in every way to honor and love them."

John jumped from his chair, laid his guitar down and raced outside to the porch. "Heavenly Yahweh," he wailed, racing down the steps and into the street, "have I failed thee so miserably because of my own strong will? But, oh dear Yahweh, it is so difficult to honor Blanche and Patrick."

John's head rang with the decibels ripping through his brain. He ran down the street, then stopped. Had he been trying to escape the voice of God? Yes, he admitted, and the thought engulfed him in waves of icy fear. He who loved Lord Baby, Spook and Papa, had been trying to turn his back.

At the edge of the cement road, he threw himself to his knees, looking into the blinding headlights of a car which veered to the left with a screech and a blare of horns. John thought to move back but realized that as long as he lived a life of love, righteousness and compassion, Papa would protect him.

He bowed more deeply, touching his forehead to the cement. The fear had departed, leaving in its stead a calmness serene, a feeling of surrender. Another car shot past blowing its horn. For only if a person surrendered to the will of Yahweh could he find peace.

John was a peaceful man, a man consumed by love, not hate. Love even for his asshole father and fucking bitch mother. "Oh, dear Yahweh," he prayed, "forgive me for I knew not what I did." Again, the fear touched him. He must be totally open and honest. Maybe he did know; maybe he did realize that he was disobeying a commandment. Though how could he not disobey it? Despite how hard he'd tried, he could not love his mother and father. No one could love Patrick Shit O'Shaughnessy and his whore wife Blanche. "Be with me, Lord Yahweh," he cried, "for I would not spend eternity in the realms of Lucifer but in Thy Holy Presence. Guide me, oh Papa Yahweh," he prayed, "to absolute love."

"If that is what you wish, my son," the voice now told him, "then you must make a journey."

"A journey, Papa?" he asked, feeling a sense of wonder. For it seemed there was hope, even for the lowest of Yahweh's children, the worst of earth's sinners.

"To Pittsburgh, John, without delay, to find your mother and father."

"How am I to get there, oh Papa?" he asked. "My automobile is undependable; I have barely money enough for the necessities. I can't get it fixed. I can't afford a ticket on the Greyhound—" John broke off. One didn't give excuses to Yahweh; one simply obeyed his commands.

"Yes, my son, I see you've discovered the error of your ways." Papa's voice was kind now, a loving father with a wayward child. "Seek them out, John. Find your parents for through the years they have never stopped thinking of you. Even though they abused you and shit upon you and fucked you up, they love you."

John was surprised. How could they love him? It didn't seem true. Yet, he knew Papa Yahweh never would lie. He raised his head. He'd always wanted the love of Blanche and Patrick, but he never thought he'd had it. He'd worked so hard to please them, to do as they wished. Now Papa Yahweh had told him they loved him. Had they always loved him?

"Of course, my son. Always. Even at their shittiest; for doesn't the mother bird care for her children? Doesn't the father bring them sustenance? And aren't these actions proof of love? Thus is there evidence of your mother and father's love. They fed and clothed you. Patrick worked long, hard years at Bethlehem Steel; Blanche prepared meal after meal for you."

"All these years—"

"Yes. Baby, Spook and I hoped you'd recognize the manifestation of your earthly parents' love for what it was. But you failed.

And now before it's too late, you must visit them. They've lived in pain for nearly a decade. Therefore on the morrow, your journey must begin."

"Yes, Papa," John answered. "But ..." He'd been going to ask again about the means for his journey, but his head was empty now of Yahweh's presence. A stillness, a quietude filled the earth. Only the humming of night insects disturbed the perfect stillness.

John rose, dusted off the knees of his trousers and trudged up the road. As he neared the O'Jenkins household, he heard the strains of "The Old Rugged Cross" wafted gently on a caressing breeze. He was at peace; for the first time in nine years at peace. He realized the wisdom of Yahweh's plan in seeking out those who were tied most closely to him by bonds of blood and clay. At this thought, the strains of another hymn came to the forefront of his consciousness. "Have thine own way, Lord. Have thine own way. Thou art the potter; I am the clay. Mold me and make me after thy will. While I am waiting, yielded and still."

The peace that passes understanding had truly entered John's soul. Even the strange looks he received when he walked through the front door didn't disturb his composure.

He grabbed his guitar from the chair, sat down and joined in the hymn the group was playing: "Softly and tenderly Jesus is calling, calling oh sinner come home." How appropriate he thought. For John was securely enfolded in the arms of the loving Lord Baby. He had come home.

When they finished the hymn, Dan said they'd be playing for revival services at the Christian Church the following week.

John walked up to him. "Dan," he said, "I have to go to Pittsburgh."

"To Pittsburgh?" He sounded surprised.

"Yes. I think it's time I went back to see my mother and father."

"Isn't this rather sudden?" Dan asked. He took the top off a music stand and folded it, then folded the bottom. The others gathered up their music and put their instruments away.

"I've felt guilty all these years, even though I didn't think they'd care."

"But you've changed your mind."

"Lord Yahweh works in mysterious ways."

"Yes, He does," Dan said. "Any idea how long you'll be gone?"

"No. But I'm leaving tomorrow morning."

"Taking the Greyhound?"

"Either that or hitchhike."

"I could take you to Reels Corner if you'd wait till I'm home from work."

"Thanks, I appreciate it. But I want to get an early start." He picked up his guitar case, set it on the chair and laid the guitar inside.

"Good luck," Dan said.

John nodded. He looked around for Martin. He must have gone upstairs. "Okay if I say goodbye to Martin?" he asked.

"Of course," Dan said.

Helen sat in the kitchen reading. "I'm going to Pittsburgh tomorrow," he told her. She nodded, barely acknowledging him.

Martin sat at his desk writing in a notebook.

"What are you doing?" John asked.

Martin turned around. "Writing."

John laughed. "I see that. I meant what are you writing?"

At first Martin didn't answer. "I write my thoughts sometimes. Things I want to remember. Stories I make up."

"What kind of stories?"

"They're dumb."

John sat on the bed. "They're not dumb, Martin. Lots of people keep journals. You can write in them whatever you want."

Martin shrugged.

"Anyway," John said, "I came to tell you goodbye. I'm going to Pittsburgh."

"To stay?"

John chuckled. "Of course not. Just to talk to my mom and dad. I haven't seen them in years." He stood and walked to the desk. "You take care," he said. "Try to get along with Dan and Helen while I'm gone." John ruffled Martin's hair. "I'll see you before too long." For a moment John felt a tinge of doubt about abandoning the boy.

***

The man in the Ford pickup dropped him off downtown. For some reason he felt frightened. Mingled with the fright were a myriad of other feelings. It was good to see the city again after all those years. He'd missed it. Missed the bustle, the sidewalks filled with people. Missed his friends, his classmates.

Yet it seemed unreal, like stepping into another person's life. He'd often thought that he had in effect had three lives, first with his mother and father, a life filled with turmoil; second, the seminary, almost entirely divorced from what he'd previously known; finally, his life in Cranston and even that broken by his hitch in the Army. The first two lives he remembered distinctly, but the people who populated them were so alien as to be almost unrecognizable.

That was craziness, he thought. Or maybe it was craziness to listen to the voice he'd heard the previous evening. For hadn't the false god often spoken to him as well?

He walked down the streets, feeling sunshine on his face, seeing tall buildings, familiar places. The Buehl Planetarium. The Joseph Horne Company store. Gimbels. In nine years not a lot had changed, yet everything had changed. He thought differently now; maybe not better but differently.

He came to Fifth Avenue and walked back over to Forbes before he got up the nerve to take the Mount Troy bus. Maybe his mother and father wouldn't let him in, wouldn't want to see him.

Did he really want to see them?

He caught the bus, dropped his money into the coin box and took a seat. His heart pumped hard. Maybe he should turn around and go on back to Cranston.

No! Yahweh had told him— But was it really Yahweh? Well, so what if it hadn't been? For was the advice so wrong? One should honor his parents, not abandon them. Anxiety knotted his stomach. How could a false god be right? Only Yahweh was right.

A moan escaped his lips; he glanced back to see if anyone had noticed. The other passengers looked out windows or straight ahead. The further up the hill he rode the worse he felt—sweaty, his mouth dry, his head aching dully.

The bus neared the intersection of East Beckert Avenue. He almost didn't let the driver know he wanted off. He almost continued on up the hill.

At the last minute he yanked on the cord, leaped from his seat and tore through the opened door. He stood on the corner, looking neither to right nor left, eyes unfocused, trying to control his breathing.

Blanche and Patrick O'Shaughnessy. His mother and father. The bastard and the bitch. The fucker and the cunt.

He took a final deep breath, and looked up. The first thing he noticed was that the deli was gone, the deli where Grandma and Grandpa used to take him for big dill pickles encased in green wax.

Despair ripped his gut. It was as if the years had all dropped away, and they should be still alive.

He looked through a dirty window. Broken shelves and old newspapers littered the floor. He continued on up the street, past Felco's. He wondered what Tony was doing now. Then past Patsy Stern's and on through the next intersection. He stopped and stared at the house. It looked the same, except the paint was faded and peeled in splinters from the window frames.

Was he ready for this? he wondered. He walked around back, licked his lips and rang the bell.

A woman in her thirties, with black hair and a shapeless cotton dress opened the door. "Yes?" she said.

"I'm—I'm ..."

She started to close the door.

"Please," he said, "please, I used to live here. I'm looking for my parents, Mr. and Mrs. Patrick O'Shaughnessy."

"Who?"

"The O'Shaughnessys."

"I think you'd better leave." She started to close the door once more.

"They're my parents. I came to see them. I haven't seen them in years."

The woman seemed to make up her mind. "Okay," she said. "We've had this house for four years now. We bought it from a man named Schultz. I don't know anything about the O'Shaughnessys."

"I can't believe this."

"They're your parents, you say?"

"Yes." He felt even more a sense of unreality than when he'd arrived downtown. It was like a nightmare, like he'd been lying to himself all these years, inventing a background that he found didn't exist.

Hadn't he lived here for nineteen years, except for seminary? He felt tears in his eyes.

"I'm sorry," the woman said. "Maybe some of the neighbors would know." She closed the door.

Some of the neighbors? he thought. Who could he ask? He turned, crossed to the next house over and pounded on the door. No one answered. He pounded again.

He couldn't understand. Yahweh had directed him here. Unless ... unless they'd simply moved to another house in the area.

He raced back to the street and on to the next house. The Phillipi's. He pounded on the front door. Finally, old Mrs. Phillipi answered. "Who is it?" she asked.

"It's John," he said when he saw her face, wrinkled, old, the eyes lacking light. She looked like she'd aged a hundred years. "John O'Shaughnessy."

"Johnny?" she asked. "Johnny O'Shaughnessy?"

"Yes, yes," he said.

"Well, do come in," she said. "I'll put the pot on for coffee." She turned and started toward the kitchen

"I'm looking for my parents."

She turned back, her face filled with shock.

"You didn't know ..."

"Know what?" he asked.

"Why, about your father."

John felt panic rising, choking him, snatching away his breath. "What about my father?"

"Oh, Johnny," she said. "You've been gone so long."

What is it, damn it? he wanted to shout. He wanted to grab her shoulders and shake them, make her tell him. "You've got to tell me."

"Are you sure?"

"Of course, I'm sure."

"Why your father's dead, Johnny. He must have died five ... no, six years ago. It would have been the early part of 1944. January or February. No, it was February, just before St. Valentine's Day."

"Dead?" he asked.

"Come in for coffee. You need it if I'm any judge."

"How ... how did he die?"

"Shot himself; twelve-gauge shotgun, my Ralphie said. Put the barrel in his mouth and pulled the trigger."

"Oh, my God." John sagged against the door frame. "Oh, my God." He sank down and sat on the stoop, the cement burning through his pants.

Mrs. Phillipi reached toward him and stopped. "I'm sorry," she said.

He glanced up, barely able to speak. "Why?" he asked. "Why would he do that?"

"I suppose it wouldn't be gossiping if I told you."

"What, for God's sake!" He leaped to his feet. Mrs. Phillipi threw a hand in front of her mouth and took a step back.

"It was your mom."

"Please, Mrs. Phillipi. Please."

She patted the bun at the back of her head. "Oh, my," she said, "I never expected ..." She looked at him then, eyes filled with compassion. "I guess you have a right." She took a deep breath. "Your ma, she had this child. Some said it was Father Quillin's. You remember Father Quillin, don't you?"

"Where is she? Where's my mother?"

"She left. Soon after your father's ... accident. She up and sold the house and left. Took nothing with her but the clothes on her back and the little baby. She hasn't been heard of since."

"But—"

"Some say she went to California. Me, I've never been sure. I only hope she's happy." She looked into John's eyes. "I'm sorry, boy."

John turned, ran down the street, just as he had the last time he'd been home. He continued to race until he felt he would drop.

Then he sat on the curb and cried.

June, 1949

Dan had decided to coach a baseball team for boys. John didn't know why; it was as if he cared about all the kids in town except his own son.

It was the day after getting home from Pittsburgh, and just for something to do, he went to the ball field and sat on a log between third and home plate. He glanced up to see Martin pedaling fast toward him. His bicycle was a big, old heavy thing. He leaned it against the ash tree behind the diamond.

"Hi, Martin," John said.

Martin smiled and waved. Then Martin's gaze met Dan's. His father turned away and began to talk to three or four kids who were crowded around him.

Dan had said there'd be an interteam scrimmage and chose the kids to be on each side. Martin's side took the field first, while Cyril Reitz, the oldest boy on the team, was at bat.

As John watched, two kids struck out, and the third hit a fly to the first baseman. Martin trotted toward home while Cyril went to the pitcher's mound.

Cyril said something John couldn't hear. Martin turned and strode back toward him. Cyril's glove lay on the ground; Martin placed his heel in the center and slowly twisted. "Go to hell, you son-of-a-bitch!" he said and turned away.

Cyril grabbed his shoulder and spun him around. "What did you say?"

"You're a fucking son-of-a-bitch, and I want you to leave me alone."

Martin jerked free and raced toward the make-shift backstop, running head-on into Dan.

"Don't use that kind of language again!" Dan said.

Martin tried to step around him, but Dan grabbed him under the arms and carried him to his bike, propped against the tree. "I won't have you shame me," he said.

With no warning he slammed Martin down on the seat of the

bike.

"Oh, God," Martin screamed. "Oh, God!" The seat broke sideways, spreading his legs, throwing him onto the metal pipe that had supported the seat. Dan turned immediately and strode back to the field.

"Oh, Jesus!" John raced toward Martin as the boy staggered backwards. "Forgive him," he said. "Forgive him."

He knelt beside Martin, afraid to touch him, not knowing what to do. In that moment, no matter what he'd told Martin, he could have killed Dan. He reached toward Martin.

Still doubled over, the boy jerked away, flaring with anger. "Get out of my way, John." He tried to go past him, yet John saw he could barely walk.

He glanced toward Dan. He wasn't even looking at Martin but out toward the field where the kids took their positions. Some of them looked toward John and Martin and grinned; others had no expressions.

"I love you, Martin," John said. "I know it's difficult, but I love your father, too. You must never stop loving your father."

"I wish he'd drop dead."

"No, Martin. God put us here to test our mettles. Here on earth, I mean. We have to find our purpose and endure."

And in that moment John knew beyond the slightest doubt that his sole purpose was to save Martin O'Jenkins.

Martin picked up his bike and limped away.

John hit a fist hard against his thigh. Dan had done so much for him. Dan was a good man! Yes, he was. Except if that were true, then John's own father had been a good— He couldn't finish the thought.

"Martin," he called. "I love you, Martin."

He'd do something to stop all the pain. Johnny and Martin were both good boys. If they lived together, John would never hurt Martin. He'd do anything for him.

Tears formed slowly in John's eyes, spilled over, tickled his cheeks.

John hoped Martin wasn't hurt bad. That metal piece on the bike could have done some awful damage.

Sounding Brass

* * *

Martin's bike lay like a wounded animal, handlebars twisted sideways, cuddled against the fence. John followed the half-rotted boardwalk around to the back of the house and knocked on the screen door.

Helen appeared inside. "Hello, John."

"I thought I'd take Martin for ice cream or a hamburger. Is that all right?"

"If he wants to go. But I don't think he's here. He's probably still at the ball field."

"I see," John said. He turned abruptly and ambled down the steps. That was funny, he thought. Where could Martin be?

Maybe in the vacant lot across the street. Martin used to climb up in the tree there, when he felt bad. John knew that, though he didn't think Martin knew he knew. It was because he cared so much about the boy. He knew where he often went after Dan beat him or Helen shit on him.

John loped across the street and up to the tree, a maple thick with light green leaves. He peered up among the branches. "Martin?" he called, trying to make his voice soft and soothing. "Martin, are you up there?"

John couldn't see anyone, but it was hard to tell. "Martin?" he called. "How about going to The Grill? What do you say? My treat."

He paused a second or two, then started to shimmy up the tree. Just as he reached the lowest branches, he heard someone out on the sidewalk.

"Well, John," a voice said. "Aren't we just a little old for that sort of thing?"

It was Mrs. Brodski from the post office. A busybody if ever there was one.

"Is it really your business?" John answered, his voice pleasant, lilting. That would get the old bitch.

"Well, I never!" she exclaimed.

"And you probably never will!" he yelled back, continuing to climb. Just as he expected, no one was up there.

He climbed back down. "Where could he be?" he asked aloud, as if someone might answer. "Oh, I know," he said. "He's probably down by the railroad tracks." On the other side from the ball field were thick bushes, with paths in and around them, worn there by kids playing hide and seek.

John started to run again, his wet shirt becoming wetter still as perspiration flowed down his back and sides.

"Martin," he called as he neared the place. "Martin!"

There was no answer, so he began to push through the bushes. "Martin?"

"What do you want, John?"

John laughed gleefully.

"What's so damned funny?" Martin said.

"Oh, Marty, I'm just so glad you're here. I looked for you. At your house. At the vacant lot."

"What for?" His voice sounded surly.

"What for? Because I love you, Martin. You don't realize I really do love you."

"I don't know what you're talking about."

"About your being a child of Yahweh, like I am. And so you're my brother."

"Go away."

"I thought we'd go to The Grill. You can get whatever you like."

"Jesus Christ Almighty, John. Don't you know what just happened?"

"Yes, Martin, Lord Baby is almighty, and, yes, of course, I saw what happened."

"Oh, man," Martin said and his voice cracked. "Oh, God."

The bushes were thick here, but John dropped to his hands and knees and scooted in among them. When he reached Martin, he held out his arms. For a moment the boy hesitated.

"I love you, Martin," John said. "Yahweh knows how I love you."

Suddenly, Martin's body sagged, and he started to cry. John put his arms around the boy and drew him to his chest.

Martin's breath caught as he released himself from John's grasp and tried to smile.

"I know," John said. "I know." He suddenly realized something. Martin was his best friend, his very best friend in all the world.

"I was worried about you," he said. "I figured I might find you here. Offer some moral support."

Martin stood and brushed off his dungarees.

"How about going to The Grill?" John said.

"Okay." Martin smiled, then grimaced.

John could tell the boy was hurting. "You all right?"

Martin nodded and moved out toward the railroad tracks. "Want to go this way?" he asked, looking over his shoulder.

"Whichever way you want to go," John said, swinging up beside him along the railroad ties. They could go out to the cement road and then on up the hill. John knew that by going that way they wouldn't have to pass the baseball diamond.

They walked in silence out to the road, the sun beating down, the sky free of clouds. They turned up the hill past the grade school. "No matter what," John said, "you shouldn't despair. Our Heavenly Father loves you. I love you with a very special love. Not like I love the preacher or Dan and Helen but much more than that."

Rev. Hoffman stood on the parsonage steps. "Martin," he called. "How are you? And you, John?"

"God loves me, Rev. Hoffman," John said. "And so I'm feeling good."

Rev. Hoffman laughed. "Okay," he answered.

"Nice man," John said. "If hadn't already joined the United Brethren Church, I might consider the Lutheran."

"We used to go there," Martin said. "When I was a little kid."

They were past Third Street now, across from Miller's Restaurant.

"You mom said it's okay to get a hamburger," John said. "I have the feeling you don't want supper at home."

Martin looked at him with surprise.

"You know, Martin," John said, "you may think it's none of my business. But I understand how you feel. Does that surprise you?"

"I don't know. I don't see—" He broke off.

"We'll order whatever you want and sit in the booth back by the juke box." He looked for a sign of agreement. "There are things that I want to tell you." He'd tell Martin how alike they were, how

---

similar their feelings. He was sure Martin felt ashamed. He always had, as if it were his fault for not being what his mom or dad wanted, for making them mad, for their not caring about him.

Two high school girls stood at the counter looking through movie magazines as John led Martin to the booth and slid in opposite him. Mrs. Stanislaw had her back to them, washing dishes. Mr. Stanislaw, a heavy man with an accent, picked up menus and two glasses of water and brought them to the booth.

Like his wife, he dressed in white. A T-shirt and pants.

"Don't believe we need those," John said, indicating the menus. "Right?"

Martin shrugged.

"Two burgers, two orders of fries, and later maybe some desert. And a couple of large Cokes."

Mr. Stanislaw scribbled on an order pad and waddled back to the counter. John watched as he slapped two patties on the grill. He turned to Martin. "I understand what's been going on, and I don't like it."

"What do you mean?" Martin asked.

"I told you I understood." He took a sip of water. "My father used to beat me too. When he wasn't beating me, he beat my mother." He looked into Martin's eyes. "Love is all important. We have to change ourselves into people who love."

Martin picked at his paper napkin.

"I was going to be a priest," John said. "Did you know that?"

Martin looked shocked. "A priest! Then how's come you go—"

"To the United Brethren church?"

"I guess so," Martin said.

"They tried to drive me away," he said. "Away from Papa Yahweh and the Lord Baby. And they almost succeeded. Until I met your father."

"Yeah, right," Martin answered. He took a drink of water.

"Martin, each of us is a complex being. Maybe you can't see it—I certainly couldn't and still can't where my mother and father are concerned—but no one is completely good or bad. We're sinners. All of us sinners. It's only through God's mercy ..."

Martin had stopped listening. With all that had happened, John chided himself for not realizing that the boy was in no mood for sermons.

"I'd like to help you."

"Sure," Martin said, rubbing at a circle of water his glass had left on the table.

John knew he didn't believe him. But when the time came, when the time was right—

Mr. Stanislaw brought their orders.

Early August, 1951

For years John had known he had to help Martin, had to take him away to Pittsburgh. But then what? He didn't know what to do and wasn't even sure talking to Martin about it was right. He trusted God to show him the paths he should follow.

The weeds were high beyond the baseball diamond; nettles grasped John's blue slacks, stuck to them as he walked along thinking. He came to the railroad tracks, followed them out to the open space near the bushes where Martin liked to come to be alone.

A group of younger children, seven or eight years old, were playing hide and seek there. They'd have to leave, John thought. His mission had to be given priority. He had to be alone to think.

He raced toward them, yelling and clapping his hands. "Scat," he shouted. Scat, scat, scat."

As they ran off, he forced his way through the thicket, found a worn spot where no grass grew, and scooted backwards to hide there. The bare earth felt cool and damp.

"Dear Yahweh," he prayed, "Lord Baby and Spook, be attentive to my pleas. In your wisdom, you saw fit to allow Dan and Helen to be assholes in their treatment of their son. Assholes, yes, but in only that one respect. Otherwise, a goodly man and woman. Since they are not likely to change, I ask for your holy guidance in saving Martin. For truly he must be saved, as Thou seest fit to save sinners."

John felt calm, serene, here in this primeval quietude, away from the scurry and commotion of life. He felt the presence of the Three-in-One as strong as ever he'd felt it.

___

"If Thou see fit, show me a sign that what I seek to do is right."
He peeked out from among the bushes, the sky alight with the rays
of the sun, shining down through a cloud, John's own personal
sunbeam. And he knew it was the sign he sought.

He scooted out from under the bush. It was settled then. There
was no doubt. Yahweh had rained the sun down upon him,
anointing him, baptizing him in fire as the prophets of old.

"Thank you, Heavenly Yahweh," he shouted, running down
the center of the tracks, down toward the cement road. "Thank
you Lord Baby, and most holy Spook." He fell to his knees, as the
enormity of what he planned struck him.

He clasped his hands and bowed his head. "Your unworthy
servant, dear Yahweh, shall do his best to bring about salvation."

John had a purpose now to his life. He was going to be a father.
A surrogate father for a lonely child. But when? When should he
set the plan in motion?

Maybe he should talk with Martin, feel him out on the matter.
But if Helen were there, how could he bring it up? He'd have to
be careful; he'd have to be crafty.

He raced up the cement road past the post office and up Second
Street to Martin's house, unlatched the gate and hurried around
to the door. He banged on the screen.

Helen stood at the kitchen sink. "Goodness, John, what is it,"
she asked. "Is something the matter?"

"It's a day that Yahweh made, so what could be the matter?"
he asked.

"You're out of breath."

"Is Martin here?"

"He's in his room."

"May I talk to him?"

"Come in, John." She held open the screen door. "Would you
like a glass of iced tea? It's awfully hot in the sun."

John was hot and thirsty, but he was on a mission. Because of
this, it was his inclination to tell her no. But then, that wasn't the
Christian thing to do—to spurn an offer. Neither could he afford
to alienate Helen in any way. Certainly, she and Dan would be
happy to have someone else take Martin, but he had to approach

it cautiously. "Yes, please, I'd like that," he said.

She took a blue glass from the cupboard, deep blue like a bottle of Evening in Paris perfume. She poured him tea, offered him sugar. He gulped the tea and raced upstairs. Martin sat at his desk, leafing through a comic book.

John sat on the bed. He didn't know how to begin.

"Did you want something, John?" Martin's voice sounded tired.

"Remember when we talked about going away together? Suppose we could do that. Go away from here and never come back."

"What are you talking about?"

"About how I know you're treated."

"So what?" Martin picked up the comic book.

"You and I, Martin."

"What about us?"

He leaned forward. "I'd never do the things your mom and dad do. To you, I mean." He bit his lip. "They're good people; I love them, as I know you love them too. But Yahweh has revealed to me their blind spot." Martin didn't say anything; he looked puzzled, maybe a little upset. John rushed on. "I'd take care of you, Martin. I'd never treat you bad."

"You're talking crazy, John. Nothing like that could ever happen."

"What if your mom and dad said it was okay?"

"But they wouldn't."

"How do you know?"

"I just do," Martin answered.

John stood up. "Think about it."

Martin smiled. "It's silly."

"You'll see," John answered. "You'll see."

August, 1951

The Plumton picnic grounds covered the top and side of a rolling hill. Tall shade trees bordered the area, providing the only relief from hot sunlight, except for the enclosed line of booths that stretched across the bottom of the hill. At the far end stood the stage, a rough platform enclosed on three sides, where various acts provided entertainment throughout the day.

John knew this was where Martin had performed his magic show for the past four years. He also knew Martin didn't like to do it; it was Dan's idea. Martin hadn't even looked at the tricks for the last six months.

It was a busy enough day for him, John thought. Martin would play twice with the high school band, afternoon and evening, and in between times with Dan's orchestra.

Since John also would be playing with Dan's group, he'd spend the day, which would give him a chance to hear both concerts by the band.

He watched as Martin helped unload the folding chairs from the band bus and set them up in the thick grass at the top of the hill where there would be no protection from the sun until the shadows lengthened during the evening.

When the band started to play, several people stood nearby or sat on the grass to listen. "I'm Forever Blowing Bubbles," "Hold that Tiger," a few marches. At the end there was scattered applause.

John glanced at his watch. In ten minutes he and Martin had to be up on the stage ready to play. John was going to wait for Martin but saw he was with Bobbie Thomas from church. She played clarinet, and once in a while she and Martin played a duet for Sunday service.

John wandered over to the stage himself and helped set things up.

"Hi, John," Martin said. He climbed up on the stage. "How'd you like the concert?"

"Sounded great." He glanced out to see Bobbie sitting on one of the benches.

As people became aware of the group on stage, they began to gather in twos and threes. Dan said the first piece would be "The Hawaiian War Chant." By the time they finished it, a bigger crowd had gathered.

The group quit after an hour. Martin would stay to play the second concert with the band; John would ride home with Dan.

"See you," Martin said as he trotted down the steps from the

Sounding Brass

stage.

"Martin!" Dan called

He turned to face Dan. "Yes?"

"Don't you go running off. I have something I want to talk about."

Martin walked over to where Dan was fitting the final pieces of sheet music into a brief case. "What?"

"Mr. Miller asked if you were going to perform your magic show this year."

"Oh?" Martin frowned.

"He said it's expected. It's so much a part of the picnic that it couldn't go on without you."

"I can't do my tricks."

"Oh, why is that?" Dan zipped the briefcase shut. "I'll take you home right now, and we'll get your equipment."

"I haven't practiced since last fall."

"Whose fault is that?"

"It's nobody's fault; I just don't want to do it!" Martin looked angry and embarrassed.

John glanced out at the benches. Bobbie still sat there, her head to the side, biting her lip. He was sure she couldn't hear the conversation between Dan and Martin, but she had to know something was wrong.

"I told you before," Martin said, "I never wanted to do magic."

"And I say that's bullshit!"

Martin turned and started off the stage.

"Come back here, Martin, and I mean right now."

Oh, God, John thought. Not in front of Bobbie and everyone at the picnic. He saw Bobbie get up and hurry down the hill toward the booths.

"I'm going to take you home, and you're going to get your things and do the show. Whether you've practiced or not. It's you who's going to look silly; it isn't me."

Martin turned and ran off the stage.

"Where are you going!" his father called.

Martin turned. "I'm going out to the car, goddamn it. You said you were taking me home."

He ran up to the street and jerked open the car door. In a moment Dan sat beside him, as John crawled into the back seat. "Let me tell you something," Dan said. "I don't want to hear you take the Lord's name in vain. For the rest of the summer you're confined to your room."

John wished he weren't there.

"What about my Boy Scouts meetings and band practice?" Martin asked.

"We'll see," Dan answered.

Martin faced the window. John saw tears on his cheeks.

By the time they reached Cranston, it was five o'clock. "I have to get back by six to play with the band," Martin said. "We have another concert."

"Do you take me for a dumbbell?" Dan's face looked dark and angry. "You'll get back in time. And once the concert's over, you'll do your magic act. Understood?"

As the pulled up in front of the house, John opened the back door and squeezed Martin's shoulder. "It's okay," he said as Dan got out and strode into the house. "Your *heavenly* father loves you. And maybe your earthly father too. Maybe he just doesn't know how to show it."

* * *

It was two days after the Plumton picnic. Except for going to church on Sunday, John had done nothing except think and pray about Martin. He knew the show hadn't gone well. He'd heard Dan telling Helen how ashamed Martin had been. "Maybe it will teach him a lesson," he said.

John wondered what kind of lesson? A lesson in hate?

John hadn't had a chance to talk to Martin at church. But he thought the boy could use company, particularly if Dan carried out the threatened punishment.

It was early afternoon as he unlatched the gate and came into the yard. He stood below Martin's window. "Martin," he called.

Martin came to the window.

"Can I come up?" he asked.

"Ask Helen," Martin said.

"Okay."

John knew Martin must be down in the dumps, angry, embarrassed. He went around and knocked on the door. Dan would be at the mine.

In a moment Helen came to the door.

"May I talk to Martin?"

"I suppose so. But he does have to stay in his room."

"I know." He opened the screen door. "I just want to talk to him."

Helen shrugged and turned away. "Tell him I'm going to the grocery in Clivesville."

John climbed the steps, went in and sat in the chair by Martin's desk.

"How are you, John?"

"Yahweh loves me." John smiled. "That's enough."

"Is it?"

"Come on, it's not all that bad."

"How do you know?" Martin answered.

John moved over to the bed and sat down, his leg against Martin's. He hadn't intended that, but despite himself, he felt a thrill. He knew he should move but didn't want to. And maybe it didn't matter because as Yahweh knew, he loved the boy.

"Did you want something, John?"

"Just to see how you are. To see how it went."

"The magic show?"

John nodded.

"It was awful. Nothing went right. I was—" He turned his head away.

"It's all right. It's okay."

"I never wanted to do the damn tricks. Ever. Everything I'm the least bit interested in— My aunt gave me a book on magic when I was seven years old. I liked it, so Helen and Dan—"

"Your mom said to tell you she's going grocery shopping," John said. "To Clivesville."

"Did she?"

"Look, Martin, if you love Yahweh and realize he loves you,

that should sustain you."

John could see that made Martin mad because he scooted away. John moved closer again. He squeezed Martin's knee, ran a hand up his thigh and then back down. He loved the boy, loved him so much. If they were together, it would be like he was Martin's father. No, it would be like he and Martin were mar—

Quickly, John stood up and felt for his safety pin. "I just wanted to see how you are and to tell you I'm still making plans. One of these days soon ..." He reached out once more and ran the outside of his fingers along Martin's chin and up his cheek.

"What plans?" Martin asked.

"We can't talk about it now; things are too uncertain." He turned and left.

September, 1951

There was absolutely no question about it. It had to be done right away. If John didn't leave, he'd kill that bastard of a father. A hypocrite, a wolf in sheep's clothing.

He was in front of his house, checking the oil on the car. It was a 1939 Ford, and it barely ran. But it had to get them to Pittsburgh. He and Martin.

He'd pick Martin up after everyone else was in bed. They'd go to Pittsburgh, just as John had hoped and planned all these years.

And once they got there? What would he do then? He slipped the dipstick back into place, closed the hood of the car, and ran an arm over his forehead. It was late September, still hot.

He and Martin, they'd get along somehow. It was Yahweh's will that this be done. He'd have the whole trip to think things through. He'd pack all his belongings—hell, there wasn't much. Everything he cared about would fit into his old suitcase. Except the guitar, of course.

Maybe he and Martin could get jobs playing—John on guitar, Martin on trumpet. The boy was good—maybe even a kind of prodigy. They'd make it somehow.

John decided to wait until after dark to stow his things in the car. Maybe then the neighbors wouldn't see him, wouldn't stick their noses in his business.

He walked around the house—it was a shanty, after all, he thought, little more than a chicken coop. He wouldn't miss it. The only thing he'd miss was the gospel orchestra. And the church. He and Martin would find a church. There were lots of churches in Pittsburgh.

Maybe he wouldn't miss the orchestra. How could he ever face Dan again anyhow? After what he did. Strangling the boy, maybe actually trying to kill him.

He glanced at the kitchen clock, willing it to go faster. It was only 3:15. School wasn't out till four.

Martin had told him about going to Sam's house, then deciding to go back home because there was nothing else he could do, nowhere else he could go.

John had seen the ugly bruise marks on Martin's neck, could just imagine the boy's terror, his wanting to strike back, yet knowing it was his own father and he couldn't.

John walked to the bedroom, yanked open the drawers on the chipped dresser, pulled out his socks, his jockey shorts, his T-shirts.

He reached for the suitcase on the top shelf of the closet. He hadn't used it in years. There'd been nowhere to go, except back to Pittsburgh that one time to try to find his mother and father. For an instant, he was filled with a blinding hate, then shrugged. Maybe his mother was dead by now. What good did it do to hate the dead?

He set the suitcase on the stripped bed. He'd washed the sheets and blanket. He packed everything from the dresser, then carefully removed his shirts and then his pants from their hangers.

He'd never had many clothes. He supposed it wouldn't do to try to pack the blue gabardine suit. It would be too wrinkled.

He wondered what else he should take. The furniture was all second-hand and so he didn't care about it. How about the silverware and dishes?

Suddenly, he felt weak and sat on the edge of the bed. "Dear Yahweh in heaven," he prayed. "Am I doing right?"

"Of course, my son," a voice answered inside his head. "Someone has to rescue Martin, and you've delayed long enough."

"How could I have done it earlier—"

"Now, now, my son, I imply no criticism. I meant only that you've known nigh unto a dozen years that your path was leading you to this crossroads, and there was only one choice you could make."

"Yes, Papa," John answered, his doubts burned away by the fire of Yahweh's voice. Holy, Blessed Yahweh. He resumed the packing when suddenly he was struck with the thought that this again could be the false god, the one who directed him to Pittsburgh that last time.

"No, John, you must listen to our Papa." The voice seemed to fill the room, as if from loudspeakers hidden in every wall.

"Who ..."

There was laughter, the laughter of a young child, gleeful, unhindered. "You know me, John O'Shaughnessy. You call me Lord Baby; others call me Jesus."

John was overwhelmed; shivers ran up and down his back. Lord Baby had never before spoken to him except inside his head or in dreams.

"Of course, I haven't," the voice said. "But I now intercede on behalf of my Papa. What you do is all that can be done. You and Martin. Love, love, love."

"Thank you, Lord Baby," John said, his being filled with the pure white light of love, as the shepherds must have been filled on that night so long ago on the hills above Bethlehem.

It was nearly midnight when John let the car coast to a stop in front of Dan O'Jenkins house. He had no more doubt, no more confusion. Papa Yahweh would provide.

Within a very few moments he saw Martin tiptoeing down the steps, a suitcase in his hand. John opened the door on the passenger side, while Martin slipped his things into the back seat.

"Ready?" John asked.

"Just a minute," Martin whispered. "I have to get my trumpet and my music."

He was gone so long John began to worry that something had happened. Then there he was, his trumpet in one hand, his music in the other. "I left a note," Martin said, "telling them not to worry, though I doubt they care. By the time they find it, we'll be miles away."

"You're sure you want to do this, Martin?" John asked, praying the boy felt the rightness of it as he did.

"I'm sure." He climbed into the passenger side and gently closed the door. Martin held his trumpet on his lap, his gaze on the road ahead.

"Sleep, if you want to," John said.

"Yes," Martin answered, leaning his head back, closing his eyes. John felt protective of the boy, as if he wanted no harm ever to come to him again.

By the time they reached Reels Corner, Route 30, John could tell Martin was fast asleep.

October, 1951

John was worried; they were out of food, and there was no more money. He didn't know what to do.

Martin sat on an old crate in the corner, staring at him, not saying anything. He looked hurt, sad. He hadn't had a proper bath since they'd arrived last week; neither of them had.

They were in the old delicatessen. There was no electricity, nothing in the building but empty crates and boxes. At least the restroom worked—in a manner of speaking. The water had been turned off, but each day John found an outside faucet somewhere, filled an old bucket that had been left in the building and brought back the water.

They flushed the toilet once a day, brushed their teeth, took care of all their needs with the one bucket of water.

John didn't know what to do. He'd heard of ... well, of hustlers, male prostitutes. But that would be wrong, terribly wrong. And he was too old, and sick. A week earlier he'd noticed that he was pissing as much pus as urine. But what if Martin were— No! He didn't allow himself to finish the thought.

Suddenly, a dozen suns lit up the windows. A bull horn blared: "John O'Shaughnessy, we know you're in there. Come out with your hands up, and we won't do you any harm."

"No!" John screamed. "No."

"Is Martin O'Jenkins with you?" There was a pause. "Let the boy come out. Let him come out." The lights played back and forth across the windows.

"Martin! Please come out," Sam Holden called.

"It's Sam!" He turned to John, a look of joy on his face. "It's my Scoutmaster. I have to go out, John. I'm sorry. I don't know what else to do." He looked at John for a second, yanked open the door and raced into the glaring lights.

"Please, Martin," John called, "we'll work things out. Please. Please." There was no answer as he sank down on one of the crates. It was over. He heard the commotion, the cheers.

"Thank God," Sam said. "We didn't know what to expect."

"John wanted to help me. He just tried to help." There was a pause. "What am I going to do? I can't go back home. I can't face Dan and Helen."

"They wanted me to find you. But they agreed to let you decide if you want to live with them or—"

"I don't understand."

"I asked you once about staying with Claude and me. The offer's still open."

Maybe this was as it was meant to be, John thought. He was simply the catalyst, his part now ended. He had never mentioned to anyone that when he had impure thoughts, he jabbed a pin into his cock. Years ago, during the war, he'd lost the pin. But later he'd found another. For a long time, he'd been ill, infections spreading throughout his body, making him weak. But he'd had to save Martin. And he had; his purpose in life had been fulfilled.

He heard wondrous singing and raised his head to see angels with the whitest of wings, gold haloes encircling their heads, faces filled with compassion, hovering near the ceiling. And he knew then that Yahweh was pleased.

And suddenly there was with John a host of these heavenly angels, praising Papa Yahweh and singing "Glory to God in the highest." And Papa's voice filled the delicatessen. Why hadn't John ever noticed that Yahweh's voice was exactly like Father Quillin's?

"You, John, are my beloved son in whom I am well pleased."

"Hallelujah, hallelujah, praise to Papa Yahweh," he cried, as angels elevated and supported him. Martin and Sam, arms around each other, grew more distant but were bathed in the light spilling down from glorious heaven. And then there was Sam Holden racing toward them.

"Call for an ambulance!" Sam shouted. "We've got to get this man to a hospital!"

John smiled. Everything was OK now. Martin would have a good home, and John's mission was fulfilled. The abuse would end; little Johnny would suffer no more. And John would never again need his pin.

The End